FIVE DOWN

TOM SIBSON

Tom Sibson

Five Down

ISBN 9798326847676

Chapter 1

The remaining leaves on the trees added welcome splashes of bright autumnal bronzes and yellows to the street as Paul Dobson strolled out of the city centre towards York's medieval walls. Enjoying his surroundings, he wrestled mentally with a crossword clue that had been preying on his mind and which he'd set himself the challenge of solving before arriving at his destination.

Five down. Facsimiles of Ruby's output. Eight letters.

Digging into his pocket, he retrieved a tube of Fruit Pastilles, simultaneously trying to ignore a slight pang of guilt for reneging on his recent promise to himself to cut out sweets and biscuits. He was aware that of late, his thirty-year-old body was not as healthy as it should be, partly due to what he considered an occupational hazard of a mainly sedentary job and partly through comfort eating since ... *well* he thought, *let's not ruin a pleasant walk by dwelling on that now.* Paul hoped the bracing exercise would help burn some energy.

Licking his fingers, he turned his mind back to the crossword clue. By the time he was in a position to be mildly disappointed with himself for now having eaten half the packet, the clue was still unsolved, and he'd completed his walk. He turned off the pavement alongside the busy main road and strolled up to the austere brick building marked by a blue and white metal sign emblazoned with the North Yorkshire Police logo. The front door lay just behind an empty bicycle rack.

On entering the police station, the warmth embraced his face with a tingling glow, bringing with it a familiar scent-cocktail of stale body odour, air freshener, and disinfectant. Paul waved at the receptionist on the front desk who, looking up, recognised him instantly with a warm smile.

'Hi, Paul, is it that time of the week already? Time flies. I'll just get her for you.'

'Well, you know the old expression. In that case, you must be having fun, Debbie. Thanks,' replied Paul, returning her smile with his own. 'No rush.'

'Fun?' Debbie rolled her eyes and laughed in response. 'Right, if you say so. Just don't put it in print. We wouldn't want people thinking we were having fun in here now, would we?'

As police stations went, Paul mused, there were a lot worse than the Fulford Road station in York. Perhaps it wasn't quite as plush as the new modern station in Harrogate, but it was certainly a far sight more pleasant than the interiors of many of the decidedly grim police buildings around Yorkshire he'd visited in his career. York police station was situated next to the army garrison and by virtue of its proximity seemed to have absorbed some of its military feel. Sitting in reception, you could just as easily be in a building at almost any British army or RAF base in the world. The only obvious clue that it was a police station, rather than a military establishment, was that the slightly worn A4 posters on the wall informed you how to report a drug dealer and to lock your car at night, instead of telling you to prepare for your medical or to watch out that you didn't accidentally walk into a spinning propeller blade.

As crime reporter for the York Press, it had fallen to Paul Dobson to visit the station, a fifteen-minute stroll from his office in Walmgate, a pleasure when the weather was fine such as today. This afternoon, as with all his previous visits, he would receive a weekly crime update from the Press Liaison Officer, Detective Constable Karen Parkinson.

It was, he had to admit, a remarkably pleasant aspect of his job, a chance to get out of the office for a while, grab some welcome outdoor air, and if the sun were out, to return up the leafy banks of the River Ouse back into the city centre. He yawned as he settled into a scuffed plastic seat, which was bolted to the floor. Removing his copy of *Private Eye* from under his arm, he pulled a biro from his coat pocket and turned straight to his favourite page near the back: the cryptic crossword. He hoped Karen wouldn't be too prompt, as he wanted to take the opportunity to make inroads into the puzzle he'd been saving especially for this visit.

Unfortunately, his promising start getting four or five clues comfortably under his belt was short-lived. After only a few minutes, DC Parkinson's familiar cheerful face appeared through a door to his right.

'Hi, Paul, good to see you again. Come on through.'

Folding up his magazine he followed Karen down the corridor to their regular meeting room. Karen turned and asked the question she repeated every time. 'How are things, then, Paul? Coffee? The usual?'

'Not too bad, thanks. I'm still not used to you in your more casual attire though, after the last couple of years of always seeing you in uniform. I like your jacket.'

Karen laughed. 'Yes, it's been two months now since I transferred over to what those in uniform call the "dark side". And they still haven't found anyone to replace me in my press briefing role. Not that I mind, of course,' she hastened to reassure him. 'It's always lovely to see you every week. The jacket's from Marks and Spencer by the way. Anyway, how's your week been since your last visit?'

‘As blissfully uneventful as ever, thanks.’ That wasn’t true but Paul decided that although they had known each other professionally for a long time and got on well, this wasn’t the time or place to mention the issues in his private life.

Letting himself into the meeting room, Paul set out the tools of his trade, precisely and always in the same order, onto the table: notebook wrapped in a rubber band maintaining today’s page, pencils, and a voice recorder. Karen returned with the coffee. He was always grateful that she made the drinks herself. It was instant, but still far more agreeable than the harsh brown, lukewarm, battery acid that masqueraded as coffee from the vending machine at the end of the corridor. Taking a sip, he glanced through the reinforced window. A departing patrol car blew a pile of fallen leaves around in its wake. He focused briefly on one as it floated and settled on the sill, the setting sun enhancing its colours in the already fading afternoon light.

‘That tastes lovely, thank you. So, spill the beans. What’s been happening around these parts this week?’ He started his voice recorder, collected his pad and a pencil, looked directly at Karen and smiled eagerly.

Putting down her mug embellished with the words “Keep Calm and Let Karen Handle It”, she casually brushed away a strand of hair that had fallen across her eyes, popped open a blue A4 document wallet, and laid the contents on the table in front of her. As usual, there wasn’t much to see.

‘OK then, brace yourself for this week’s exciting white-knuckle ride. We’ve had a mobile phone stolen from a car at the supermarket on Foss Islands Road the day before yesterday at half-past five. The woman had her phone on the front seat of her red Vauxhall Nova while she was putting her shopping in the boot. A guy just ran up, grabbed it, and legged it off towards

Tang Hall. Age…maybe mid-twenties, but the woman said she didn't get a proper look. Dark grey hoodie and jeans. We've got a bit of CCTV footage from a distance, but it was already quite dusky outside and it's not great, so we're asking if any more witnesses can come forward.'

Paul noted it on his pad with a view to adding a small appeal in the next edition.

'Last night at about ten to midnight, a taxi driver got punched by a passenger he'd picked up from the taxi rank outside the railway station and he was dropping off in Acomb near the Baptist Church. The passenger then cleared off without paying – the driver didn't see where he went but said he was wearing a grey shell suit top, was about six feet tall, around thirty years old and had a short-trimmed beard. So far we've not been able to find him on any CCTV footage. Again, if anyone can help us identify him, that would be much appreciated.'

'Skin colour?' Paul licked his pencil, waiting for the answer.

'White, sorry. Finally, we have a shoplifting and hate crime committed a couple of afternoons ago in the Heworth area – an Asian shop owner set on by two lads in their late teens. He caught them stealing some cans of lager and when he confronted them, they abused him, kicked him, and ran off. He'd never seen them before. We do have some half-decent CCTV footage of this one. It's on this memory stick here.'

Paul took the device she slid across the desk and secured it beneath the elastic band. He should be able to get a couple of screen grabs to print in the paper. 'No problem. Anything else?'

'That's about it for this week. Oh, I nearly forgot. With Bonfire Night coming up, I'd be grateful if you could mention to your readers to exercise caution with bonfires. We've already had a couple set alight by troublemakers. We're having a clampdown on anti-social behaviour, particularly when it's linked to fireworks, so if any young hooligan is thinking of getting up to mischief with a pocket full of bangers, they can think again. According to this memo I've got, we'll come down on them like a ton of bricks.' She pulled a face. 'If we can find the bricks, that is,' she whispered, putting her finger to her lips.

'Thanks – new appeal from York Police – need a ton of bricks,' he said as he pretended to write it down. Karen chuckled.

Paul drained the rest of his coffee. 'So, no usual juicy international diamond heists in Dringhouses? No great train robberies on the York to Harrogate line or thefts of the *Mona Lisa* from the Woodthorpe area this week then?' he asked, the joke clear in his voice.

Karen burst out laughing. 'More likely, the nearest thing we'll get is someone claiming to their insurance company that they've had a *Mona Lisa* stolen. This is York we're talking about.'

Paul grinned. 'Well, we can all dream about a change from the monotony. See you next week, same time. Thanks for the update, Karen.'

* * * *

November the Fifth. The public displays had been and gone much earlier in the evening and the children, along with a fair number of their parents, were all now safely tucked up in bed.

The air was heavy with the smell of wood smoke. With it came a mist that seemed to cling to the streets and linger in the damp, dark air by the river. It was half-past eleven, and the skies had fallen black, but not completely silent. As ever on this night, there were always plenty of thoughtless individuals who had no issue with letting off rockets this late, and the darkness and quiet would occasionally be punctuated by a loud bang followed by a colourful sputtering shower.

Selfish gits, thought the lone figure standing in West Bank Park. Waking up little kids and frightening animals this late at night. What a city of stupid knobheads. Still… The figure smiled. It's working in my favour.

The dying cascades of sparks tumbling and burning out against the black backdrop were an extremely welcome diversion from what was now planned to happen. The occasional crackles and explosions in the sky were the very reason this specific night had been chosen, the first night, the inaugural act no less. In a night filled with what seemed a million bangs, one extra wasn't going to stand out.

A statue of Queen Victoria stood in a half-forgotten corner of West Bank Park against a hedge and surrounded on three sides by dense greenery comprising privet and cotoneaster. In the darkness, she was almost invisible. Nature had been a cruel custodian, and the years had garlanded her with moss and lichens and the pigeons had crowned her to the point where her identity could almost be in question. After an attempt at restoration and cleaning to her former glory some years ago, the moss and the pigeons had simply returned with increased fervour.

Standing carefully so as not to touch the stone plinth, the lone figure contemplated the billowing cloud of expelled breath, which ballooned grey in front of their face before dissipating into the smoky mist. The gaps between the explosions grew longer, allowing the normal nocturnal sounds to return: the distant rumble of a car, an owl calling out, and the rustle of nearby leaves. It was, however, the approaching sound of a dog and faint footsteps, which caught the figure's attention.

Around the stonework, what paucity of light pierced through the canopy of greenery shone in lines, as if trapped within the thin veil of fog. The approaching silhouette came into view, hazy and frayed at the edges, but definable. Slowly, the figure's hand reached within its clothing and removed a pistol. It was rather plain looking, the barrel just a little longer than you would typically expect, giving it the appearance of something out of a cosplayer's Dieselpunk collection or a movie prop from an apocalypse film. However, the merit of this particular gun wasn't in its looks but in its specific design to quietly kill.

The footsteps of the approaching individual and the dog grew louder. In the faint light, the silhouette transformed, and the features of a man grew out of the darkness. Both he and his Pekingese were enjoying the now relative peace and the cool night air.

The next moments contained a myriad of variations that had been mentally well-rehearsed like all the possible openings of a chess game. Maybe two bullets were going to be necessary, one for the man, that pillock of a man, and one for the dog if it got yappy. The plan was to make the least noise, but what would be would be. The gun had not earned the nickname "Hush Puppy" by Special Forces for nothing. Its ability to remove awkward guard dogs during clandestine operations was legendary.

A quick look round ensured they were alone and now the scene was set. The movement from the side of the statue momentarily startled both dog and man. There was no sound from either.

There was a "pop" and with that, the task was completed, simply and efficiently.

Unlike in films where people who are shot fly backwards, arms flailing, in reality they simply crumple and fall. As the body landed, there was a slight thud as his head hit the ground. It is doubtful there would have been any feeling. The dog's lead was now trapped under the man's right hip and the Pekingese jumped anxiously onto the man's chest. Luckily for itself, it didn't bark.

A flood of relief flushed the adrenalin away as the gun was carefully returned to inside the clothing. A swift check was conducted to ensure nothing had been left behind and, with the same attention to detail taken on arrival, the figure left.

A growing pool of blood emerged from beneath the dead man's body and like the swiftly disappearing shadow, it would be swallowed by the darkness.

Chapter 2

On his brief but tense journey from Dunnington village on the outskirts of York, Detective Inspector Gene Garland had driven briskly along a series of quiet roads and streets. Despite years of making such early starts to the day, as he passed houses with the upstairs curtains still snugly closed, he felt envious of their inhabitants.

Parking on the road which ran along the north side of West Bank Park, he jumped out of the car with a determined, athletic vigour that belied both his age and the inhospitable hour of morning, and entered the park through the rather macabre-looking wrought-iron gates that would have looked perfectly in place at the entrance to the Addams Family drive. The gateway was now strikingly adorned with crime scene tape which fluttered in the icy air, and a uniformed officer stood guard. Pulling the zip of his trademark black military combat jacket up further against the cold, he nodded a brief good morning to the officer on the gate and thrust his hands into his pockets to keep the blood circulating. He normally took a dim view of people walking around with their hands in their pockets, believing it looked slovenly – an attitude he'd acquired from a very young age from his father, God bless him, who had proudly served in the Royal Artillery.

Entering the park, he felt as though he were passing through some kind of liminal space: a portal between two separate worlds through the back of the wardrobe into some grotesque, dystopian Narnia. Disappearing behind him lay the safe and predictable world of normality, street lighting, comfortable houses, and innocent people with routine lives. Ahead of him lay another world which thankfully few members of the public got to see: a world of darkness, corpses, blood, and violence.

Any last vestiges of drowsiness evaporated as he turned the corner of the hedge by the children's play area which was still shrouded in darkness. The sight that confronted him brought his senses fully to life with his blood flowing and brain charged into action.

Under the light of the temporary illumination beside the white crime scene tent, he could pick out some faces of a few colleagues who had already arrived and who were busy pulling on the traditional forensic coveralls. He exchanged a brief good morning with them. He took a paper suit for himself with a polite nod of thanks and cursed mildly under his breath as he wrestled it on. Turning to the left-hand side of where Queen Victoria stared onto the white crime scene tent, he spied DC Parkinson who had just been tying a friendly and exuberant Pekingese dog to a nearby tree whilst simultaneously trying to look at something on her mobile. She shoved the phone in her pocket as Gene approached.

'Hi, Parkinson, I thought I recognised your Nissan Juke parked up on the road outside.'

'Yes, boss, I don't live too far from here, so I got here quick quickly.' She turned slightly away from the harsh glare of one of the lights. 'Looks like a shooting, boss. A lady walking her dog this morning found him about half an hour ago. She's being interviewed in one of our vans at the moment.'

Gene scratched his nose and wondered, not for the first time, how dead bodies would ever be discovered if not for people taking their dogs for a walk. Dog walkers in Britain found everything – corpses, World Cups, you name it. He recalled there had even been a picture on Facebook recently where some poor woman's Labrador had unearthed a discarded, luminous turquoise sex toy and refused to let it go from its mouth until it had been well and truly chewed.

'Do we know anything about the victim?'

'According to the contents of his wallet, his name is Alec Hopkins. Aged sixty-one. Lived alone on the road at the bottom of the park with his dog. That's all we know so far until we pull together a full profile on him.'

Gene Garland looked across at the crime scene tent. He would need to consult with the forensic pathologist as soon as he'd finished speaking with DC Parkinson. As much as he found the job unpleasant at a time like this, he prided himself on his rigorous attention to detail at crime scenes.

'I'll get a house search and some door-to-door organised this morning. Anything else about him yet?'

'Just one other thing so far,' said Karen. 'A quick background check revealed a conviction for a DR10 in 2003. Had a crash and the other party was hospitalised for a while.'

'Hmm. Drunk driving causing serious injury.' Gene frowned. 'What is it with people who don't have the self-discipline to watch what they drink before risking their own lives and others? Check who the victim was and where they were last night. Seems a long shot, but some people can carry a grudge for a very long time, so let's keep an open mind. We need to see where the evidence takes us. Anything else?'

'Not at the moment, boss.'

'OK, thank you, Parkinson. I'll talk to some of the others now and get a thorough fingertip search of the park underway.'

Their conversation was broken by the appearance of the forensic pathologist, Adrian "Jack" Horner, from out of the tent. Gene looked up. Jack never appeared sedately with dignified deportment, but always seemed to announce his arrival with a burst of energy like a showgirl erupting out of a Hollywood birthday cake.

'Well, a very good morning, DI Garland,' he beamed, looking far too awake and buoyant in Garland's opinion for this cold hour of the morning. 'How are things?' Without pausing for breath or a reply, he continued, 'Well, it looks pretty clear to me. Single bullet shot to the chest from the front went clean into the heart between the second and third rib. We'll recover the bullet for forensics when I get the poor old chap on my table. I'm not a ballistics expert, so you'll have to talk to the boffins about that, but from the characteristics of the entrance wound I can see, I would say it will be a small, low-velocity handgun round. I expect the bullet will be still lodged in there somewhere. As you'll see, though, it still made rather a bloody mess. Come and peek through the flap now you're suited up.' He shooed Garland towards the tent with the almost abnormal enthusiasm of a child wanting to show off a new toy to his friends.

Garland raised his hand to shield his face from the tent flap as Jack burst through in front of him. 'Time of death?'

'From the temperature measurements I've taken,' he replied, 'I'd say it was some time around midnight. I've taken care not to disturb the body too much, but without even touching him I can see there's some rigor mortis developing in his face.'

With a sweep of his hand, he gestured at the victim's grim, cadaverous face, which gazed blankly up at the roof of the tent with a macabre rictus grin. 'One of the technicians has already taken plenty of photographs for you.'

'I see what you mean, Jack,' muttered Garland, looking down at the body from the entrance to the tent. 'Anything else?'

'I've noted some livor mortis, too. That's when the blood stops being pumped round and settles to the bottom of the body. You see it as a purplish discolouration to the skin. As you can see, I didn't want to start disturbing a lot of clothing right now. I'll remove the clothes properly back at the mortuary but from here I can clearly see the giveaway colour on his hands which supports the fact that death was between five and eight hours ago. It all depends on outside temperature too and it was cold but not freezing last night.'

'Any other injuries?'

'Looks like he cracked his head on the ground with quite a wallop when he hit the deck, but otherwise, no. No other marks that I can see, no frenzied stab wounds or anything like that. And from the position of the livor mortis on his hands, I'd say the body's not been moved. I've taken some fingernail scrapings for the forensic team, but I can't see any obvious evidence of any physical contact. I'd say he was simply shot where he fell. Can't see any gunshot residue on his clothing with the naked eye, but I reckon he was still probably shot at quite close range. Your forensics guys will be in a better position to inform you all about that. Obviously, I'll be able to tell you more myself when I've had a proper look at your old fellow on my table.'

'Thanks, Jack,' responded Garland earnestly. 'You know I appreciate this.'

Garland held the tent flap open for Horner as he stepped back out into the cold damp air and then turned towards the statue and looked up at its stony visage. 'Come on then, Your Majesty,' he pleaded aloud to Queen Victoria. 'It looks like you're one of only two witnesses.' He glanced down. 'You and this dog here.' The little Peke just looked back across at him with an inscrutable gaze and gave a short, solitary bark, and

Queen Victoria simply continued to glare down on the scene with her unaltered stare.

'Well, she's certainly not amused, is she?' Jack Horner started to peel off his coveralls. 'Oh, by the way, Gene, before I go. Are you still coming to the football match when York next play at home?'

'Yes, I was certainly intending to,' replied Garland, still slightly amazed even after all the years in his career that a pathologist could switch seamlessly from examining a freshly murdered corpse to nattering about football.

'I'll give you a call during the week and we'll arrange something. Unless you want to come to this chap's post-mortem, and we'll arrange it then. You're cordially invited, as always. I'll even arrange coffee and chocolate digestives, your favourite. Can't say fairer than that.'

Garland smiled and raised his hand in a gentle denial. Post-mortems were not his thing, and Jack knew it. 'It's OK, thanks.'

'Take care, old pal. Good luck with everything and remember, I'm only a phone call away.' Jack slapped him warmly on the shoulder, gave a brief smile, picked up his case, and strode away from Garland, out of the park and back into the normal and predictable world.

Chapter 3

The morning had started just like every other recent day for Paul Dobson. The cheap radio alarm roused him from his unsettled sleep – he still wasn't completely accustomed to the sound of traffic so close to his windows. This was followed by an almost somnambulistic traipse across the hall into the little kitchen to put the kettle on. It wasn't a long walk.

While the water was coming to the boil, Paul continued his well-perfected morning routine. Squeezing past the clothes horse, which was full of his damp clothes, he stepped into the bathroom. 'Oh, how the mighty have fallen,' he muttered to the world-weary reflection in the mirror above the washbasin. In the bedroom of his previous house, a rather spacious well-to-do three-bedroom detached in the nearby scenic village of Nether Poppleton, there had been a convenient en suite attached to the master bedroom. He considered the irony that it had actually been a longer walk from the bed to the en suite in his old house than the walk from his bed to the separate bathroom in the new one.

How had the letting agent described this one? Deceptively compact? Something like that. Still, it was clean, presentable, convenient for work, and above all, it was affordable while he got the issues in his personal life sorted out.

Turning on the shower to produce its decidedly unenthusiastic spray of water, he'd learnt from experience not to step into it straight away, but to give it a good couple of minutes to heat up to something tolerably above lukewarm. Hearing the kettle click off in the kitchen was his usual cue that sufficient time had elapsed, so he took off the old T-shirt and boxer shorts he used as nightwear and stepped into the bath under the showerhead. Just as he'd got nicely soaked and lathered up, he heard his mobile ringing on his bedside table.

Despite his frustration, he shook his head and smiled. This kind of thing had happened to him so often that in the York Press offices he'd unintentionally become the creator of what his colleagues dubbed his eponymous "Dobson's Law", which states that a mobile phone which has lain silent for hours will immediately ring when you've left it behind in another room.

Trying to rub the shower gel from his eyes without making them sting, he padded his way back to the bedroom, his feet flapping on the floor like a bedraggled penguin as he tried to get to the phone before it stopped ringing. He saw with surprise that it was DC Karen Parkinson's name on the display.

'Karen. Hi there. This is a surprise. What's going on?'

'Good morning Paul. Just thought I'd let you know your parting wish from our meeting earlier this week has come true.'

'I'm sorry?'

'I couldn't arrange a jewel heist or a train robbery or a *Mona Lisa* for you, but will a cold-blooded shooting in a York park do?'

'What?' Paul quickly tried to gather his thoughts. 'No way. Seriously?'

'I thought I'd give you a call because we're probably going to need the press's support on this, and I knew you'd like to hear it from me first. There's not much I'm cleared to tell you right now, but I know I can trust you and I'm allowed to reveal some details. It was late last night in West Bank Park. Sixty-one-year-old gentleman shot in the chest. He lives locally. The park is still taped off and people are starting to wake up and are walking and driving past, so before long people are going to know that something is up, anyway.'

'Any idea of a suspect or motive for it?'

'Sorry, Paul, I can't comment on that yet, but I promise you, I'll let you know more as soon as I can.'

'Thanks,' replied Paul. Anything I can do to help, let me know. Should I call in and see you? Do you know at this stage if there will be a press conference?'

'There's no press conference planned,' responded Karen. 'and this morning I'm going to be in and out of briefing meetings, and then I'll probably get sent out to either do some door-to-door work or some follow-up enquiries. I'll call you later with anything more I can tell you. Wish me luck, I'm in for a busy day.'

'Good luck, and thanks again for letting me know so promptly. As ever, you know the Press will do all it can to help if you need requests from the public.'

With his head still swimming from Karen's call, Paul returned to the still-running shower, his mind in a whirl and his body still covered in lather, only to discover that in his absence the hot water had all gone, and the shower was running ice-cold.

* * * *

Incident Room 1 at York Police station had clearly been designed with spartan functionality in mind. At the front of the room was a flat-screen television which could be plugged into a laptop, and which was currently displaying the North Yorkshire Police logo and the time of 08:45. Beside the screen were two large whiteboards, upon one of which several photos were already attached. Garland's team filed in clutching their notepads and pens. There was an animated buzz of conversation in the air.

‘OK, keep the chatter down in this room,’ DI Gene Garland called out. Since his early start, he’d managed to grab a quick shave with the electric razor he kept in a drawer in his desk and had squeezed in a hurried spruce-up. He ran his fingers through his short flat-top hair.

‘Thanks all for being prompt,’ he continued as they each sat down in one of the equally utilitarian meeting room chairs. ‘So, folks, this is what we know so far. The victim was found several feet in front of the Queen Victoria statue in West Bank Park.’ He indicated several photographs on the whiteboard and with a wiggle and click of the mouse on his laptop, brought one of them up onto the television screen.

‘He’s Alec Hopkins, a sixty-one-year-old man who lived alone just a couple of hundred metres from the bottom of the park. He was born in Selby, then moved here in 1980 when he got a job at what then, for those of you old enough to remember it, was called British Rail. After that, he got a job as a manager in the accounts department for a local building contractor and spent the next twenty years there working his way up to finance director. Did very well too and took early retirement last year. DC Palmer’ – he gestured towards a young man in jeans and a casual jacket standing by the window – ‘can you get in touch with his ex-employers? The details are in the file. Find out whatever you can about his employment, any reason for a colleague to hold a grudge, and so on, and see if they know of any surviving family and follow that up.’

‘I’m on it, boss.’ Palmer made a note.

‘The pathologist at the scene revealed a gunshot wound to the heart from close range. The cause of death will be confirmed at the post-mortem but I believe it will be a direct result of being shot. No evidence of moving or tampering with the body.

Estimated time of death is around midnight. The post-mortem is later this morning, and we'll learn more then. DS Jamshedji,' he nodded towards a studious-looking man in a crisp suit and striped cotton shirt. 'I'd like you to do the honour of attending.'

The officers in the room exchanged sly smiles with each other. They loved and respected DI Garland dearly, but his aversion to attending post-mortems was legendary. Garland continued.

'The body was found this morning by a Mrs Alison Hill who was taking her Cocker Spaniel for an early morning walk round the park at around quarter to six. She found the body lying in a pool of congealed blood and called 999 straight away. She didn't know the victim and unfortunately doesn't seem to have anything more to add. One thing we do know about the victim is that back in 2003, he had a conviction for drink driving. He crashed and put another driver in hospital. Probably unrelated, but let's not rule anything out. DC Parkinson, I'd like you to track down the other party with DC Snow and interview them, please.'

In the corner of the room, Karen nodded and smiled across to DC Dave Snow, an affable and intelligent young detective with whom Karen got on well, save for what she considered his appalling taste in heavy metal music.

'I'm expecting there to be a bullet retrieved at the post-mortem which should go straight off to ballistics and I will be chasing a report back on that as soon as possible. DC Ward and DC Goodier, I want you two to attend a forensic visit to the victim's property this morning, his address is in the file, and follow up with house-to-house interviews in the area. There's no CCTV whatsoever in the park, but if we're lucky, a house in the neighbourhood might have one for security and if so, maybe one of them picked something up, so please check that out, thanks. If not, work outwards from the park to see if any cameras have picked up anyone approaching or leaving the area.' The two of them looked at each other, gave a thumbs-up, and nodded.

'A fingertip search of the scene this morning is still ongoing but has so far revealed nothing, save for a till receipt which was found under a nearby bush for a recent purchase at a corner shop. I'd be amazed if it was connected to this, but DC Portland, you can check it out. They may even have some CCTV footage from the time and date of purchase if they've not erased it yet. You will also all want to take note of what we didn't find. There was no spent ammo casing found at the crime scene. Nor have we been able to get any footprints and so far we've not found any DNA evidence or fibres.

DC Hayward, I'd like you to do some more digging around into the victim's life and background, look into his personal affairs and financial transactions, his bank statements and phone records, and consult our HOLMES database to see if anything else significant shows up. Anybody got any questions or thoughts you want to share at this stage?'

His eyes alighted on DS Jamshedji again. 'Dattaram, you look thoughtful. Penny for them?'

'My first line of thought,' mused DS Jamshedji, 'was whether the victim had deliberately come to meet his killer in a pre-arranged meeting or was just in the wrong place at the wrong time. That's two very different scenarios.'

'Yes, that's bugging me too. The statistics say that only a fifth of male victims are killed by strangers, but then again, not many murders are shootings in a public park. We need to see what digging into his background throws up, so let's all crack on with that as fast as possible.' Garland scanned the silent faces, deeply aware that there was a sense of foreboding lying heavily across the room about this one. No apparent motive, a killer that vanished into the night without leaving a trace, and the only witnesses were a stone statue and a dog.

'Come on, you're a great team and I've got real faith in you,' he said in an attempt to motivate the room. 'I know this is going to be a tough one, but we're off to a good start.'

Everyone picked up their things and filed out of the room. On her way back to her desk, DC Karen Parkinson called into the ladies' toilets down the corridor. Inside the cubicle, she checked her phone, which she'd turned to silent for the briefing, and frowned at the missed call.

* * * *

Right at that moment, DC Parkinson wasn't the only one looking at her phone. Paul Dobson's stroll back up Walmgate from the sandwich shop where he'd called in to purchase his morning's bacon sandwich had been interrupted by a jingle from his pocket, informing him of an incoming email. Fumbling with his half-eaten sandwich as he retrieved his phone, he swiped his slightly greasy finger up the screen to read the contents.

Let's have fun; look out for my rhyme
Can anyone solve the race against time
to get there before me to the scene of a crime?

He froze to the spot for a second. The sender's email address wasn't one he recognised. He gave the screen another look before decisively stuffing the phone back into his pocket, shaking his head, and walking on.

Crank emails now. Just what I need, he thought as he entered the inviting warmth of the York Press offices and bounded up the stairs to his desk.

Chapter 4

The rest of Paul's morning kept him occupied. Karen had called him again, giving some more details. The victim's identity had been released after York Police had informed his only known family, an estranged son. West Bank Park had not reopened and so Paul had been forced to resort to finding some old library photos of the Queen Victoria statue in the press photo library for his article. That weird, crank email was best put to one side. *What the hell was the matter with some perverse folk?*

From his window, he casually observed the comings and goings of the citizens in the street below, carrying their shopping bags and occasionally entering and leaving the barber's shop and fast-food takeaway opposite. He rubbed his temples with his knuckles to try to relieve a cracking headache which two paracetamol and two ibuprofens hadn't even touched. Checking the time in the bottom right-hand corner of his laptop screen revealed that it was now quarter to one, which meant that according to the instructions on the packets of tablets, he could look forward to swallowing some more in half-an-hour's time. With a sigh, he remembered that there was also the issue of the depressing manila envelope which was awaiting his attention on his coffee table back home. He told himself he needed to stop procrastinating over its contents and so made a resolution to do something about it as soon as he felt mentally up to the effort.

His headache-distracted reverie was temporarily broken by the appearance of Sue Webb, the office manager, along with her accompanying strong waft of perfume into his office. The smell always seemed to forge ahead of wherever she was going to announce her imminent arrival. 'Hi there, Paul. How's it all going today?'

'Well,' replied Paul, 'I've certainly known less eventful mornings. I didn't expect all this would be going on.' He waved his hand at his laptop screen. 'I've just about finished writing up this article about last night's murder. What do you think? I wondered if it sounded a bit too dry and bland. It's times like this that I envy our sports writers being allowed at least some florid artistic licence – last week one of them even managed to crowbar a passage from Tennyson's "The Charge of the Light Brigade" into his copy. And to top it all, it was an article about a snooker match.'

Sue started giggling. She came round to his side of the desk to read the screen. 'Trust me, it looks great. Now, what's not so great are these.' She held up one of the packets of paracetamol accusingly. 'Are you sure you're OK?'

'I'll be fine. A couple more coffees and I'll be back on top of my tree.'

'Well, I'll go make you one specially now,' responded Sue brightly. 'Frankly, you look like you need a Jack Daniels and a lie down in a corner. Anyway, I just called by to remind you to make sure your weekly expense form goes in. You know what they're like in accounts. Now, about that drink…'

Plucking Paul's prized *Vulcan Bomber* mug from his desk, she gave him a friendly smile and turned round to head off to the staff kitchen. As she did so, she bumped straight into Jane, one of the York Press photographers, who happened to be walking past holding a handful of papers which were scattered to the floor in the collision.

'Oh, good grief. So sorry, Jane, didn't see you there. You're not hurt, are you?'

'No, I'm fine, I'm fine.'

'I'm not doing very well this morning. Let me pick these up for you. Oh dear, so sorry.'

'It's all right, it's all right, honestly, I can—'

From the doorway, Sue and Jane's flustering conversation was immediately truncated and their heads both snapped round at the sound of Paul's loud exclamation: 'Well bloody hell fire.' Rising up from behind his desk, he ran both his hands in a distraught fashion over his hair.

* * * *

DC Karen Parkinson parked up at the side of the road behind a navy-blue Mercedes, put the handbrake on, and turned off the car stereo.

'Thank God for that.' DC Dave Snow, in the passenger seat, let out a long-protracted exhalation and slumped in his seat. 'One more minute listening to Nicki Minaj or Rihanna and I'd have climbed out of this window. Seriously, I've been willing you to put your foot down and get here ever since we reached the outskirts of Harrogate.'

'Stop overreacting.' Karen grinned. 'Does it make it any better if I tell you I have no idea how they got onto my playlist? Anyway, I actually quite liked those songs.'

'That last song, whatever it was and by whoever it was, sounded like it's listened to by girls who nick stuff from car boot sales,' Dave moaned.

Karen laughed. Dave was only in his late twenties, just a few years younger than herself, and yet she knew his tastes in music were completely different. She'd seen a denim jacket of his embellished with a Whitesnake logo on the back when he'd worn it once to work. She did a quick mental calculation. If

"Fool For Your Loving" had been playing on the radio in the delivery room while Dave was being born, it would even back then have been on a "nostalgia" music station. She smiled across at him. 'Come on, let's get this interview done with and if it goes well, I'll see if I can find some AC/DC or Mötley Crüe to play on the way back if it makes you happy.'

* * * *

Gene Garland stared down at the blank A3 sheet of paper on his desk, retrieved a trusty black Sharpie pen from his top drawer, and set to work on what he always did in situations like this, which was to draw a mind map. It was a technique which had served him excellently for at least the last two decades. Pursing his lips, he carefully drew a large oval in the middle and neatly wrote "West Bank Park Murder – Alec Hopkins" in the middle.

He surveyed the paperwork in front of him which summarised the information he had got back so far. The initial ballistics report showed that the bullet was a hollow-point 9mm. Although no spent case had been left at the scene, the ballistics lab had done some very thorough work and the report indicated the bullet was probably fired from a Parabellum cartridge. Frustratingly for Garland, this didn't narrow things down much at all. It was one of the most popular types in the entire world, having been around so long it had actually been used in the First World War. It was a testament to its success and longevity that even to this day, about one in every four handgun rounds sold was a 9mm Parabellum and was used by just about every army and police force in the Western world. *Hell*, he thought, *even the British Police Force firearms unit's own Glocks fired them*. He meticulously drew a line on the mind map from out of the central bubble.

The full post-mortem results – he took a quick glance at his rugged G-Shock watch under the cuff of his white cotton shirt – would be along later that afternoon. He'd already spoken with DS Dattaram Jamshedji on his return to the station for a top line debriefing, who had confirmed the cause of death was from the gunshot wound. Jamshedji had smelled strongly of Vicks Vapo Rub, the giveaway sign of someone trying to stop the cocktail of post-mortem smells upsetting their stomach contents. Garland drew another line on the mind map.

The victim only had one surviving relative, a son who lived in Cumbria. Apparently, he'd not spoken to his father for twenty years following a family dispute when his mother died, and he hadn't appeared particularly distressed at the news about his death. Parkinson and Snow should now be on their way back from Harrogate where they'd been to talk to a Nigel Edgerton, the man who'd been hospitalised in Hopkins' drunken car crash. Garland had requested that swabs from Edgerton's fingers be taken in the unlikely off chance they might contain some gunshot residue and link him to the crime scene.

Garland turned his attention briefly back to his laptop screen to scroll through the photographs from his team's visit to Hopkins' house earlier that morning and frowned. Nothing of any great significance leaped out at him although he was experienced enough to know that what may at this stage of the investigation seem irrelevant might turn out later to be of importance. A photograph took pride of place on Hopkins' mantelpiece which depicted him in York railway station in front of a steam locomotive. Garland zoomed in a little on the photo and noted that the locomotive was called the Evening Star –

something to get one of the team to look up later. Hopkins was smiling, holding a bottle of wine in one hand whilst the other hand was employed in shaking hands with some worthy and official-looking gentleman. On Hopkins' coffee table had lain a recent magazine about military aircraft which had contained recent news on the Red Arrows display team and an article about the Blackburn Buccaneer in the 1991 Gulf war.

Frustratingly, it appeared that Hopkins enjoyed a technologically-free lifestyle. No computer had been found at his house and his only telephone seemed to be a landline, thus denying Garland and the digital forensics lab some potentially bounteous sources of his lifestyles, activities and contacts.

Gene's instincts had told him that the till receipt found under the bush looked like it was going to be unrelated to their case and indeed that had turned out to be the case. He still had a mountain of information for his team to sift through from the door-to-door enquiries, the victim's background, and whatever CCTV footage they could get in the area.

Replacing the cap carefully on his pen – he couldn't abide people who didn't put caps back on pens and tops back on bottles – he headed out of the stuffy building and over to the staff car park to get some fresh air and a can of Coke from the glove box of his car.

Leaning back against the car boot, the rear suspension squeaking and complaining slightly as he rested his middle-aged, but still quite muscular and healthy frame on it, he took a long refreshing swig of the Coke, which despite having been in his car all morning was still quite cold. Despite it only being early afternoon, the pale watery sun was already starting its descent over the adjacent York Garrison buildings, which he could see through the chain-link fence at the bottom of the car park.

Pulling the can away from his lips, he gazed at the garrison buildings and pondered for a moment the fact about the 9mm Parabellum being used by nearly every army in the Western world.

* * * *

'Well, that all went smoothly,' noted DC Dave Snow as they got back to Karen's car. 'I do believe we've deserved ourselves some AC/DC.'

'Go on then. I did agree to that didn't I? '

Karen eased herself into the driver's seat. The interview had gone well. Their interviewee, Nigel Edgerton, had seemingly, or so he said, not even remembered the name of the driver who had caused the car accident all those years ago and had told them he just wanted to put it all behind him. As a pleasant coincidence, his son, who'd been a teenager at the time, was now a police officer working for West Yorkshire Police in Leeds.

On the bypass, heading back to the A59, Dave settled back comfortably, turned up the volume on the stereo and started singing along in loud, off-key accompaniment to AC/DC's 'Thunderstruck'.

'Hang on,' shouted Karen. 'Call coming through.' Dave pulled a miserable face as Karen took the call and Paul Dobson's voice from out of the car speakers brought an end to Dave's raucous vocals and blistering air-guitar solo.

'Paul? Hi there, can you call me back? I'm in the car heading back into York. Can't really talk right now.'

'No, listen. Come straight to the York Press offices. There's something you have to see. It's urgent.'

* * * *

As Paul barked frantically down the phone to Karen from inside the York Press main meeting room, he and some of his colleagues sat round the central table, fixating their eyes on the screen of Paul's laptop which was displaying the contents of his latest email.

So that you have proof that I'm not one to jest
I know it was nine millimetres in the chest
Now, not in some park on the outskirts of town
But right in the dead centre is where the next one goes down

Chapter 5

The rest of Karen and Dave's journey had passed in anxious silence, save for one rather tense phone call to DI Garland. Karen pulled up to a jolting stop outside the York Press offices and was out of the car almost before the engine stopped turning. She and Dave were ushered to the meeting room where a serious-faced Paul introduced them to Sue, still radiating scent, and the very smartly dressed and, Karen thought, rather aptly named, Linda Reader, the editor. In the corner, a young fellow with a ginger mop of hair and sporting a Che Guevara T-shirt was introduced as Steve, the IT technician.

'So, just to confirm,' Karen summarised. 'Your work email address is in the public domain?'

'Yes,' confirmed Paul. 'It's on the York Press website.'

'And you've had no other dodgy-looking emails apart from these two?'

'No.'

'Nobody else received any emails, phone calls, letters, text messages, or anything else suspicious this morning?'

Everyone in the room shook their heads.

'It could be just some sad crank,' Karen said. 'You get them coming out of the woodwork at times like these. To be honest, I'm surprised you've not had any calls from spiritual mediums claiming to be able to solve the crime. We usually get dozens.' She gave a slight shake of her head, then continued, a serious tone entering her voice. 'I'm concerned about this email, though. There is mention of the calibre of bullet and where the victim was shot which, unless it was a lucky guess by a hoaxer, is something that only the killer would know. I'm therefore going to ask you all to keep it to yourselves. The last thing we want right now is to throw the city into a mad panic until we've checked it out further, and of course, none of this goes in the newspaper.'

'Yes, of course.' Linda nodded her agreement. 'I completely understand.'

'I had a look into the email headers,' said Steve, standing up and brushing some biscuit crumbs from Che Guevara's face. 'But I couldn't find any useful information in there. I can tell you it's come from an anonymous email account, and if the person using it is deliberately routing their internet traffic around the world to disguise their IP address, it's going to be impossible to trace it back to anywhere or anyone. It's how hackers and criminals who want to surf the Dark Web remain untraceable.'

'So it takes quite a bit of technical knowledge to do this?' prompted Karen.

'No, on the contrary,' Steve replied. 'Ten minutes of research and some basic IT knowledge would make you proficient enough. It's all very user-friendly point-and-click. You don't need any great technical skills at all. I could teach my twelve-year-old nephew to do it. In fact, knowing what twelve-year-olds are like these days, I wouldn't be surprised if he already knew.'

'Great,' said Karen. 'Not ideal. I'm sorry to say, Paul, I need to take your laptop with me. Our digital forensic team might have some tricks they can use to take Steve's discovery further.'

'Yes, fine,' said Paul. 'I was expecting you to say that.'

DC Snow bagged up the laptop as Karen continued.

'I'm looking at the name on the email address the sender has used, which is *test.article@...* Does the name or phrase "Test Article" mean anything to any of you?'

There was a shake of heads all round.

* * * *

Incident Room 1 was full for the second time that day as Gene Garland stepped up to the front and the background noise of murmured conversation died down to a silence.

'I know this has already been a long and eventful day, but there's been an important development on our case within the last hour.'

'Everything we have learned today is all now documented in the files so I need you all to endeavour to read through it. I want to use this time now to share something urgent with you.'

He pointed to an enlarged screenshot on the television screen at the front. 'It's an email received today by the crime correspondent, Paul Dobson, at the York Press. Some of you might have seen him in the waiting room when he comes in for his weekly briefing session with Karen.'

There were nods, but you could have heard a pin drop.

'We don't know if it's genuine or crank. But you can see the sender talks about a nine millimetre to the chest. This is significant because the calibre of the ammunition involved was 9mm but this fact has not been released to the public. So unless it's a completely lucky guess by a hoaxer, this is something that only the actual killer would know. We absolutely need to take this seriously.'

He gritted his teeth and paused for composure. It was days like this when he felt he earned his salary. His next set of decisions could literally mean life or death for an innocent person, and the crushing weight of that responsibility was pressing extremely heavily on him. He straightened his back, squared his shoulders, and continued.

'Dobson's laptop has been taken to our digital forensics' laboratory at Northallerton. For now, though, our early indication is that the sender has been very diligent in covering their tracks.

'I believe at this stage we should not let this information get out into the public domain. We have no concrete evidence yet that it's from our killer and I certainly don't want to send an entire city into meltdown on the basis of one email from a weirdo. I've also mandated a press blackout on it. What I've requested is an immediate, significant boost in both foot and car patrols in the city centre starting this evening. I want to maintain a highly visible police presence, particularly around the Coney Street, Parliament Street, and Davygate areas in the city centre.

'One more thing, which is absolutely critical. We need to get onto the council right away and make sure every single CCTV camera in that area is switched on and working. If any cameras are out of action, I want them fixing with urgent priority, and I mean fixing this afternoon if possible. I don't want a murder taking place in our city under the lens of a non-functioning camera. From the Place de l'Alma on the night of Princess Diana's accident to the camera outside Jeffrey Epstein's prison cell, history is already filling up with far too many "Significant Events Not Caught on Camera" and I absolutely do not intend this to be one of them. Are we all absolutely clear on that?'

* * * *

Well then, let's see what the night brings.

The shadow tiptoed gently around the front of the building and past four ornate stone columns that supported its mock-

Roman structure. Designed architecturally like a miniaturised replica of the Temple of Portunus in Rome in some bizarre, cosmopolitan attempt to bring some classic Mediterranean flair, its ill-fitting appearance looked as if it had been uprooted from a baking hot vineyard by a tornado like Dorothy and Toto in the *Wizard of Oz*, carried across Europe and the North Sea and unceremoniously dumped back down into a bitter, black, and drizzly Yorkshire night. It now sat here among some unkempt grass at the end of a line of trees. The building almost appeared to be missing a warm home, shivering in the cold.

The figure crept past the corner with the blue plaque on the wall. It was far too dark to make out any lettering, but the figure knew from previous visits it was dedicated to the building's architect, James Pigott Pritchett.

Pompous up-his-arse git with a pompous up-his-arse name. The figure smiled. For Christ's sake, it even sounds like a mixture of prig and prick. Sums up this city though to a tee, good and proper.

A quick pat of the pocket in the hoodie confirmed everything was in place and good to go. The black branches of the spidery trees around the building shook as a sudden, biting wind carrying the faint smell of the grimy, bug-filled pond round the back of the building stirred them to scratch the starless night sky.

Footsteps...

Excellent. Concentrate now.

In another tingling adrenaline burst, the figure gently removed the handgun and noticed that their hand wasn't trembling anywhere near as much as the first time.

For what seemed like an age, the advancing person was invisible against the dark backdrop of the row of foliage with only the irregular sounds of uneven, stumbling footsteps heralding their arrival. Then, in the very dim light, an outline came into view. It was staggering slightly, weaving from side to side through the fallen leaves up the path towards the building.

Come on, come on, hurry up you dozy tosser. I want to get this done.

Arriving in front of the building, it momentarily wobbled and paused to regain its balance. A stationary target.

The shadow slipped out of its place of concealment and onto the path. As with last time, the victim was oblivious to what was coming.

Pop.

The person's body folded. Another dull thud as they hit the floor.

Two down.

Chapter 6

Gene Garland had been brutally roused from his bed for the second morning in a row. It had been an anxious, disturbed night, and he felt he'd barely slept at all. When the call, just after six o'clock, stirred him from his fitful slumber with the news he'd been dreading, his heart had sunk. Now, his BMW drove through the almost deserted early morning route he'd driven a thousand times along Fulford Road, home to the police station, his regular place of work. This morning, though, he carried on past the police station, forking off into Cemetery Road, and through the wide entrance gates into York Cemetery.

The short road through the entrance was just comfortably wide enough for his car, which, tyres crunching on the fallen twigs, led him to the top of the cemetery through rows of headstones picked out in his dipped headlights. Up ahead, through the windscreen wipers, he could already see the glaring, white tent illuminated under strident electric lights. Behind the tent rose the stone columns that supported the classically styled façade of the Chapel of Rest. Shadows of bustling figures in forensic coveralls created a magic lantern display reminiscent of a Son et Lumière concert he'd once attended in the grounds of a stately home in France. Garland got out of the car and the side of his face was instantly greeted by a slap of cold, windy drizzle. He walked over, zipping his faithful black combat jacket right up to the top, and tucking his trusty old York City scarf round his neck.

DS Jamshedji had already arrived and was standing a few yards away, organising people in forensic coveralls into conducting a search. In among the thousands of thoughts racing through Gene's head, he couldn't help but marvel at how

Jamshedji managed to look so smart and crisp at this godforsaken hour.

'Same again, Jamshedji?'

'I'm afraid so, boss.' Dattaram Jamshedji looked glum. 'Seems like a carbon copy of the murder in West Bank Park. Jack Horner's been in the tent to view the victim, and from what I've learned it's just like the last one. Bullet at short range.'

'Found by a dog walker?' Gene could guess the answer before Jamshedji gave it. Who the bloody hell else in the world with any common sense would be walking through a cemetery at this god-awful hour of the morning in the piss-wet freezing drizzle?

'He's being interviewed in our van. The poor man got an awful fright.'

'Damn and bloody blast.' Gene kicked himself. For all his best efforts getting city centre patrols and CCTV cameras organised, it looked like the same killer had struck again, and in a location where the only witnesses were the stone angels atop the graves.

He called over to Horner who was trying to take whatever shelter he could underneath the entrance to the chapel while he reviewed some photographs on a large digital SLR camera. Horner looked up at Garland and Jamshedji and bounced over with jovial bonhomie.

'Morning all. Well, this is twice in a row I've seen you in the early hours of the morning, Gene. We really must stop meeting like this.'

'I wish. What did you find?'

'Well, the sight is unpleasant, but at least it's dry in the tent,' Jack said cheerily. 'We'll know more at the post-mortem, but from what I can see, it's just like the last time – low-velocity bullet to the chest, probably a hollow-point as before, as it's made a similar hole but didn't go through the torso. The body fell where it was shot. This time, our victim is a woman, about 165 centimetres in height…' He paused. 'Sorry, that's about five foot five inches in real money. She's about sixty years old, medium build. Forensics have taken her handbag to try to identify her, but she has this rather distinctive tattoo on the side of her neck which will help get her identified. We'll take her DNA, of course.' He held up the camera, the rear screen facing them, and used his other hand to try and shield it from the drizzle. 'Have a look at this photo.'

Garland and Jamshedji peered at the image of the victim's faded tattoo, which consisted of a black rose and a dagger with a snake coiled round it.

'So there we go, Gene. Same as last time, no sign of any struggle, no obvious signs of disturbance or tampering with the body. No other injuries. Time of death, again, sometime around midnight.'

They walked together round the corner of the chapel to try to find somewhere out of the wind to talk, and were hit by a biting drizzle. Gene pulled his scarf even more tightly round his neck.

'What is it, Gene? Something's up, I can tell.'

'This is between you and me, Jack, because it's not public knowledge yet and I don't want it to be. A reporter at the York Press received an email yesterday claiming to be from Alec Hopkins' killer. It warned us they would strike again and here we are the next morning with another dead body.'

Jack frowned. 'Oh. Bloody hell. Any other information in the email?'

‘That’s the whole crazy thing. The mail said that the next killing wouldn’t be on the outskirts, it would be, to use their words, “right in the dead centre” of York. So I’m thinking’ – he rubbed his eyeballs – ‘either the email can’t have been from the killer at all and was from some hoaxer, or the killer’s just played us for fools by deliberately diverting our attention to the wrong place.’

‘Oh no, no,’ said Jack. ‘No, not at all. From what I can see, the killer told you precisely where they would kill again and fulfilled the promise to the letter.’

‘Sorry?’

‘Look around you, Gene. Think about where we are.’ He straightened his right arm and swept it around over the hundreds of gravestones and stone crosses that surrounded them. ‘Where are we standing, if not indeed, pardon the pun, right in the *Dead Centre* of York? You get it?’

‘Oh Christ.’ Garland felt his stomach tie in a knot as the penny dropped and he considered the implication of what Jack had brought to his notice.

Jack’s face softened and he looked at Garland with a concerned expression on his face and briefly rested a hand on his shoulder.

‘Blame my warped sense of humour for being able to see the pun in the clue. Anyway, must crack on. I’ve got this morning to write up and then prepare for the old girl when she’s delivered for me and my table. I’ll report back as fast as I can. See you at the match, old lad, if you can make it. Take care.’

Jack gave Garland a friendly parting slap on the arm, then picked up his bag and strode off towards his car.

* * * *

Once again, Paul Dobson's day had started as a benign replica of all his other recent mornings. A short trot across to the kitchen to switch on the kettle, then head into the bathroom to turn on the shower and listen out for the sound of the kettle clicking off to alert him as to when it was warm enough to enter.

He climbed under the showerhead, hoping that the indifferent trickle of warm water might start his mojo working and he could try to align himself at one with the world. Just as he was fully lathered up, he heard the sounds of his mobile phone ringing on his bedside table. He scrambled hastily out of the shower, dripping wet, with a sudden memory of the film *Groundhog Day* in his head, and a heavy and sick feeling in his stomach.

* * * *

Garland pushed to the front of Incident Room 1 where a second whiteboard now accompanied the first. Even though it was now nine o'clock in the morning, he'd not had time to stop for a drink, let alone breakfast, since being summoned from his bed to the cemetery, and he was feeling decidedly not his best.

'OK, we've all been busy this morning, so the first thing I want to do is make this a chance for everybody to report back in turn to the group what they've learnt so far.' He cast his gaze over the assembled faces. 'So, let's go "round the horn." Jamshedji?'

'Just like the last one, boss, the fingertip search doesn't seem to have come up with anything. Like the Hopkins shooting, there was no spent ammo case recovered here either. We've taken some swabs from the victim at the scene but as before, we've not been able to find any other forensic evidence. The post-mortem is later on today if you'd like me to attend?'

'Yes, please. Palmer?'

'Door-to-door revealed the identity of the victim. She's Alice Morton, aged sixty-three, born in York, and lived round the corner from the cemetery near the allotments.'

The silence in the room reflected everyone's thoughts. The victim's house was only about a few hundred yards as the crow flew from the incident room in which they were now sitting. So close.

'She spent most of her life working as a sales assistant in various stores in the city centre, moved to Leeds in 1987 when her husband got a job there, but when he died ten years ago, she moved back.'

'OK, thanks. Goodier?'

'She's known to us, sir. Nothing huge, but there have been some incidents of rowdiness with neighbours – both when she lived in Leeds and since coming to York – following binges of alcohol. Sad, really.'

Garland furrowed his brow. A possible alcohol connection? 'Ward?'

'I've arranged in advance for any bullet retrieved from the post-mortem to go straight off to ballistics. I'll chase it up throughout the day. A very basic mobile phone, one of the really old fashioned flip-phone types, was found in her handbag so we can start looking at numbers in the contact list and any recent texts or phone calls.'

'OK thanks. Hayward?'

'No CCTV cameras anywhere near the scene, boss, and so far, we've not caught anyone on any footage who might be the killer. However, one of the cameras going up towards the city centre has caught images of someone who might be Alice walking down towards Fulford Road at around half-past eleven last night. If it is, it's the last known footage of her alive. Maybe she'd been drinking in town and was walking home.'

The thought ran through Gene's mind that if she'd stuck to the main, well-lit road, it would only have added another minute to her journey. He didn't dwell on it. 'DC Snow?'

'The dog walker's been interviewed, boss. Has a regular six o'clock walk through the cemetery with his Jack Russell come rain or shine. Found the body in front of the chapel. Other than that, I don't think he's had anything of particular value to add. It's all in the file.'

'Parkinson?'

'I've already spoken with the team and started entering information into HOLMES. So far, I've not found any direct connection with our first victim, and nothing jumps out yet about her life which would give anyone a motive for murder.'

'Thanks. Right, let's get on with what we still have to do. Top priority for me is to dig deeper into the backgrounds of both today's and yesterday's victims. Compare phone records and see if they've called each other or have any recently dialled number in common. Go through both their bank statements with a toothcomb. Find out where they went socially, where they went to school, even where they went to the dentist. I want you to be thorough and leave nothing unturned. Seriously, if they even attended the same pantomime at the same theatre ten years ago, I want to know about it."

His words were met with serious nods all round.

'Despite our best efforts at boosting up security and patrols in the city centre, it looks like our killer got one over on us. True to their word in the email, the location of the cemetery is indeed the *Dead Centre* of York. '

He paused to let the revelation sink in, which drew groans from a room of exasperated faces as the penny collectively dropped. He continued, 'Yes, I know, I know. Don't think I'm not kicking myself either. Paul Dobson's laptop is up at digital forensics. However, the latest news isn't great. It looks like the killer has completely covered their tracks in their emails as well. Apparently, it's not very difficult. The techniques are well known among hackers, internet criminals, and most branches of the security and armed services.'

As he considered his last sentence, he looked out of the rain-spattered windows onto the buildings of the army garrison next door.

* * * *

The words from Karen's phone call from his second consecutive interrupted shower played over and over again in Paul Dobson's mind throughout the morning. As with the day before, she'd not been in a position to divulge too much information, but that which she could had been shocking enough. His heart had sunk. The email had been genuine. A second person had been killed.

The laptop on his desk in front of him, which Steve had given him as a temporary replacement, was ancient and grindingly slow. Upon switching it on, it had decided it was the perfect moment to run a lengthy Windows update, which it had now been doing for over half an hour. As Paul waited, gritting his teeth in frustration, his mobile buzzed to inform him an email had arrived. He picked it up.

As he read the mail, a horrified shiver shot through his spine.

The path that winds up through the leaves and the twigs
Surely leads to the place that perplexes the pigs.
In front of the chapel, another lies dead.
What will be location three? Oh my word, I've just said.

Chapter 7

'Come on, people, quick as you can, please. Things to do.' Gene Garland was waiting impatiently at the front of the incident room as his team piled in for the second time that morning.

A part of him was exhausted, both body and mind having felt continuously pummelled since his early morning call, and yet strangely he'd never felt more energetic and alive. The next few minutes could be crucial.

'Shut the door please, Hayward. We've had another critical development. A new email to Dobson. This one arrived just half an hour ago. I need you all to take a close look at it here.' He gestured to the screen on the wall on which the latest email was projected. A murmur rippled round the room and Garland saw everybody crane forwards.

'Right. Now you've all seen it, I want to know your immediate thoughts, so whatever comes to mind I want you to call it out. You know the rules, but I'll repeat them, anyway. No suggestion, however off-piste, is to be ridiculed. No pulling rank. And we support each other as a team on this. Understood? OK, go.'

DC Goodier was first, a sporting and studious young man. Garland liked him, although, like most senior detectives, he worried about the effects of the job's relentless workload on the life of a family-oriented member of his team.

'I can see it's from the same email address as the last one and it also accurately describes the location of the killing at the cemetery with "the path that winds up through the leaves and the twigs" to the "front of the chapel". I don't believe this is a hoaxer.'

'I agree,' concurred Garland.

Garland knew he didn't have to remind a single person in the room of the now infamously disastrous debacle during the seventies in their neighbouring cities of Leeds and Bradford. This was an era when the hunt for the Yorkshire Ripper was seriously de-railed by the police barking up the wrong tree resulting from very credible letters and tapes they'd received from a hoaxer. Such certainty had been placed on their authenticity that the real killer was able to slip through the net to kill several more times. Such a waste of innocent life and such a humiliation. The real identity of the sender remained a mystery for decades until finally, advances in DNA technology allowed them to be traced to a north-eastern man who had sent them as a cruel prank and had nothing to do with the murders at all. Garland was determined not to make the same arrogant error, yet the evidence in front of him was chillingly compelling.

DC Portland shifted in his seat, stroked his trim dark beard briefly in thought, and spoke up. 'The killer is taunting us, boss. Getting an obvious kick from laughing at us and mocking us being one step behind.'

'Correct.' Garland nodded, recalling parallels with the hoax Ripper tapes. He could recall with clarity the mocking tones and the lilting Sunderland accent in the hoax tapes from his childhood years. "I see you've had no luck catching me". There had even been a telephone number for the public to ring and listen in the hope that someone could identify the voice. He had a flashback to being a young schoolboy sitting on the floor of the living room swooping his toy model of *Thunderbird 2* in the air, while his mother and father sat on the sofa, the handset of their Trimphone pressed between their ears while they listened.

He shook it out of his head and addressed the detectives. 'My advice is, however personal this gets, and it could get worse, do not under any circumstances take it personally. Keep a cool, rational head, and your judgement, however difficult.'

DC Palmer spoke up next. 'It suggests to me some kind of personality disorder. Maybe we should think about getting in a psychological profiler, if that's the case.'

'You're right,' agreed Garland, grateful for the comment and not offended in any way whatsoever that a younger, junior colleague might be suggesting to him how to do his job. This wasn't the time for standing on ceremony and in any case, this wasn't how he and his team delivered results. Unknown to Palmer, Garland had already been on the phone organising a forensic profiler that very morning.

'Any reason why the killer sent the mail to the York Press, boss?' asked DS Jamshedji. 'It seems a bit odd if the aim is to taunt the police.'

'I wondered that myself.' Garland put both his hands on his hips. 'The best I can suggest so far is that we just have a general-purpose email address here at the station, whereas Dobson's email address is specifically for him and is shown on the York Press website. Maybe the killer is angling for publicity. We shouldn't discount the possibility they have other, bigger ideas planned going forward, if we let the bastard get that far, which I don't intend to do.'

When DC Snow spoke, it was with an anxious tone in his voice. 'I'm reading that last line as a clear indication that the killer is going to strike again, and we know once that promise has been made, the murder won't be long in coming.'

'Exactly,' said Garland, his right index finger in the air. 'So, if we are going to act on this, we have little time. It could come as soon as tonight.'

He squared up his shoulders and took a breath.

‘OK, think about this. The first email talked about “solving rhymes” to “race against time to the scene of a crime”. The second email, in which the location was given in the verse. Then apply that thinking to this email.’

Sitting in the corner taking notes for herself, Karen Parkinson looked up and spoke. ‘The next killing, boss,’ she exclaimed eagerly. ‘It’s telling us that the location is hidden somewhere in the verse.’

‘Absolutely. I think the killer got a huge buzz out of telling us where they were next going to strike in the first email and then fell around laughing when we got it so wrong. So in this email, they’ve done it again.’

The silence in the room was broken only by the faint hum of one of the fluorescent lights as the detectives absorbed Garland’s words.

‘Let’s read that last line again.’ His hand smacked against the screen with a resounding crack. ‘‘What will be location three? Oh, my word, I’ve just said.’’ He cast his eyes over the sea of faces with a steely gaze. ‘Somewhere in that email the location of the next murder is hidden, and we have possibly only until tonight to find it before we have a third dead body. This is a direct challenge from the killer to us to crack the clue and get to the next location before they do.’

A frantic babble immediately broke out around the room. Gene Garland raised his hand quickly to restore silence.

‘What’s more, you can bet your last pound they won’t have made it easy. They won’t want us to crack it in time, so they’ll have made it tough and I can promise you this will be a serious intellectual challenge. I’ve arranged for a copy to be sent to each of you. It will be ready and waiting in your inboxes when you get back to your desks. I know you’re all investigating a hundred things already, but I want every one of you to spend serious, quality time looking at it. Give it your finest brain power and see if you can crack the killer's clue and get us one step ahead. I don't need to remind you of the time pressure on this one. If I'm right, the killer doesn't want to risk giving us too much time to crack it. We'll meet again back here at seventeen hundred hours to share ideas and brainstorm. Good luck.'

* * * *

Last out of the room, Garland returned to his office and seated himself behind his large wooden desk. Being a generally practical sort, his desk didn't contain much in the way of personal decoration. A postcard-sized photo frame containing a picture of his wife, his son, and his daughter sat in one corner next to a an old and lightly scuffed but otherwise well-preserved model of *Thunderbird 2* he used as a paperweight. Picking up *Thunderbird 2*, he turned it over and over in his hands as he concentrated on a printout of that email.

Chapter 8

DS Dattaram Jamshedji stood beside the post-mortem table that afternoon, his body bathed in the aroma of a foul combination of disinfectant and general, stomach-churning bodily unpleasantness. He took a sniff of the smear of Vicks VapoRub he'd rubbed on his top lip and wished that he'd not worn one of his best cotton shirts that day. He knew from experience the pervasive smell would even contaminate the blazer he'd carefully hung outside the door.

'Thanks for fitting this in so promptly. Gene asked me to tell you again he's ever so grateful.'

'Not a problem,' Jack replied across Alice Morton's body on the post-mortem slab. 'As you can see, I've already removed the clothing and bagged it. She wasn't one for wearing lots of jewellery – just a necklace with a crescent moon pendant on it which I've also bagged up for you. Now we can start on the interesting stuff'

Having carefully examined the cold, white body from all angles, taking several photographs in particular of the bullet entry wound, Jack had proceeded to take a blood sample and then open up her chest in the customary wide "Y" shape to expose the internal organs. Despite having attended many post-mortems, and barely twenty-four hours having elapsed since attending that of Alec Hopkins, Dattaram Jamshedji still grimaced as the scalpel went in.

'And here we are.' Jack Horner beamed triumphantly, grabbing some stainless-steel tweezers with a disposable-gloved index finger and thumb. Holding one of the lungs to one side to assist with access, he reached inside Alice's chest cavity.

Dattaram sniffed at his top lip a little more urgently and persuaded himself to lean forward.

'Got you.' Jack retrieved the tiny, blood-congealed bullet and dropped it into a metal kidney bowl with a loud clink. It was smaller than a blob of toothpaste, making it hard to imagine how it could have such a fatal effect. 'Well, I'm no ballistics expert, but for now I'm going to stand by my view this morning that it's your same killer, Dattaram. Not that I thought you really doubted that, anyway. I see you've already organised a courier to pick this up to run it round to your ballistics chaps and they should be able to tell you more.'

Jamshedji shook his head. 'Look, I know this is a bit unconventional, but Garland asked me if I could ask you another favour. But it's not to go any further.'

'Go on, I'm all ears.'

'We've had another email. We're not telling the public about it at this stage, but Garland wondered as you were so quick at deciphering the last one if you could let us know what you think about this one. We're convinced the killer has left a clue to the next location in it.' After fishing in the pockets of his chino trousers for the printout of the verse, he read it out while Jack continued to forage around among what looked to him like random, reddish-brown items of offal.

'Well, the only thing striking me as a medical chap is this word *perplex*. In medical terminology, the word plexus refers to a branching network, like a branching network of nerves or blood vessels. The reason we call this bit the solar plexus' – he pointed to the appropriate spot on the corpse in front of him – 'is because it's from the Buddhist or Hindu concept of this region of the torso being the centre of branches radiating as from the sun.'

He paused and shuffled, suddenly aware of being unsure of Jamshedji's religion and he became immediately embarrassed at the thought of explaining something Jamshedji possibly already knew better than himself.

Jamshedji, on the other hand, showed absolutely no offence whatsoever. In fact, he was keen to know more. 'Go on.'

'I believe it's from the Latin word meaning "braid",' Jack continued, rather relieved. '"Learn Latin." my parents told me, "it'll help you in medical school". Anyway, yes, so a literal translation of the phrase "per plexes" or "per plexus" would mean "by the braid" or "by the network."'

'Thank you.' Jamshedji had a pen in his hand and was furiously writing it down.

'They're just my first thoughts, mind. If I think of anything else, I'll let you know.'

He reached once more into the corpse, removed another lump of offal, and carried it over to the scales for an accurate measurement. Returning, he held it in front of Jamshedji's eyes. Jamshedji's brown brogues inadvertently backed away half a step onto the tiled floor.

'See this, Dattaram. This is her liver. Look at the state of it. Shouldn't look like this. It's been totally ravaged by years of alcohol consumption. It's a warning to us not to get addicted to the demon booze. Causes a lot of harm to us and unfortunately often to others, too.'

* * * *

DC Ward and DC Snow shook hands with the police constable standing at the end of Alice Morton's short driveway before donning disposable overshoes and thin nitrile gloves and entering through the paint-peeled front door. As he went through, Ward's head involuntarily drew back.

'Whoah, get a noseful of that! What a rank smell from in there. It reminds me of when I was in uniform and sometimes used to do the early patrols round the backs of the nightclubs and it stunk of stale cigarette smoke and age-old lager.'

Snow followed Ward into the hallway.

A couple of forensic officers were already in the untidy front room. One of them was equipped with a camera and was busy taking photographs from every angle prior to anything being removed for evidence. Atop the scuffed carpet in one corner, a pile of evidence boxes had been stacked on a space on the floor that wasn't already occupied by an empty beer can or cigarette packet. Ward and Snow briefly exchanged greetings with the forensic officers.

'How can people live like this?' muttered Ward irritably. 'Just look at it – all these empty cans of lager down by the sofa. Disgusting!'

Snow crouched down and took a closer look at one of the cans. 'Oranjeboom.' he observed. 'That's not a brand name I recognise.'

'It used to be very popular back in the eighties but you don't see too much of it now. They even used to have a TV campaign with a jingle "Oranjeboom, Oranjeboom, it's a lager, not a tune".'

Snow shook his head blankly.

'The tune was like the one they used for a popular detective show back then, what was it called? Oh yes, *Van der Valk*, that was it. Set in Amsterdam.'

'Sorry, I don't remember at all. I'm too young to remember either the advert or the detective programme.' As the words escaped Snow's lips, he realised he'd been undiplomatic towards his older colleague.

'Well,' remarked Ward drily, 'in any case we need to start looking around this place for anything that could suggest a motive for Alice's death. Oh, and if you find anything that you don't know what it is because you're too young, let's say for example, a *cassette player* or a *soap-on-a-rope* or a *typewriter* then make sure you ask this old fart to help you identify the *antique* in question.'

* * * *

Paul Dobson dropped down into the orange plastic canteen chair somewhat harder than he'd anticipated, with a loud noise that caused several nearby diners' heads to momentarily turn.

'Shush,' Karen said in mock-chiding tones. 'You're not supposed to be here. But I think you deserve at least a mug of tea and a bacon butty for coming in straight away. Red or brown?'

He rubbed his eyes. 'Sorry?'

'Sauce.'

'Oh, er, red. I was miles away.'

'Here you go.' She reached across to the table next to them and picked out the least-encrusted bottle of tomato ketchup. She dropped her voice to a hush. 'I haven't told you this yet, but DI Garland believes there is a cryptic clue to the next location in the email. Don't think I've not seen you in reception doing the *Private Eye* crossword, you know, us detectives are taught to be highly observant. I've also noticed you look a bit worn out. Are you OK?'

'I'll be fine. It's all been a bit hectic for me recently.'

'Garland's asked if you can come to his office when your stomach's full because he'd like to talk through how the press are going to handle this and what we might or might not want to say.'

'Yes, that's fine,' Paul responded. 'And thanks for the tea and butty. Does that mean I owe you a drink and a meal now?'

Karen grinned. 'Anything you say may be remembered and given in evidence.'

* * * *

Garland looked up from the papers on his desk as Karen knocked on the door. 'Paul Dobson to see you, boss.'

'Ah, thank you. Sit down. No, please stay, DC Parkinson, pull up a chair.'

Paul sat down, and from force of habit, pulled out his notepad with the trusty elastic band round it still in place. He blushed slightly at the sight of the memory stick Karen had given him still sticking out like a red and black plastic sore thumb. He quickly justified it to himself that he'd had a rather chaotic recent last couple of days to say the least.

Garland shook his hand in a firm but friendly grip and then leant back in his chair.

'Thanks for coming in so quickly. I really appreciate this. I'd like to ask for your cooperation in how the press handles this. Who knows about this third email apart from you and your editor?'

'Just Linda and me,' Paul replied. 'I didn't think anyone else needed to know. I just made my excuses and came round here as fast as I could.'

'Excellent. That's what I hoped you'd say. Now some good news, at least for you.' Garland leant forward in his chair. 'Our computer forensics guys pass on their thanks to you for giving them your email login details, which means they can now check out this email and any future ones without depriving you of your phone or any more laptops. But in return, we would appreciate some discretion on this latest email business.'

'I take it you're not going to go public on this?'

Garland picked his Sharpie pen off his desk and twirled it in his fingers a couple of times before speaking.

'I'm asking for a temporary blackout on this one. I don't want to go through all the bureaucracy of issuing a formal notice at this stage but will if I have to. I've already spoken with your editor, Linda, and we have come to a sensible understanding, and Karen here has assured me that I can trust you completely.'

Outside, the pale sun was already low in the sky and, as it shone weakly through the skeletal trees, Garland shifted slightly in his seat to look out through his office window. It wouldn't be long until darkness fell over the city and then the carnival could start at any time. He turned back to Paul.

'I've had to weigh up a very difficult balance. The last thing I want to do is cause un-necessary panic. If only we had a sample of handwriting or something more concrete to show then it may be different…'

A flourish of images of the hoax Yorkshire Ripper letters flashed through his mind. Garland was once again jerked back to when he was a young boy peering out of the rear window of his father's Ford Cortina on a drive into Leeds. One of the letters to the police had been posted on a large billboard by the roadside.

'If, and I mean if, then there would be some mileage in getting the public to help us identify this person. But we haven't got that, so all we risk is sending the city into an uncontrolled mass panic for no gain. Do you see where I'm coming from?'

Paul nodded solemnly. 'Of course.'

'But what I would like you to say, and I can't ask this enough, is that the press advises everyone, as a general piece of advice, to take extra care when out and about. In particular, to stay away from poorly-lit areas, not to go out late at night, and not go out alone if at all possible. It's a sensible precaution which I'd like to implement without causing hysteria.'

Garland placed his pen back on his desk. 'Now before you go, there is one last thing I wanted to speak with you about, but knowing Karen here, I'd be amazed if she hasn't already mentioned it.' He smiled in Karen's direction and her return of the smile was slightly nervous. 'She tells me you're a cryptic crossword buff. Now, I'm looking at the idea that the killer has deliberately left a cryptic clue to where the next murder will take place somewhere in that email. And I'm not too proud to ask for the help of anyone I think might be of value.' He waved his hand over his desk, upon which were several A4 pieces of paper with pen scribblings all over them. 'I've been trying for hours but can't find a bloody thing.'

He gazed down at several pieces of paper before picking a couple of them up, screwing them into a tight ball, and aiming them at the bin in the corner of the room. One of them hit the rim and bounced out onto the carpeted floor and lay there, looking up accusingly at them all.

The moment was broken by the staccato noise of Karen's personal mobile. 'Oh shit, sorry, I should have put it on silent.' She yanked the phone out of her pocket, silenced it with a brisk swipe of her finger, and shoved it back deep down in her pocket as fast as she could.

‘Best let you go. I’m sure your afternoon is going to be almost as busy as mine. Thanks for the help. And remember – if you work anything out, please get straight in touch.’ Garland shook Paul’s hand once more.

Karen escorted Paul back to the reception area to say farewell. As she walked back down the corridor, she stole a swift glance up at the wall clock and did a quick mental calculation. Maybe she could grab some time to attend to that phone call before the meeting with Garland at five.

Chapter 9

Garland drummed his fingers impatiently on the white gloss-painted window ledge of the incident room and stared out, the daylight now fading fast. Like King Canute trying to hold back the tide, he found himself mentally willing the impending darkness to ebb away. The fluorescent lights in the room were all on, no two of them emitting exactly the same shade of white, and one of them still giving off an irritating hum. A glance at his watch. Sixteen fifty-five.

One by one, his team filed in like students entering the classroom for a lesson. He smiled and acknowledged each person as they entered and waited until they were all sitting.

Good afternoon class. Today we're going to do differential calculus. Or the formation of oxbow lakes. Or French irregular verbs. If only.

Grabbing a whiteboard marker pen and holding it aloft, he lifted himself over from the window, glad to move away from the gathering darkness outside, and over to the large screen on the end wall which was displaying the latest email.

The path that winds up through the leaves and the twigs
Surely leads to the place that perplexes the pigs.
In front of the chapel, another lies dead.
What will be location three? Oh my word, I've just said.

'Thanks, team,' he called out. 'I want to hear every single idea no matter how off the wall. OK, who's going to start me off?'

DS Dattaram Jamshedji was first. Garland noticed that for the popular guy that he was, none of the rest of the team had chosen to sit immediately next to him this time, then he recalled where Jamshedji had returned from earlier that day and he understood.

'I picked Jack Horner's brains about it,' he said. 'And from his medical knowledge he noted that the word "perplexes" sounds like the Latin phrase "per plexus" meaning "by the braid" or "by the branching network"'.

'Great stuff,' Garland said, writing these phrases down on the whiteboard next to the screen. 'What could this suggest?'

Jamshedji continued. 'I googled York Braid but nothing obvious came up. But the idea of "network branching" has some strong possibilities, though. There's a spot where the River Ouse and the River Foss branch from each other just south of the city centre at the Blue Bridge. Although it's quite residential, there are some well-shaded, leafy areas where a killer could hide and get a shot in.'

He paused to adjust his shirt cuffs under his tailored serge blazer without getting his nose too close to the cotton fabric while he considered his next sentence.

'But to me, boss, the most obvious answer is in the branches of the railway lines. York is a railway town. The area to the west of the city centre is packed with a colossal network of railway lines. Not all of them are easy for members of the public to gain access to. But I looked on a map and there is one major branching network at Leeman Road Millennium Green. I went and checked it out and it would be the perfect spot for the killer. Nice green space where walkers come, plenty of trees to hide behind and muffle any noise, and very much in keeping with the two previous sites. And literally "by the branching network". Look. I took some photos.' He pulled out his iPhone, gave a couple of taps and a swipe with his finger, and passed it around the room. There were appreciative murmurs from the team. Jamshedji was absolutely right.

Garland noted it on the whiteboard. 'Superb work, Jamshedji. OK, excellent, off to a great start. What else have we got?'

DC Hayward consulted his notes. 'I've been looking at this word "pigs",' he said. 'Of course it's a derogatory word for the police, but I've been having a see if I could maybe read more into it. There are no pig farms near the centre, but there is a pub with the word "Hog" in its name. Most importantly, though, we have the street Swinegate right in the heart of the city. It would be a minor change in modus operandi for the killer, as it's a shopping street, but the pun on the name is just too strong to not mention it.'

'Good one.' Garland noted that down. The whiteboard was starting to fill up.

'And I also found out,' Hayward continued, 'that the symbol of the boar was used for the personal badge of Richard of York. According to Wikipedia, the boar may be a pun on the old Roman name for York: "Ebor". So anywhere with a Richard of York connection or displaying blatant Richard of York symbolism could be a possibility.'

More ink went on the whiteboard.

'And finally,' he concluded, 'I found out that the medieval city street The Shambles gets its name from an old word meaning "meat market". So in the fourteenth century, The Shambles would have been lined with pigs' carcasses.'

'This is absolutely top-class research. Thank you.' Garland's pen was writing furiously now. 'Portland, what have you come up with?'

'I couldn't make anything meaningful out of the message, boss,' answered DC Portland. 'But Ward and I have been having a think about the email address that the sender used: *test.article@...*We found that "test article" is a term used in industry for a prototype and could suggest the author might have used the email address for a dry run. We should put some feelers out to see if anyone in the force or the press has had any emails from it before.'

'Yes, I agree. Can you get onto that?' requested Garland, writing it up on the board.

'And one more thing,' DC Ward said. 'It looks like this term is used particularly in the aerospace and food production industries. It might have been through working at one of these places the killer has heard the term.'

'Excellent. Excellent.' Garland was writing furiously. 'DC Snow, have you got anything?'

Dave Snow reached into his jacket pocket and brought out a piece of A4 paper. 'I've been thinking about York being a Roman town and wondered if there was a Latin connection. I admit this one is way off, but I'll mention it, anyway.'

'Fine. All crazy ideas accepted.'

'I took the first syllable of the word "perplexes" which is "perp" – the abbreviation for perpetrator, well, not so much in Yorkshire just yet.' He raised his hands quickly in mock defence. 'But then again, most civvies probably pick up their crime terminology from American TV programmes. The wife used to love watching one called *CSI: Las Vegas*. It drove me mad.'

Garland smiled and nodded. 'Me too. Go on.'

'So if you use that as a marker for the next bit of the message and then say the next few words in Latin, running on a bit past the end of the line you get...hang on, it'll be better if I come up and write it down so you can see.'

He jumped up out of his chair and Garland proffered the whiteboard marker with which he wrote:

Perplexes the pigs. In front of the

PERP: Lex este p. ig. sin fronto f. te...

'Which, if you excuse a bit of clumsy grammar, translates from Latin as "Perp: The police are quietly ignorant if quickly and strongly I..."' He gave a bit of a shrug. 'Admittedly, I had to squeeze in some abbreviations, like "p" the abbreviation for "piano" which means "quietly" – although technically that's Italian rather than Latin – and "ig" – the abbreviation for "ignarus" and "f" for "forte". I had to massage it around a bit but then I fizzled out and didn't have time to see how the rest fitted together because we didn't do Latin at my secondary school and I had to use Google Translate but still—'

He broke off, aware that he was starting to ramble. His cheeks went slightly pink. Suddenly, the room broke out into a spontaneous ripple of applause.

'Superb work.' exclaimed Garland. 'It might sound like so much of a stretch we'll need some pain-relief gel for our muscles afterwards, but I'm impressed and convinced enough that I'm going to locate a Latin academic tonight to pick through this and see if they can shed any more light onto the rest of the translation if there is one.'

'Thank you, boss,' Snow said as he made his way back to his seat, hands slapping and punching his arm as he went.

'Any more for anymore? Goodier, you look like you have something on that pad of paper.'

'Not much,' replied Goodier, frowning. 'I tried taking the first letter of each word and just got a meaningless string that started TPTWUTTLATT. I then tried it backwards and still just got senseless nonsense. Then I thought about the phrase "I've just said" and wondered from that if the clue was to do with certain words in the poem that sound like other words.'

'I believe the technical term is a homonym,' Garland said. 'That's a really excellent idea. Did anything come out?'

'That's where I came unstuck. I identified "place", "leads", "chapel", "lies" and "what" as words in the poem that have identical sounding words with different meanings. "Place" could be "plaice", as in the fish, but there's no obvious location in York with a fishing connection strong enough to make that a clue. Then there's "Leeds" as in the city twenty miles down the A64. A "chappal" is a type of sandal, "lyes" are types of soap, and a "Watt" is a unit of power.'

As he was speaking, Garland studiously wrote down the words PLAICE, LEEDS, CHAPPAL, LYES, and WATT in large capitals.

'This is absolutely excellent stuff. Thank you, Goodier. Anybody else?'

Karen raised a finger. 'I might have something, boss.'

'Let's hear it please, DC Parkinson.'

'Well. You know Paul is a bit of a crossword expert? In some of our meetings I had a chat with him about it. I was curious to work out what all the clues had to do with some of the answers he'd come up with.'

Garland nodded solemnly, but around the rest of the room there were a few raised eyebrows which Garland made a deliberate point of ignoring.

'Well,' Karen continued, 'in the cryptic crossword world, words like "perplexes", "confuses", "muddles" and so on possibly point to the fact that the next word or words is an anagram. So I took the letters of the following words "the pigs" and tried to make anagrams of them. I'll write up what I got.'

Garland passed her the marker pen as she made her way to the front. On the remaining bit of space on the board, she wrote:

GET SHIP

PEG THIS

GET HIPS

Then she stood back so that everyone in the room could see.

'Looking at the first one, that could be a reference to the boats tied up on the river. To narrow it down, I looked in the rest of the poem to see if there was any reference to a specific name of a boat, but so far, I've not found one.'

'Maybe we can work it backwards,' suggested Garland. 'A couple of us can go out after this meeting, get the names of all the large craft tied up on the Ouse in York, and see if we can retrospectively fit any of them with some of the other words in the poem. Keep going.'

'There was a ship called the *HMS York*, but it looks like it was scrapped many years ago. Then we've got PEG THIS and I've been racking my brains trying to think of any large piece of fabric in York that could be hung, like a tapestry or a flag which is lying down and needs to be "pegged up" on a line. Alternatively, it could refer to the angling term for the point on a riverbank or side of a lake where you go fishing. There are a few possible sites. Here, boss.' She handed Garland a piece of paper upon which she'd written a list.

'Which then leaves us with GET HIPS. Now, I found a private hospital in York which has a reputation for doing hip replacements. You might know it, it's near the Forensic building and there's a large grassy area behind it, screened by trees which stretch all the way from the road down to the river. It would be an ideal spot for an assassination. And finally, there're hips as in Rose Hips. There's a spot near Naburn Lock, which is famous for rose hip picking. So, if you wanted to GET HIPS, that's where you'd go.' She sat back down to another round of congratulatory smiles, nods, and mutters of 'nice one.'

Garland smiled appreciatively. 'Can I just say that whatever happens tonight, I just want to let you know I'm proud of all your efforts and glad to have you in this team.' His eyes, looking around the room, caught the rapidly advancing wall clock, relentlessly counting away the seconds into the advancing night.

'Right then, before we leave this room, we still have some work to do. We need to tighten up who's going to be responsible for precisely what follow-up actions we need to take to protect the good innocent people of York.'

Turning towards the windows along the side of the incident room, he noticed it was already dark enough outside for him to see nothing through the window, merely his own worried reflection caught under the fluorescent lights looking anxiously back at him.

'We may not have much time.'

Chapter 10

It was the end of a long, exhausting day. After an early start, followed by a busy afternoon conducting Alice Morton's post-mortem, Jack Horner wasn't working late. Throwing on his coat, he headed straight out into the cold damp evening and, with a satisfying clunk of the car door, settled himself into the welcoming soft tan leather seats of his Audi. With a quick press of the ignition button, the engine roared into life and the soothing sounds of Ralph Vaughan Williams washed over him from the six stereo speakers. Time to head home to a comfortably padded armchair and relax with a fine glass of Scotch in front of his beloved and outrageously expensive hi-fi system. His one love – his one *remaining* love, he reminded himself – he'd painstakingly assembled over years to become his pride and joy. Despite being regarded as the life and soul of any party, in private, Jack felt he never really understood other humans, which was ironic given that he spent most of his working life looking around inside them. But you knew where you were with a good hi-fi, he thought.

Tonight, though, he had something pressing on his mind. Amends to be made, and he couldn't put his mind to rest until they were done.

Taking a diversion from his customary route home, the silver-grey Audi turned in the direction of Fulford Road. Continuing down, tapping his fingers on the steering wheel gently to the accompaniment of Vaughan Williams' *Pastoral Symphony*, he pulled up at the familiar gates of York Cemetery. He parked up at the roadside, pausing to regain his composure. The police tape had now all been removed from the entrance and the forensic tent and temporary lighting at the top of the slope long since dismantled, and the chapel now stood in complete darkness. He got out of his car and walked up through the same entrance gates which, just twelve hours earlier had seen him pass through to attend the body of poor, cold Alice Morton.

It was a couple of minutes' walk until he reached the spot he'd visited so many times. The distant street lamps washing over the gravestones with a foggy haze weren't strong enough for him to read the words on the headstone, but that didn't matter. He knew exactly what they said. He reverently squatted down and placed his right hand lovingly on the side of the stone.

'I'm so sorry I didn't stop to say hello to you this morning,' he whispered aloud. A slight lump came to his throat. 'I was rather taken with attending to business and in any case, I didn't want to make a fuss. So I did what I had to do and put a bit of a jovial front on.' He stifled a cough. 'I'm afraid that's what everyone expects. Nobody wants a morbid pathologist, do they?'

His voice was barely audible over the distant sound of the traffic on the main road. But he only needed one person to hear what he was saying. He gripped the side of the headstone.

'Forgive me for not stopping by. But you were in my mind all the time. I couldn't rest until I could come and make it right. I hope you understand.'

The tears pricked the corners of his eyes as he stood up slowly.

'But I'm making it right for you. Trust me, I'm making it right.'

* * * *

Garland stuck his read round the door. Karen was still engrossed in her computer screen. 'Working late again? I know you've not been with us long, but you're an absolute credit to the team already.'

'Thank you. I'm still ploughing my way through this mass of information to find something to connect these first two victims.'

Garland frowned. There was a heavy implication in the phrase *these first two* that Karen, like him, was expecting there to be at least a third. Possibly even tonight.

'Anything?'

'Sorry, boss. So far all I've got is that they had the same electricity supplier.'

Garland lowered himself into an empty swivel chair beside her, which emitted a small squeak as he did so, and he peered over at the name of the supplier on Karen's notepad. 'Same one as me. Nothing connecting them from the forensic house searches at all?'

'Not a thing so far. Apart from being of a similar age, they were quite different people in terms of their interests and lifestyles. We've not found any dialled telephone numbers in common between Alec Hopkins and Alice Morton and none of the neighbours we've spoken with about each murder claims any knowledge of the other victim.'

'Damn. Anyway, I've got extra patrols organised tonight in the areas of all our suggestions from this afternoon's briefing, so fingers crossed one of us was right. I'll carry on here. You get yourself off home.'

'See you tomorrow.' With what she hoped was a comforting smile, Karen left and walked down the corridor to retrieve her rucksack from her locker whereupon she pulled the back of her hair from out of its neat scrunchie, which she threw into the bag with some considerable ardour. Taking her mobile phone out of her pocket, she saw she'd had another missed call.

With a sigh, the phone went the same way as the hair tie, hurled into the depths of her bag where it could stay for a while and give her some peace and quiet to think.

Making her way out into the staff car park, her mind was still in a spin. Would anyone put the jigsaw together in time?

She flung the rucksack onto the passenger seat as she climbed into her car. Well, tonight would tell.

* * * *

Nigel Edgerton hated the local evening news programmes on television. After watching the main news, which covered major world-changing events like wars, political upheavals, and leading world figures, they then switched to the local Harrogate area news which, heralded with an optimistic 'And now for the news in your area', inevitably covered a dreary agenda of depressingly parochial items such as a new park bench in town, an otter spotted in some pensioner's back garden, or an infant school that had raised money for dental health awareness.

'Sod this,' he said to his wife Lillian on the worn but comfortable sofa next to him. 'I'm going to make a cup of tea while this is on. You having one?'

'Please,' she smiled. He winced as he raised himself up and Lillian gave him a concerned glance. 'Oh dear. Is that hip of yours playing up again?'

'It doesn't seem to like these cold autumn nights,' he replied. 'But given that the doctor's told me a replacement might do more harm than good, I guess I'll just have to wait until spring.'

'I'd hoped it might have got better. That car crash was so many years ago. Speaking of which, have you heard anything back from the police? Any update from them about the driver who was found dead?'

'Not a thing. I guess they're too busy. They're so under-resourced aren't they these days? Our lad David says so and he should know. He's been a policeman in Leeds for … how many years is it now?'

With a groan, he walked into the kitchen. Lillian strained to listen to the local news above the sound of the boiling kettle and rattling cups emanating from the adjacent room. Suddenly, a news item caught her attention.

'Nigel, get back in here quick. Look at this, look, look.'

'All right, I'm not as fast as I was.' Poking his head through the living room doorway. 'What is it, love?'

'Another one found dead in York. Alice somebody or other she's called. Look, they're showing her photo. There.'

Nigel looked at the photograph being shown on his television screen of a woman in a summery outfit sitting on a beach, smiling at the camera and making a 'peace' sign with her right hand. She had a large eye-catching tattoo on the side of her neck. 'No, love. Who is she?'

'I recognise her. Didn't she live next door to our David when he was living in his first house in Leeds?'

He shook his head. 'I don't remember, sorry.'

'You do. You do,' persisted Lillian with the perseverance of a woman convinced that their husband is wrong, which in Nigel's experience happened rather a lot.

'Remember that time we were having a barbecue in his back garden, and she stuck her head over the fence, mouthing off about the smell and the noise. Right fishwife's mouth on her. Dreadful woman.'

'Ah yes, I remember that now you mention it. But I couldn't put a face to her.'

'I'm sure it's her. Sure it is. Look.' She pointed at the screen. 'That nasty looking tattoo on the side of her neck is a right giveaway. And I don't think it was the first or only time our David had some serious run-ins with that cow. He didn't like her one bit.'

She grimaced at the TV screen

'No, he couldn't stand her at all.'

* * * *

Paul turned the key in his door, pushed it open, paused to pick up yet another manila envelope from off the mat, and sighed.

How different it must have been for my parent's generation in the days before the internet, he thought. The sound of something coming through your letter box could have prompted a wealth of pleasant possibilities: a letter or a card from a distant friend, a birthday, Christmas, or Easter greeting. Maybe a love letter to stir the heart, read, and then cherish forever, hidden away in an old biscuit tin in the loft. Nowadays, all his birthday wishes came via a message on his Facebook wall, correspondence from friends and family came via texts, and he couldn't remember ever having received a love letter in his whole life. Which left the Royal Mail to distribute all the bad stuff: bills, final demands, stomach-sinking and heartily undesirable bits of government bureaucracy, and unwelcome items like the envelope he was currently holding.

Tossing it onto his coffee table along with all the others, he went into the kitchen and threw open the fridge door only to find it almost bare. With everything going on, he'd forgotten to go shopping again. Deciding that he couldn't be bothered with another takeaway, he rummaged in the cupboards, and found two bags of salt and vinegar crisps, a packet of custard creams, and a curry Pot Noodle.

'Tonight, I shall dine like a king,' he spluttered to himself through a mouthful of biscuit, his pledge to himself to eat more healthily once again put on hold for another night. Returning to his compact living room, he was aware in the quiet of the night just how the place echoed. The laminate floors, empty magnolia painted walls, and paucity of soft furnishings seemed to make every footstep reverberate. He kicked off his trainers so at least each step of his socks on the floor wouldn't remind him of how hollow the place was.

He pulled out his notebook, removed the elastic band from around it, and opened it at the page where he'd written the contents of the day's email. One Pot Noodle, half a packet of custard creams, and several hours later, he was still playing around with the words, desperately willing them to give up their secrets.

His personal laptop on the coffee table cast a glow onto his face. Several tabs on his browser were open. One for Google, one for Wikipedia, one for a crossword anagram finder, and one with a Google Earth satellite view of York. It was getting late. Earlier, he'd spied just enough milk to make a cup of tea. He would have one last drink, call it a day, and head for bed. Whatever secrets the email held, it wasn't going to give them up tonight.

Getting up to the window to close the curtains, he picked up a small canvas frame from the window ledge and laughed to himself cynically as he read the words in it.

Live. Laugh. Love.

Written in sparkly silver text in a large cursive font. He couldn't remember how it had ended up in his possession after the split, or what had made him put the tacky thing on the window ledge. He did, however, remember the day his wife Amanda had been shopping and bought it. He recalled how he'd chuckled and teased her over her taste for kitschy glitz until eventually she'd hit him over the head with it. Probably in jest. Well. Maybe in jest. Maybe. And now Amanda was gone and the only time he heard from her was via a manila envelope.

They'd been together for many years and shared a lot together. The canvas was a cruel reminder of the three simple things they'd lost the ability to maintain. The failed areas of their marriage summarised in three words. Three simple words.

What will be location *three*? Oh my *word…*

Hang on. A thought hit him. He tossed the frame back onto the window ledge and sat back at his laptop, all thoughts of eating any food forgotten.

A few clicks of the mouse. No. Taps on the keyboard. Click search. *Not that. Try again.* A few more clicks. Search. *No, not that either.*

Try again. Search.

Oh shit. Jesus Christ.

He scooped up his mobile with trembling hands and scrolled to Karen's number which was still on his recently dialled list. Hitting the *call* icon with his finger, he waited, heart pounding in his throat, for the call to connect.

'Paul? What on earth's going on?'

'Karen, listen. I've not got time to explain, but I need you to get some squad cars over to Hull Road Park. I repeat, Hull Road Park. Now. Trust me on this, I mean it.'

He was almost shouting.

'NOW.'

Chapter 11

Gene Garland might have just turned fifty, but he was still fit and agile. He sprinted from his car down the short path through Hull Road Park; his pupils adjusting to the enveloping darkness could make out the shapes of two uniformed officers in distinctive hi-vis jackets standing over a lump on the ground.

Bloody hell fire. Too late.

'We got here as fast as we could,' said the taller officer. Garland recognised him from the station. A bright young lad in the uniform division, PC Charlie Atkinson. His colleague, WPC Gabby Janowski, stood over the corpse.

'I know.' Garland stopped running and sagged. 'I'm not blaming either of you. Sometimes shit happens.'

So, this was it. Another night, another failure to get in front. Now an innocent person had just paid with their life due to the police's inability to crack the clue in time. Garland felt the weight of this job landing heavily on his shoulders.

Come on, Gene, he told himself, shoulders back. Chin up.

'Ambulance is on its way, boss.'

Garland reached into the pocket of his jacket and pulled out his torch to illuminate the body of a young, slight woman in a powder-pink tracksuit. Leaning carefully over the pool of blood emerging from under the body, so as not to leave any blooded footprints on the path, he pressed two fingers of his right hand on the side of the lifeless form's neck. He sighed deeply and shook his head slowly as his heart sank.

'Tell them to come in quietly. This poor girl is past any help and I'd rather preserve as much as we can for the forensic guys to look over. I'd rather not have an ambulance turning up with blues and twos going ten to the dozen attracting attention. In the meantime, we're going to need to get the whole park taped off and then we can get to work without being disturbed. I take it we've got some more squad cars on the way?'

An affirmative nod. 'Yes, sir. There was a young bloke here just before you arrived. Said he was called Paul Dobson. He was out of breath, running. Said he knew you. We took his contact details and Janowski got him to leave the park straight away so he didn't contaminate the scene. He left about five minutes ago.'

'How was he?'

'Shocked. He saw the body on the floor and nearly collapsed himself. I thought he was going to throw up. His knees were practically buckling underneath him.'

Garland turned to the young woman in the stab vest and yellow hi-vis jacket standing by the body. 'Quick thinking. Thank you for that.'

'No problem, sir.' She smiled. 'I was worried he was going to vomit all over any vital evidence, so I got him out of the way as quickly and delicately as I could.'

'Excellent,' said Garland. 'You did well.'

Looking back up towards the road, Garland now saw the bright red brake lights of several more police cars piercing through the darkness of the night, lurching to a stop at the side of the road outside the park entrance. As for a sight of Paul Dobson, there was none. The thought nagged at him incessantly – how the hell had he managed to work the bloody poem out?

He turned off his torch so as not to attract attention until at least the crime scene tape was in place and the forensic tent and floodlights appeared. A surge of emotion rose up, almost overwhelming Garland, making him want to howl at the sky. The rage and frustration coursed through his body, flooding from his temples down to his toes, and he gripped his hands tightly into fists waiting for it to pass.

Again. Un-bloody-believable.

Taking a long, slow pull of the cold damp air into his lungs to still his nerves, Garland looked around and took detailed stock of the situation. Leading through the gates from the road outside was a path about a hundred yards long, which led to a pavilion building, a squat, functional structure. The heavy steel anti-crime shutters rolled down securely over every door and window didn't do anything to enhance its appeal. There was a faded and peeling poster on the side which had a picture of a top hat and a wand on it advertising a magic show in the park sometime back in the summer. Some scrote with nothing better to do had sprayed graffiti in illegible writing on the brickwork near it.

To the right of the pavilion, a short path ran alongside a mesh-fence-enclosed basketball court. Garland knew straight away it was a basketball court, as ten feet above the body on just the other side of the wire mesh, a basketball hoop was silhouetted against the grey cloudy sky like a detached halo floating up away from the body. At the far side of the basketball court, he knew, was a small river, which the locals called Osbaldwick Beck.

He considered how the events might have played out. It would have been a simple matter to come up from the quiet, darkened safety of the narrow path that ran along the bank of the river, under the cover of the evergreen trees with no CCTV cameras for miles. A little turn up the side of the court would reach the pavilion. Hidden from view, this would provide the perfect spot to wait for an unsuspecting victim, then simply emerge, take a single shot, and then head back down to the sanctity of the river bank to vanish into the night.

Garland zipped his jacket up a bit further as a biting breeze flung some soggy fallen leaves into the air, one of them landing on top of the corpse. Clearing his mind of all distractions, he started to work on his strategy, which would keep him busy right the way through beyond sunrise.

* * * *

As Karen's Nissan Juke jerked to a halt outside the park and she started to get out, her car door practically hit Paul as he rushed towards her. Noticeably shaking, he grabbed hold of her shoulders.

'I saw your car pull up. We're too late.'

Karen slumped. 'No. I don't believe it.' She gave the driver's side front wheel of her car a hearty kick in frustration. A pause. Then another.

'DI Garland's already here. I waited just down the street and I saw him go into the park. You OK? You look out of breath.'

'I'm OK, Paul. My heart's pounding a bit but I'll be fine.' She led him to under a nearby street light so she could observe him better. 'More to the point, are you all right?'

'Not really. I drove as fast as I could and ran down here from my car like Linford Christie but didn't get here in time. I legged it down the path into the park. Two police officers were already there. And the body. I saw the body, Karen. I saw the frigging body.'

Karen put her hands on his shoulders to calm him down then stepped back again into the glow of the street light. 'You were brave,' she said. 'Not to mention incredibly foolish. You had no idea what was down there and "there for the grace" and all that it would have been you lying there in the park. You realise that now?'

Paul nodded glumly. Karen held up a warning finger.

'Well, don't you forget it. I want you to promise never to do that again. Do you hear me?'

'I promise.'

'Right. Well, it's going to get frantic around here very, very quickly. I can already see lights coming on already in some of these houses, so this park is going to get taped off very soon and then a lot of things are going to start happening. There's nothing more you can do so get yourself home and try to get some sleep if you can, although I know that's going to be difficult.'

'I'll try,' he lied.

'And then tomorrow morning you can come to the station and I'll treat you to another cuppa and the finest culinary delight our canteen's exquisite menu can offer if you tell me how you cracked the code. Is that a date?'

'Thanks.' Paul smiled, his sense of humour briefly returning. 'I'll have steak tartar with truffles followed by lobster Thermidor.'

'We're on.' grinned Karen. 'Although it might be cottage pie, peas, and apple crumble. Got to go now. Take care of yourself, Paul.'

'I'd better let you get on. You've got a busy night ahead. See you at lunchtime.'

Paul staggered back to his car, his body numb and his mind buzzing full of noise like a radio stuck on full volume. Pulling out his car keys, he cast a glance back over his shoulder. Karen had just flashed her badge at the uniformed police officer now standing at the park entrance. As she passed through the gates to disappear into the park and what lay ahead, she cast a glance back over her shoulder, too.

Chapter 12

Paul tucked into his battered cod with chips and mushy peas with gusto as Karen looked on in amazement. He was eating with the enthusiasm of someone who'd not eaten properly for several days. Then again, Karen chided herself, it probably was because he hadn't eaten properly for several days. Despite being of a very similar age to Paul, seeing him like this gave her a rush of maternal instinct towards him.

'You enjoying that?'

Paul politely waited until he'd swallowed his current mouthful before replying. 'Yes, thank you, it's delicious.'

Karen smiled. Well, that's the first and possibly the last time I've ever heard anyone call the food in here delicious she thought.

'Sorry we're out of steak tartar, truffles, and lobster Thermidor today,' she quipped. 'The chef told me the usual delivery from Fortnum and Masons didn't turn up this morning. Honestly, at this rate, they're going to take away one of our Michelin stars.' She sipped at her can of Coke. 'So go on then, don't keep a girl waiting. How did you do it?'

'I'd been looking at it for ages,' Paul began, 'and then I just got this flash of inspiration. The clue was hinted at in the last line with the words "*what*", "location *three*" and "my *word*". It struck me as unusual that it said "What will be location three" rather than "Where..." Maybe being a journalist I'm sensitive to English grammar. The clue was all based on a geolocation service called *What Three Words*. Have you heard of it?'

'I'm extremely familiar with it,' Karen replied. 'It's common knowledge across all the emergency services. We even had a training session on it a few years ago. The world is divided into a three-metre by three-metre square grid, and each one is referenced by a unique set of three words. It's particularly handy for the emergency services when you can't easily give a street address, like if you're injured while climbing or horse riding in the middle of nowhere.'

She took another sip of her drink. 'We even learnt – get this – there's a building in South Korea with the grid reference "Electric Light Orchestra". Perfect for Jeff Lynne to retire to when he wants to hang up his guitar. So what were the three words in the clue?'

'Twigs surely leads,' Paul explained, waving his fork on which was speared a huge chip. 'The centre of the square referenced by the three-word phrase "twigs surely leads" is almost slap bang beside the hoop on the basketball court. When I saw the body it was up against the chain wire fence that separates the court from the path, half under the little privet hedge there with her head below the hoop.'

'Wow, well done. The clue stated exactly where the killing was going to be.' Karen paused. 'Pudding by way of extra thanks? I think the kumquat and guava pavlova with champagne sauce is off as well today, but they do a vaguely digestible jam roly poly and custard.'

She'd just started to rise from the table when Garland walked in, spying them immediately. He gave them a hearty wave and came straight over. On close inspection, he looked drawn and fatigued, having been up for most of the previous night, but he still managed to give Paul a hearty slap on the shoulder.

'Hope you're treating our VIP guest well, Karen.'

'It all depends… Is this going on expenses?'

‘If we’ve got a return on our investment, then you can have a dessert as well. Do we know how it was done?’

‘What Three Words,’ said Karen. ‘Twigs surely leads.’

Garland turned to Paul. ‘Amazing work. I’ve got to take my hat off to you. I’d never have got that in a month of Sundays.’ He bit his lip to stop himself from adding, ‘if only you’d got it fifteen minutes earlier’, realising it would sound ungrateful, which he wasn’t. In fact, he was incredibly impressed.

‘It was just a thought that popped into my head,’ Paul explained modestly. ‘Just lucky, I guess. If I hadn’t—’ He was rudely broken off by a noise and vibration from his mobile phone in his pocket. ‘Sorry, I’d better get this.’ He swiped his finger across the screen. ‘Hang on, it’s an email,’ and then he went silent. ‘You need to see this.’

He turned his phone around and Karen and Garland leant forward to read the words on the screen:

In the dark of the night, I stand there half hiding
Laying in wait for my prey to come striding
Fumbling stupidly, you’ve not got the mettle
To work out my clue and just grasp the nettle

Paul looked up. The colour had drained from Karen’s face and Garland looked particularly grim.

‘If you don’t mind, can we skip the dessert, and all get straight up to my office?’ he said

* * * *

‘Listen up, everyone, we’ve had another breakthrough.’

As Garland's words cut across the incident room, everyone sat up straight in their chairs and turned to face the front. 'First, I want to run you through the events of last night. The victim is a twenty-nine-year-old woman called Kirsten McNally. She lived alone locally. We've traced her parents and informed them of her tragic death.'

What Garland didn't mention was that earlier in the day he'd visited Mr and Mrs McNally at their home in Bishopthorpe to deliver the news personally. He hated that part of the job more than anything else in the world, and despite his tough exterior, always felt incredible, almost unbearable, surges of anxiety when doing it. Seeing the anguished reactions of people knowing that their loved ones were not coming back was almost too intolerable to bear, yet he felt he owed it to the victim's family. Besides, he believed it would be a coward's way out to delegate the duty.

'We have no idea what brought her to Hull Road Park at that time of night, so perhaps it was just a late-night stroll and she was in the wrong place at the wrong time. We will need to check CCTV footage of the area to see if we can determine her exact route. Post-mortem has been arranged, but the attending pathologist, Dr Horner, said from what he saw at the scene there's no reason it isn't the same killer. Door-to-door enquiries are being followed up, but it appears that our invisible ghost has come and gone without anyone seeing or noticing a thing. Now pay close attention to the next bit.'

DC Goodier, who was about to pop a chocolate digestive into his mouth, paused and put it back on the desk in front of him.

'Last night, Paul Dobson cracked the killer's code, which specified exactly where the killing would take place.

Unfortunately, we were about fifteen minutes too late to prevent the murder and catch our killer.'

The electricity that shot round the room was almost palpable. Karen looked across at DC Snow sitting next to her and noticed that the hairs were standing up on the back of his neck.

'After all our excellent efforts, I'm sorry to say that none of us was right in our thinking this time, including me. But I don't want that to discourage you in any way. Now, as I'm sure you're all keen to know, the key to cracking the code lay in the What Three Words app. Three consecutive words in the poem gave the exact geolocation of the killing.'

A collective groan went round the room. Garland knew no detailed explanation was necessary as he was aware everyone had already been trained in the app and was very familiar with it. Garland had mixed emotions; he was delighted the riddle had been solved but was desperate not to demotivate his team. He allowed himself the luxury of a smile. The next bit of news should hopefully really cheer everybody up.

* * * *

Maureen McNally raised her red-eyed, tear-stained face to gaze at her husband. The television in the corner played out silently into the grief-stricken living room. She looked longingly at the photo of Kirsten in the frame on the mantelpiece. It had been taken on a family day out to Alton Towers when she was fourteen. She was wearing blue jeans and a T-shirt with a kitten on it and was giving a cute, pretty smile to the camera.

'Our girl. Such a lovely girl. So many years of a bright future ahead of her.'

Her husband, Roger still couldn't understand, as he often never did, his wife's unflinching, rose-tinted spectacles in the face of what he considered such obvious evidence to the contrary. After their only daughter had dropped out of school having failed all her exams, she'd fallen in with the wrong crowd. It was, let's face it, nigh impossible, he thought, to reconcile her reckless lifestyle choices with his wife's phrase "many years of a bright future".

After moving out before she was practically thrown out by her increasingly exasperated parents, in and out – and, far more often, out than in – of occasional dead-end jobs, his daughter's life, so far as Roger could see, consisted of smoking weed, watching tacky reality shows on television, and reading those ghastly celebrity gossip magazines with the lurid pink covers. The last time he'd called round, just a few weeks ago, her front room had been cluttered with them and her kitchen had been so bad you almost needed to put on a biohazard suit before you went to put the kettle on.

He came and put a comforting arm round his wife's heaving shoulders.

'She should have stayed here with us,' she wailed. 'I'll never forgive myself now.'

Roger was lost for a reply. If she'd stayed, if she'd not left the day when they'd fallen out for the umpteenth time over her behaviour, then maybe it could have all turned out different. But in his heart of hearts, he knew that would simply have been impossible. As if Maureen would have been able to tolerate Kirsten's lifestyle. He'd not mentioned to his wife what he had seen on his last visit to Kirsten, when, excusing himself to go to the toilet upstairs, he'd peered through a bedroom door that had been left ajar. Looking into the room he had seen, stacked up to almost ceiling height from the cheap orange curtains at one end to the doorway at the other, dozens of shrink-wrapped cases of booze and cigarettes.

He'd recalled the time he'd called unexpectedly to find Kirsten chatting to three dodgy looking blokes in a Transit van. They'd all been sporting baseball caps and had been covered in tattoos. It didn't take a genius to work out how Kirsten and her dubious friends were supplementing their benefit money. The Tang Hall estate was, he was sure, grateful for the unofficial off-licence.

'Who would want to kill our lovely girl?' sobbed Maureen.

Roger thought back to the commercial enterprise going on from Kirsten's upstairs bedroom but kept his lips tightly closed.

Chapter 13

Garland was fizzing with energy as he triumphantly lifted the sheet of paper in his hands and clamped it to the board. The sounds of the magnets striking the whiteboard rang out loudly, bringing immediate silence to the incident room. 'We've had another email,' he barked to the assembled room. All eyes locked onto the enlarged printout of Paul's most recent email.

The room broke out into a mixed cacophony of expletives interspersed with excited grunts. After several seconds, Garland held up his hands and called for quiet.

'Listen up and pay attention, this is important,' he commanded when order had resumed. 'When I arrived at the murder scene this morning,' he continued, 'the two attending officers, Atkinson and Janowski, who were the first to see the dead body, informed me they'd seen nobody else around at the time. I then asked DC Parkinson, who was next on the scene, if she'd seen anyone else on the road outside when she arrived. Parkinson, over to you.'

Karen cleared her throat. 'The street was empty of pedestrians apart from Paul Dobson, who'd called in with the riddle's solution. I spoke with him briefly, then sent him straight home. I didn't see any other members of the public. I spoke with PC Janowski who'd been taping up the park entrance on Alcuin Avenue and she said she hadn't seen any rubbernecks either.'

'So, I worked on the basis,' Garland continued, 'that after having fired the lethal shot, our killer quickly and quietly disappeared into the dark and spirited themselves off well away from the scene not to return. I've checked the morning's papers and press releases and there is nothing in there which indicates the specific time we found the poor woman.'

Jamshedji beamed. 'If that's the case, boss, then it means the killer might still think the body was discovered in a similar fashion to the previous two, in which case they wouldn't know their code had been cracked.'

Garland thumped his fist on the desk. 'Excellent. Go on, Jamshedji.'

'Which may mean,' continued Jamshedji, 'they've used the same code this time around.'

'Yes,' agreed Garland, 'my thoughts exactly. So, in my office just now, I've sat with Parkinson and Paul Dobson and we've sifted through the new email on exactly that premise. Let's take a look.'

And with his whiteboard marker, he pointed out the words in front of them all.

In the dark of the night, I stand there half hiding
Laying in wait for my prey to come striding

Fumbling stupidly, you've not got the mettle
To work out my clue and just grasp the nettle

'This is what we found,' explained Garland. 'Most three-word combinations didn't yield a location at all or were too ridiculously irrelevant. For example.' He pointed with his marker pen. '"Striding fumbling stupidly" is in the middle of the South Pacific.' He picked up a face-down piece of paper on the desk and some more button magnets.

'But this phrase' – he indicated – '"Half hiding laying" is massively significant. It points to a geolocation right here. Look.'

He clamped the second piece of paper to the whiteboard and then stood back so that everyone in the room could see the map.

'Saint Nicholas Fields, About a ten-minute walk from the site of our last murder.'

'I know those fields really well,' DC Goodier spoke up, recognising them straight away. 'I used to take my kids there quite a few times when they were younger. It's a beautiful place in the summer, lots of trees and flowers. That little curved building in the middle of your map is called the Environment Centre. They use it for educational purposes to teach the kids about nature and plants and stuff. The square you've marked is on a path at the side of that building.'

'Indeed,' said Garland. 'The perfect spot for a killing. Well, not tonight.'

* * * *

After the meeting with Garland, Paul was feeling uplifted. It looked like the killer had finally blundered. As a result, they'd been able to crack the next location and for the first time since the whole tragic business had begun, the police would be one step ahead instead of on the back foot.

Sworn to secrecy about the clue, he'd started walking back to his office to write up his article on Kirsten McNally's murder for that night's edition. Halfway through his walk he'd been seriously tempted to make a small detour to do a reconnaissance visit over to St. Nicholas Fields and check out the location for himself, but had decided that he wanted to neither tempt fate nor jeopardise any operation which might now already be underway.

He looked around in a brief anxious moment, realising how little attention you normally paid to who might be watching you.

Relax, Paul, stop feeling so paranoid.

Back at his desk, he set to work on his article. Garland had given him some strict guidance about what facts he could and couldn't mention and he was determined to keep his own side of the bargain, as an innocent life could now depend on it. When he was finished, he flopped back in his chair, his brain filled with a heady mixture of sheer exhaustion and excitement. He looked up to see Linda Reader walking into his office.

'Come on, Paul. You look done in. You need to get back home, have a shower, a beer, and a sleep. In whatever order you fancy. Go on, off you go.'

'Honestly, I'll be—'

'Off with you.' she insisted. 'Tomorrow's another day.'

The tone of her voice suggested she didn't want a debate, and in fairness, she did have a point. But as for tomorrow being another day? Somewhere in among St Nicholas Fields, some very busy people were going to have to get through the night.

* * * *

Garland double checked the safety catch and gently placed the Glock into the concealed holster under his jacket. As an officer who was fully firearms trained and certified, he wanted to be part of whatever happened that evening. On top of that, he was conscious that he would be asking his fellow firearms officers that night to be putting their lives at risk. The memories came flooding back of the times that his father had instilled in him that you should never ask anyone to undertake any risk or difficult task that you wouldn't be prepared to do yourself.

As he was the only officer in his team who was firearms qualified, he'd needed to request extra resources from the firearms unit. Beside him, also holstering their checked-out pistols, were officers Goddard, Ollerenshaw, and Hancock. Pete Ollerenshaw and Jim Hancock were both large muscular figures with wide shoulders and Garland had watched them both play on the Fulford Road police rugby team. Mike Goddard, by comparison, was tall and athletic and ran the occasional marathon. Garland knew them all reasonably well in a professional capacity and felt confident he could rely on them. There was a strange calm in the air that always seemed to precede these kinds of operations; a quiet professional matter-of-factness that eased nerves in readiness for the serious job in hand.

From off the counter beside him, Garland picked up the spare pre-loaded magazine to place into a compartment in his bulletproof vest. Inspecting the magazine one last time for damage and to verify it was properly loaded, he reflected on the thought that it also contained 9mm Parabellum ammunition.

* * * *

Trying desperately to switch his mind off back at home, Paul changed out of his works clothes into jeans and a T-shirt, sprayed some deodorant under his arms and decided he'd pop out for a takeaway pizza in a little while. Not the healthiest of food, he thought, but it was all he could be bothered with. He was hungry and if he walked to the take-away, the stroll would help distract him for a while.

In the meantime, there was that other issue to deal with which wasn't going to go away. With a sigh, he braced himself. He carefully laid out the contents of the manila folders from his estranged wife's solicitor. The turn of each page seemed to lay out even further Draconian demands to a long and growing list in their impending divorce.

There was a time I believed you wanted us to enjoy the world together, he thought despondently. Now you won't be happy until you see me living on the streets.

After skimming through the paperwork with barely half of it registering, he forced himself to look through it once again, hoping that the words would make more sense to his unwilling brain a second or third time around.

How did it end up like this? he asked himself, as indeed he had done regularly over the last several weeks. He suddenly felt very melancholic.

Opening the photo library on his phone, he didn't have to scroll very far back to find the last pictures of Amanda from when they had been on holiday together in Barcelona. Was it really only earlier this year? She stood in front of La Sagrada Familia, the hot Catalonian sun bouncing off her gorgeous blonde hair; her sunglasses were masking her beautiful blue eyes, but nothing could mask her captivating smile. A small lump came to his throat, and he hastily sniffed back the emotion. He scrolled forward through the library. There she was again in several photos on the very last morning he spent with her, at Madame Tussauds on a short break in London. She looked so lovely and carefree as she playfully posed next to models of various celebrities. Who would have known it was all about to go horribly wrong and they would end up like this?

Paul tossed the phone down on top of the solicitor's letter. His appetite had disappeared, and he wasn't really hungry for that pizza. In any case, there were more important things to worry about tonight. For someone who prided himself on not being superstitious, he was surprised to realise he had his fingers crossed on both hands.

Chapter 14

The evening was chilly but mercifully dry. Round the front of the timber yard that backed onto Saint Nicholas Fields, Garland didn't show any tension as he double checked the operation with his three colleagues. Beside them, the locked and chained security gates of the timber yard creaked a little whenever a wind blew up. Whenever this happened, the breeze would send a faint aroma of wood and sawdust into the air and rattle the discarded drinks cans which lay in the puddles by their feet.

Ollerenshaw stared down the lane past the timber yard towards an unlit narrow entrance to the fields. 'I always wondered why they were called fields, when they're all trees and woodland.'

Goddard grinned. 'Don't sweat it,' he chuckled. 'These trees might make for good hiding places for the killer, but they also make for great opportunities for me to get around unseen. I know these woods very well. And the chances are, the trees weren't here when it was named…'

'I'm with you on that,' agreed Garland. 'This feels more like my home territory than the killer's. We'll use it to our advantage. We're the alpha wolves hunting tonight, lads.'

'Too right.' Hancock, the officer in charge of the night's operation, nodded. 'So, to confirm one last time that we're happy with what we agreed on back at the ranch. We'll each go in and patrol the following areas: I'll take the back of the industrial estate coming up to the stream. Goddard, you go to the east behind the car park. The avenue which runs east to west along the northern end of the fields is quite lengthy, so Ollerenshaw, you take the westerly end that backs onto the concrete plant.

Garland, you can cover the easterly end up from the rear of the electricity substation. Are we all clear on our areas?'

Silent nods all round.

'OK.' Hancock checked his watch, pressing a button on the side to illuminate the face. 'It's twenty-one thirty. All the dog walkers and people cutting through the fields to get home will be back in their living rooms with their cosy feet up in front of their televisions. This means that anyone entering the fields after this time of evening stands a more than fair chance of being either a killer or a murder victim. One last radio check, guys?'

They checked their radios and nodded. Hancock continued.

'We'll check in with each other with clicks on the radio. And remember that we're all authorised under Section 60 to stop and search anyone in here tonight given that they may be carrying a handgun. If in doubt about anything don't hesitate a second to radio immediately for backup, and make sure you capture the faces of anyone you see with your body cams.'

Garland unzipped his jacket a little and gave his holstered Glock a comforting pat.

'OK, folks, it's show time.'

* * * *

Karen unlocked her back door, took off her gloves and her black tracksuit top, kicked her trainers off and nudged them under the radiator by the door. After an eventful day at work, and then having to go out again to attend to a few things, she was ready to sit down and try to relax.

She had a couple of personal phone calls to catch up on first, though. She walked through into her living room where she'd left her mobile phone on the sofa and picked it up from where it was lying next to the TV remote and a copy of *Pride and Prejudice* she'd been struggling to read for the last fortnight. The bookmark, placed less than a quarter of the way through, not only reminded her of her lack of reading progress but also of her lack of progress in finding a Mr Darcy of her own. Frankly though, at this stage in the novel she couldn't see what the fuss with him was all about. Those Bennet sisters and their gob-on-a-stick mother were all welcome to him, she thought, as she pushed the book to one side.

Flopping down on the sofa she dialled the first number.

'Karen. Are you OK?' Paul's voice sounded worried as he answered the call. 'What's happened?'

She allowed herself the luxury of a relaxed smile. 'Nothing's up, Paul, nothing that I've heard about, anyway. I just wanted to check that our code-cracker-extraordinaire is all right this evening. I feel like I owe you a bit of a duty of care at least.'

'Yes, I'm fine,' lied Paul. In truth, having to deal with the divorce papers had knotted his stomach into agony. In retrospect, maybe looking at the photos of Amanda in Barcelona and London had been a huge mistake. Too late, it was done now. More concerning though, was the thought that the police knew the next location, and he was willing them with every fibre of his body to succeed in catching the killer.

'I hope Garland's going to be OK. I know I've only just met him, but he seems like a decent guy.'

'Be strong and have faith,' assured Karen. 'Garland will be just fine.'

* * * *

Roger McNally had been restless all evening. His tearful wife was devastated, but he had something urgent on his mind. He needed to see Kirsten's house one last time to put his mind at rest before he could say goodbye.

Making an excuse that he needed to get out and clear his head for an hour or so, he left the house, his feet crunching on the slate chips that carpeted their expansive driveway. He clicked the button on his key fob to open the remote-controlled garage doors and slid into his Land Rover Discovery. He reversed out of their driveway, being careful not to scratch the immaculate paintwork on an overhanging rose tree. Then he was away out of the charming village of Bishopthorpe and on to the outskirts of York.

Some twenty minutes later he pulled up outside his daughter's house. A plain building, constructed with cheap modern beige-coloured brick and lacking any architectural features which might have threatened to increase the building cost in any way, it sat at the end of a short concrete drive and a scruffy handkerchief of calf-high grass that served as her front garden. A remnant of police tape tied around one of the gateposts fluttered in the evening breeze. Somewhere in the background, he could hear youths shouting and kicking something against a metal door, and the noise of a distant revving car engine. His overall impression of the neighbourhood wasn't improved as he alighted from the Land Rover to be greeted, as he had been every time, by the ever-present aroma of recently smoked cannabis blowing down the street.

He fumbled in his pocket and retrieved a key. He hoped Kirsten had not changed the locks since their falling out and that it still fitted so he could look around one last time.

Approaching the peeling wooden gate, he suddenly realised he was not alone. There was a dark figure in front of Kirsten's front door trying to peer through the letter box.

'Hey! What are you doing?'

The figure stood up slowly and turned around to face Roger; the streetlight caught him and revealed a dark-haired man wearing what looked like a very expensive black leather jacket. As Roger strode up to him, a grin spread across the man's unshaven face.

'Who the hell are you?'

'I don't have to tell you, old man.'

'This is my daughter's house. Who are you and why are you here?'

'I'm not here for a discussion. You don't need to know that.'

The emotions of the day suddenly bubbled up like raging lava inside Roger. Although he was a good thirty years older than the stranger, and not in as good health as he had been, his years of fitness while serving in the Royal Air Force stood him in excellent stead. In a snap of anger, he let fly with his right fist, knocking the other man several feet back down the concrete drive.

'That was a seriously bad move.' Wiping the blood from his mouth, the man grabbed hold of Roger's head by both ears and smashed his skull straight into Roger's nose. Keeping hold of Roger's head, he then crashed Roger backwards into the front door frame. However, he'd not counted on Roger's adrenalin levels running quite so high. He'd also not realised Roger was holding a Yale key in his right hand. With a howl, Roger summoned his strength and drove the pointed end of the Yale key below his attacker's left eye.

Kicking Roger's legs from under him, the attacker knocked him to the ground, raised his right foot, and prepared to stamp on his head with full force, when a York Police patrol car screeched to a halt at the end of the drive.

* * * *

Garland, Hancock, Goddard, and Ollerenshaw made their way under the cover of the trees. They could hear the trickling of Tang Hall Beck running in the darkness nearby. To the right of them, just discernible through the dense foliage, three white silos from the concrete plant towered over them, their ghostly outlines illuminated by the street lights in the distance. Nature and heavy industry were sitting side by side here.

According to a website Garland had studied that afternoon, the woodland boasted a varied and engaging diversity of flora, yet from what he could discern in the dim light, the only plants on either side of the path were thistles, and some kind of nondescript large-dock-leaf type plant of which he had no idea of the name.

After a few minutes walking in silence, the four of them reached the Environment Centre building in the middle. Constructed in the 1990s on what had previously been a landfill site, the building was small but pleasing on the eye. A small patch of land to the side of it had been cleared to form a neat garden with a pond.

Aware that at any moment they could be unknowingly in some hidden assassin's gun sights, Garland and the other officers checked carefully and quietly round the building. To their relief they found nothing amiss. Hancock beckoned them over and spoke in a hushed voice.

'We'll split up in a moment but keep within a hundred yards of this building. It provides the perfect cover, especially with its shape, for our killer to lie in wait. Positioned just over there' – he pointed at a spot tucked round the inner corner of the building – 'it's perfect to pop out of hiding and get a clean shot at almost point blank range.'

He looked up at the other officers. 'Garland, can you show us the exact spot?'

Following Garland, the officers made their way about ten yards up a path which led from the side of the building up into the trees.

'According to my map,' announced Garland decisively, pointing down the path, 'the spot which is indicated for the killing is exactly right there.' With that, he stepped along the path, trying to locate the exact place and stand on it like an actor finding his mark on the stage at the beginning of a scene.

'Hang on, there's something there on the path. What the bloody hell is it? I nearly stood on it.'

Just visible in the dim light, the object in the middle of the path looked like a dimpled, almost spherical rock. Garland went to pick it up, then suddenly thought the better of it.

'Unholster your guns and take a good look around you,' he whispered. 'I don't want this to be an ambush or a trap.'

When they'd checked the coast was clear, Garland retrieved a disposable glove from his jacket pocket and slipped it on. He switched on his torch to take a closer look at the object, and as it became caught in the dazzling beam, he was surprised to see it was bright yellow.

He squatted down beside it to take a close look. It was a lemon.

A bloody lemon!

A lemon - the slang term for a useless dud. Rage coursed through him, and he had to fight the urge to fling it with all his strength into the trees. Picking it up in his gloved hand, he straightened up to show it to his three colleagues. As he held it aloft and turned it in the beam of his torch, he noticed the words written in black marker pen on the lemon's skin, which left no doubt as to what it was meant to infer:

THIS IS YOU. HA HA HA.

Chapter 15

Garland faced a set of downcast and melancholy faces as the sun rose over the gloomy incident room as he gave his team feedback on the previous evening's disappointment.

'The lemon's gone off to forensics to see if they can pick up any latent prints or contact DNA, but I'm not holding my breath. A forensic handwriting examiner is also giving it their finest attention but with only a few words to examine, they don't have much material. After that, the lab might be able to do some chemical analysis of the ink from the pen. And I know we've already started looking at CCTV footage around the area but there are no cameras near where the lemon was found, and as we are all aware, a lemon is not exactly a cumbersome thing to smuggle in either.'

A photo of the lemon complete with derisive slogan, blown up to huge proportions like a rounded yellow Hindenburg zeppelin, seemed to mock them all from the screen.

Oh, the humiliation, thought Garland, subconsciously paraphrasing the emotional "Oh the humanity" quote from the original Hindenburg disaster.

'So, we've got two main possibilities.' He squared his shoulders and continued. 'One – we have a leak in either here, or the York Press offices and the killer found out we were onto them. I believe I can trust you all though. We've worked a long time together as a strong team. And as far as I know the only person at the York Press who is aware of this level of information is Paul Dobson, who did after all crack the last code himself.

'Or two – which is the one I'm drawn to believing – the killer either saw us arrive at the scene from a distance or alternatively suspected that once we discovered the last body, we would be able to retrospectively work the location back into the last clue and crack the method. On that basis, the idea of planting the lemon, the symbol of uselessness and failure, was deliberate all along. The intention was an elaborate ruse to set us up and ridicule us for believing we were in front when they were ahead the whole time.'

Jamshedji spoke up. 'Boss, I was wondering if the killer would plant the lemon, wait until you'd left, and then come back and carry out a killing on the same spot after you'd gone.'

'You're on the ball yet again, Jamshedji.' Garland nodded approvingly. 'It occurred to us too, so we stayed on patrol all night up until six o' clock this morning. Just to be on the safe side, I've also organised some officers to patrol there again tonight. I'm not expecting anything, but we've been surprised before.'

He realised this was all depressing.

'Come on, chin up everyone,' he said. 'As I said before, don't take this personally. It's what the killer would want, and we are not going to give them that satisfaction. Look on the bright side. Nobody died last night, and to me a life that gets to continue is worth a ton of our embarrassment. Let's now spend some quality time before we go, deciding what we do next and who will be responsible for doing what. Let's take full advantage of the fact we don't have a cryptic rhyme currently occupying us, which means we can give full attention to the bread-and-butter work – phone records, background checks, CCTV, and so on.

We've received the last victim Kirsten McNally's phone and sent it off to digital forensics. We all know what we need to do with the phone records, so keep at it. We've not found any direct connection between Alec Hopkins and Alice Morton but that doesn't mean that Kirsten McNally couldn't be the connecting bridge between them.

We've also found some social media apps on the phone and can confirm she did have an Instagram account which I want you to examine with a microscope for any connections to the previous two victims. Other than that I've been informed there was a horoscope app on her phone and also a game of *Pokémon Go*. I don't have time for mobile phone games myself, but the younger ones of you may already know that this is a game where you win points by finding virtual creatures in various real-life locations. Kirsten may have been playing this game and on her way to try and earn some points when she walked through the park to where she was killed. I need you to look into this.

Your files have also been updated with the photographs taken from the forensic visit to Kirsten McNally's house. The photos of her spare bedroom are the most illuminating. You'll see it was filled with boxes of cigarettes and beer, and if a customs official has ever clapped eyes on any of it before now, I'll eat my hat. It was all made up of foreign beer brands like Kronenbourg, Krombacher and Oranjeboom. I'd like to ascertain which of her friends were involved in this little unofficial enterprise, not just for smuggling, but in case they're connected to these murders.

Snow raised his right index finger slightly in the air for attention. 'Boss, before we go any further, I just want to make everyone aware that her father Roger McNally was involved in an incident outside her house last night. According to the sergeant in charge of the custody suite, he had a fight with another man and was picked up by a patrol car that had been called out for something else earlier. They've both been arrested and are in the cells downstairs ready to be questioned later this morning.'

'Really?' said Garland, raising his eyebrows. 'Well, despite the fact I'm well and truly knackered, I think I'm going to stay awake and attend these interviews. Anyone like to come with me?'

* * * *

'Thank you for letting me know. You really didn't need to but that's most courteous of you and I appreciate the call. Send my regards to DI Garland. Bye for now.' Jack Horner replaced the telephone handset back on its cradle and smiled at Jamshedji's words informing him there was to be no murder victim post-mortem today.

And this frees up some precious time in my working day today then, he thought, to work on the next stages of my personal project.

Peeping out of his office door to check that the corridor was empty, he returned to his desk, pulled a memory stick out of his pocket, and plugged it into his laptop.

* * * *

The frail-looking lady sat on the velour armchair opposite DC Snow and DC Hayward was unfailingly polite and trying to be helpful.

'I'm sorry I can't tell you anything more useful, gentlemen. Kirsten moved in a couple of years ago, but like I said, we've not spoken to each other much, and we just kept ourselves to ourselves.'

Snow nodded. He could believe that. A young lass who ran a booze cruise enterprise and an elderly neighbour who had a copy of "*The Dalesman*" magazine on her chair arm were hardly going to be bosom buddies.

The small sitting-room was simple but immaculately clean and tidy and looked after by someone who took pride in what they had. He mentally compared it to what he'd seen of Kirsten's property in the file and could easily envisage how this polite old dear would have little in common with the chaotic Kirsten other than the street where they lived.

'Did you see if she had many visitors?'

'Oh, all the time. Mainly young lads coming and going at all times of day and night. One of them had a white van.'

'Make or registration?'

'Sorry, love, it was just a white van to me.'

'Have you ever witnessed any trouble before at Kirsten's property? Anything that might give rise to anything suspicious?'

She shook her head. 'No. She was generally quiet. Couldn't even hear her music or telly through the walls. I was grateful for that. The last thing you want to be hearing is this loud heavy rock or metal or whatever they call it. Rubbish, isn't it? I can never understand a word they're singing about.'

Hayward shot a sideways glance at Snow who maintained a poker face.

'Last night was the biggest commotion I think we've had in a while. I'd heard some tearaways driving round the estate making a noise and so I called the police to let them know and they said they'd send someone out. The next thing I knew there was a banging-about outside Kirsten's and then a police car arrived with all its lights and whatnot.'

'Going back to Kirsten's visitors, did you notice anything unusual about any of them?'

She shook her head. 'No. One young lad looks pretty much like any other when you get to my time of life. Although I've seen that older man who was involved in the kerfuffle on the doorstep before now. I think he's Kirsten's father. He used to visit her occasionally but then for some reason he stopped coming all of a sudden and I've not seen him for about a month.'

'Did you ever speak to him?'

'No. I did once try. I was going out, and he was in his car outside with the windows down and I shouted hello to him but he never replied. I think he was far too engrossed in the crossword puzzle he was doing.'

Chapter 16

The air in the downstairs interview room was stale and musty from the lingering body odours of the thousands who had passed through before. Devoid of any windows, you could be anywhere in the world. Certainly, anywhere functional and intimidating. Garland had to marvel at how the designers had succeeded in creating something so basic and joyless in one of Britain's most beautiful cities.

The traditional twin-cassette-tape interview recorder had recently been replaced by a modern but equally black and threatening-looking digital recording device. On the day it had been installed, Garland had felt a strange nostalgic pang for the old mechanical device of the past despite being a person who made a concerted effort to be adept and up to date with computer technology. On the upside, he reflected, it meant that conducting a professional and often authoritative interview didn't take him back to his younger days when he used to record the Top 40 off the radio chart show every Sunday tea time.

On the other side of the table, which was bolted to the floor, sat a young man with stubble and a bored expression on his face. Garland looked him over. Dressed in his leather jacket and smart jeans and sporting what would normally be well-groomed hair if he'd not spent the night in the cells, he didn't look like your archetypal scratter brought in for fighting in the street. There was, however, a purple bruise and angry swelling under his left eye. Karen looked at it and pursed her lips. He'd been extremely lucky that the keys in Roger McNally's hand had missed his eyeball and the punch hadn't landed properly.

The man smoothed down his leather jacket, rolled back the left cuff, and looked pointedly at what appeared to be an expensive watch in a deliberate "get on with it" gesture.

Garland and Karen sat down. 'Just to confirm you don't want a solicitor present? You are entitled to free legal assistance.'

A deliberately protracted yawn. 'Nope.'

'I would also like to inform you that you're entitled to medical attention should you need it.'

A wave of the hand. 'Whatever. I'll be fine.'

'All right then, just as you wish, now the—'

'Let's not waste time, please. I'm a very busy man. Now, to save farting about, why don't I just tell you why you're going to be letting me out of here without charge?' The young man leant back casually in his chair and interrupted Garland mid-flow.

* * * *

Paul sat at his desk watching a compelling documentary about the Dark Web on his laptop in an attempt to understand more about how people could avoid detection on the internet, and also to take his mind off what may or may not have happened the previous night. The documentary turned out to be extremely interesting and enlightening. In 2011, a notorious website called Silk Road had appeared out of nowhere. It sold every hard drug imaginable, guns, crime tutorials, criminal services, and many other illegal items. The FBI had been on the case trying to shut it down for years, but it was hidden on the Dark Web. The beauty of the system was that neither buyers nor sellers could be traced via their internet IP addresses, and payments were made with untraceable crypto currencies. At its peak, it was claimed that it was making sales of nearly one and a half million dollars a week.

Despite the efforts of the FBI, the case was solved by a civilian government tax inspector, who, using a combination of dedication, ingenuity, and straightforward everyday internet search tools like Google, was able to do what the whole of American law enforcement had failed to accomplish. He identified the mastermind behind it all who was subsequently arrested and was now serving life without parole. Paul began to wonder if a York journalist, using equal dedication and initiative, could do the same.

* * * *

'Well, there's a turn up for the books,' Garland said as he and Karen stood outside the incident room. 'As if this whole thing wasn't weird enough, we now have police informers turning up at the house of our latest murder victim.'

'Where do we go from here?'

Garland's face broke into an exhausted smile. 'I'll tell you where… I'm off to brew up a coffee so stiff you can stand a teaspoon up in it. Between you and me, I'm knackered. This is bloody relentless.'

'There's one good thing anyway, boss,' said Karen sympathetically. 'From what I can gather, neither our informer here nor the murdered woman's father are interested in pressing charges for last night. They'll both bandage up and go home.'

They walked together down the corridor that led to the kitchen.

'I still need this informer checked out further,' insisted Garland. 'The reason he's not been on our radar is that he lives in Leeds and is handled out of one of the police stations there.

The one at Stainbeck Lane. He says he knows Kirsten McNally from when he lived down the road from her three years ago. A simple check with the council on that address should verify that. He also says he was unaware she had died and he was making a social visit, which I suppose is feasible since Kirsten's name hasn't appeared yet in any media to my knowledge. I'm also keen to see if there are any text messages sent to him from Kirsten's phone. And given that so far he's the only person we've brought in relating to these murders, I'd like you to run his name through the HOLMES database just in case some connection does come up.'

'I'll get his finger-swabs sent off for analysis this morning,' Karen said. 'Although given he didn't put up any objection to us taking them, despite his initial abruptness, I'm not hopeful.'

'Me neither,' grunted Garland. 'Bloody hell, I'm worn out. What an exhausting time that was last night and all for a lemon. And forensics have even taken that away so I can't put it in a vodka and tonic.'

Karen put a spoon of instant coffee into each of the two mugs beside the kettle. She paused and on second thoughts, scooped another spoonful into Garland's mug.

'So then,' Garland continued, 'I'm going to get onto this guy's handler at Stainbeck Lane and if it all checks out, we'll let him go. There's something about his handler's name though – DS David Edgerton. The name rings a bell somewhere, and I don't mean in that copy of *Wuthering Heights* you keep telling me you've been trying to read for the last month.'

'It's *Pride and Prejudice*, actually.' Karen poured the steaming water into the two mugs. 'And the family in *Wuthering Heights* is called Earnshaw, not Edgerton. But yes, boss, it struck me too. The chap Dave and I interviewed who'd been in Alec

Hopkins' car crash was an Edgerton and he mentioned his son was a police officer…'

* * * *

Paul finished watching the documentary on his laptop and pulled out his ear buds with a renewed sense of resolve. Half-past eleven already. Desperate to learn about what had happened at St Nicholas Fields the previous night, he wondered whether he should call Karen again or just sit tight and wait for her to call him. The suspense was becoming unbearable.

A ping from his laptop informed him he had a new email. As soon as he opened the mail, his dilemma was resolved.

Since the beginning and up to the end; you're surely destined to fail once again

Feeling the pressure, you now realise how it's ironic the lemon's your prize

Can you crack my message, my symbols, my clue; reporters and coppers I'm looking at you

Have fun every one of you trying. By the end of tonight, the next one will lay dying

Chapter 17

As the detectives filed into the incident room for the afternoon briefing, they were surprised to see three fresh faces sitting at the front. Garland stood to one side, so that the screen at the front displaying a blown-up screenshot of the latest email could be seen by everyone.

'OK, settle yourselves down,' Garland instructed. 'This is the mail which was sent to Paul Dobson today. Based on the previous emails, we know full well that hidden somewhere in this verse is a location. From the last line of the verse, my understanding is that this will be the location of a murder tonight, so the pressure is really on us all to get this cracked in time. On that basis, I'd like to introduce you to three excellent people who I've brought in to help give us some specialist advice.'

The detectives' eyes scanned the three visitors. The first on the left was a pleasant slim man in his fifties in a denim shirt, with long, slightly greying, hair tied back in a ponytail. He gave a cheery wave to the assembled room. In the middle, a mild looking gentleman who, brushing crumbs off his tweed jacket and stroking his sandy moustache, gave everyone a brief nod before removing his wire-rimmed glasses, giving them a quick wipe with a handkerchief, and then putting them back on again. On the right, a young woman in a bright blue floral blouse and a striking vermilion Alice band in her blonde hair gave everyone a quick smile.

'I'll just give these good people a few words of introduction,' continued Garland. 'On the right is Professor Dawn Robinson. She divides her time between acting as a consultant to our digital forensics lab and being a part-time lecturer at York University specialising in' – he quickly consulted a Post-it Note on the desk in front of him – 'computational mathematics. She's also head of the local MENSA society, and I reckoned with that pedigree, she'd be a fantastic asset to helping us crack these clues. I'm sure you'll give her a warm welcome.

'In the middle here is Jason Brown. We go back many years when I first knew him as DCI Brown when he was in the Leeds squad. He's been retired for five years now and lives in York.'

At this piece of introduction, everyone in the room sat up just that bit straighter and put their shoulders back. It was an entirely involuntary response, but Garland noticed it, as indeed did Brown. They briefly smiled across at each other in mutual recognition of a shared observation. *You can take the man away from being a Detective Chief Inspector*, thought Garland, *but you can't take a Detective Chief Inspector's human observation skills away from the man.*

He continued. 'Since his retirement, he's become a genius in local history and is a walking encyclopaedia on anything and everything related to the architecture and history of York. Some of you might have even seen his latest book on the Roman invasion of York in one of the bookshops.'

A wide smile broke out under Brown's moustache. 'Glad to be of some use again, Gene. I was getting bored anyway, growing tomatoes.'

'And on the left here beside me is criminal profiler Doctor Luke Tennant. He has a long career history in solving many high-profile cases and joins us fresh from his transatlantic flight from the Behavioural Science Unit in Quantico, Virginia. We'll start with you, please, if that's all right, Dr Tennant.'

Luke Tennant got to his feet, brushing a strand of his long wispy hair out of his eyes. 'Good afternoon, everyone, thanks for having me along.'

Fully expecting an American drawl from his introduction, everyone was immediately surprised to hear a strong West Yorkshire accent emerge from his lips. Sensing the reaction in the room, Dr Tennant gave a disarming chuckle. 'Yes, I know. Even lads from Huddersfield can get training at Quantico nowadays if you save up enough cornflake packet tops. But it's good to be back in God's own county. Anyway, let me run you through some initial thoughts I've had, now that DI Garland has brought me up to speed. It's a common complaint about criminal profilers that we spend a lot of time and a lot of money to stand here and tell everybody the bloody obvious. If you can bear with me for five minutes, I'm going to once again risk that criticism today. Just don't say I didn't warn you.'

His humble demeanour brought smiles round the room.

He's very modest, thought Karen, but I'll bet they don't send blokes from Yorkshire all the way to Quantico unless they're really, really good.

'Please feel free to ask questions at any time.' He spread his hands. 'The first place to start in building up a profile of the killer is to classify their murders in terminology we call "organised" or "disorganised". The organised serial killer is disciplined and plans the murders in advance, often to the point of being meticulous. This is as opposed to the disorganised type, the ones who opportunistically strike at random. The FBI profile of a classic organised killer is that…' at this moment, Dr Tennant noticed everybody's pens poised to make notes as he counted off the points with the fingers of his left hand. '…they personalise the victim, the murder has elements of exerting control and torture, and the body is frequently hidden after the event in an attempt to cover up the crime. I've seen no evidence of these things in your cases. By contrast, the FBI profile of a disorganised killer is one where the victim is killed quickly, without emotion, with minimal interaction, and the body is often left in plain view. Which is exactly what we have here.'

He placed the glass of water carefully back on the desk and raised his index finger to make his next point. 'The crazy thing is that everything in this case flies in the face of conventional criminal profiling wisdom. Organised killers are typically intelligent, whereas the disorganised ones are often unintelligent or uneducated. These cryptic clues have turned everything on its head. The murders have hallmarks of disorganised killings, yet the cryptic clues are clearly the product of an intelligent mind, and this means we should be looking for someone with strong organisation skills.'

'OK then,' Garland said. 'Do you have any idea what the motive behind all this could be?'

Dr Tennant paused a moment to consider the question. 'Some killers are just very mentally disturbed. For instance, they might believe they're following orders from God who has told them they've been specially selected to save mankind. Some, on the other hand, have such a nebulous grip on reality they believe the person they're sawing the head off is not actually a person at all but is, for example, a plank of wood which needs shortening.'

DC Goodier raised his hand. 'Does that mean we should be looking for a person with a history of mental illness as a focus of our enquiry?'

Dr Tennant shook his head. 'There are many types of mental illness and the vast majority of them are completely harmless. Some studies suggest that as many as one in six people in the

UK right now are suffering some degree of mental health problem and what they need is support and understanding through a tough time, not bias.'

Goodier nodded in appreciation. However, with his trademark dogged persistence which Garland had witnessed on the times he'd been with him in the interview room, he pressed his point. 'Fair comment. But going round shooting people and sending rhymes to the press, that's not normal, balanced mental behaviour is it?'

'No, it isn't,' Dr Tennant acknowledged, 'but we've got to draw an important distinction between people who are so out of touch with reality that they're not in control of their actions, versus those disturbed individuals who know what they're doing is illegal but do it, anyway.'

'So, for example,' persisted Goodier, determined to get to the bottom of it, 'if I were under some delusion that I was actually Dr Who and you were one of the Cybermen and I killed you in order to save the human race, that would be the kind of insanity you're describing?'

'Exactly.' Dr Tennant gave a thumbs-up sign with both hands. 'In fact, exactly this argument would be an acid test for insanity in British law. Oh and it's only the TV programme that's called *Dr Who*, the actual character is called the Doctor.'

He gave a disarming wink at Goodier who laughed and raised his hands in mock surrender. 'They taught you that at Quantico? I'm impressed.' Smiles round the room broke a little of the tension.

Dr Tennant laughed once again. 'My professional title is Doctor and I share the same surname with one of the most famous actors to play the Doctor in recent years. It would be almost criminal for me not to know.

‘Anyway, moving on. The second type of killer is possibly interesting to us. These are the ones on a mission to eradicate people from their target group in society. From this, the killer derives a sense of worth that they’re doing right by society even though they know what they’re doing is illegal.’

He paused. Hayward raised his hand. ‘Can you give us some specific examples of these target groups we might consider?’

‘It could be people belonging to a certain religion or political party, a sexual orientation, a certain lifestyle, or occupation of which the killer disapproves.’ Tennant took another sip of water. ‘Or as sometimes happens, a specific list of those people who the killer believes have wronged them in the past. Although I’ve been told we’ve found nothing striking about the political, sexual, or lifestyles of the victims, and there doesn’t appear to be a connection between them all which we’ve yet found.’

Hayward lifted his pen. ‘That’s where we’re hitting a brick wall. For the life of us, we just can’t find a tangible connection between any of the three victims. All we have so far is that one had an age-old conviction for drink-driving, one was a raging alcoholic, and one sold illegal booze. And at that point, if you pardon the pun, we ran dry.’

‘Yes, but sometimes what can appear a clear connection to a deranged killer can be totally ludicrous to the rest of us. For example, one serial killer pre-selected his victims based on the first person he saw who was wearing red that day. You’re not likely to find that type of connection in any HOLMES database.’

Hayward frowned at the realisation of the potential vastness of what he and the rest of the room were facing. He glanced across at Garland who nodded back. Tennant continued.

‘The third type is the type who kills for their own gratification, and although that’s usually a sexual one, gratification can come in many forms. If this is the case, we would need to discover what form of gratification is involved.

‘Which brings us to the fourth type, the ones who are the narcissistic types who, having lived a life of what they perceive as filled with unfair rejection and unjust underachievement, want to give some payback. If this is the case, then you’ll find no connections between the victims at all because the specific victims themselves are not the prime focus of the killer.’

He frowned as he concluded. ‘Our case here is a strange one. There’s no torture and there’s no element of control being exerted over the victims leading up to the death.’

He paused a brief moment to let his next point sink in.

‘That is, of course, if you consider the people who are being murdered as being the people the killer wants to control and torture. But how about the press and police? I mean, who in this room isn’t feeling both controlled and tortured right now?’

Chapter 18

The familiarly reassuring sounds of the citizens of York going about their daily lives filled the street below Paul's office window. He liked to think of the street below him as a Goldilocks street – not too central but not too remote, not too crowded, not too empty, but just right.

There had been a time not so long ago when he'd disliked having to get up and commute into an office, and when a pandemic had caused him, like many others, to spend time working from home, he'd initially embraced the opportunity with enthusiasm. Now, his office was his comforting place of constancy throughout his recent upheaval in a turbulent world. Working from home was overrated anyway, he thought. He sighed and rubbed a hand over his eyes. If it hadn't been for the enforced days in each other's constant company, maybe he would still be with Amanda. There's nothing like spending days in mutual house arrest for exposing the cracks in someone for whom, until it was actually put to the test, you had always thought would be the person you'd never want to leave your side for the rest of your life. When circumstances had finally allowed them to travel again, the romantic getaways to Spain and London had only exposed the cracks even further.

Sitting upright in his chair, he reminded himself that there was no time for that kind of maudlin thought as time was ticking and another person's life was on the line. He stared at the words of his latest email desperately trying to make some sense of them. On his laptop screen in front of him were pages of the York Press internal database. It had occurred to him it contained a huge amount of local information going back many years and it had the potential to yield something that wouldn't be found in police records.

A movement at his door and the appearance of a head made him reach for his mouse to minimise the window on his screen. When he saw it was Linda Reader, he relaxed, took his hand off the mouse, and settled back again.

'You OK, Paul? Still thinking about that latest email?'

'Yeah. To be honest, it's driving me round the bend. I take it we're still not letting anyone else know about this?'

Linda shook her head. 'There's only you and me here who know about this latest one. DI Garland called me about maintaining the blackout. But if you want a bit of friendly advice, it's not up to you alone to solve it. There'll be a lot of good people working on this. Don't try to take the problems of the whole world on your shoulders.'

'Thanks, Linda.' Paul typed the word *lemon* into the search box of the database and clicked the button next to it. He groaned. There were dozens of articles to trawl through, including one about the comedian Keith Lemon and one containing a recipe for lemon meringue pie.

'Talking of which,' continued Linda, 'I take the health of people round here seriously. While you've got this on your plate, is there anything I can organise to make life easier? I heard from accounts you've not put your expenses in yet, so I can do that for you and save you a job. Anything else?'

'Well, I do know I've got to get my car booked in for its MOT soon, and I could do with another meeting with my solicitor about…you know…when I can get a moment with all this going on.'

He waved his hand in the direction of some paperwork on the top of his in tray. Linda leant forward and scooped it up.

‘Right. Leave things with me. No, don’t argue. You’re valued here and you’re worth a bit of nurturing. Back soon. In the meantime, try not to go too crazy trying to solve York’s answer to the *Da Vinci Code*.’ With that, she smiled at him and disappeared back out through the door as suddenly as she’d arrived.

Paul turned his attention back to the verse on the screen. *Da Vinci Code*. He laughed to himself. He’d read that novel when it came out and had quite enjoyed getting his head round all the revelations of hidden iconography and symbolism in the book. He’d taken Amanda to see the film when it came out, but when they’d got to the cinema, some lacklustre romantic comedy with Meryl Streep had been showing and they’d ended up seeing that instead.

Symbolism. My symbols. He read the words in the verse and a thought hit him. What if the verse was all about hidden symbolism and icons? He shook his head worriedly. So far as he knew, there were not any secret societies in York. Putting his rapidly emptying coffee mug back on the desk, he allowed himself a smile at the realisation of the obvious contradiction in his thinking. Of course, he wasn’t aware of any secret societies. They wouldn’t be particularly secret if everyone was familiar with them. At that thought, an idea came into his mind. He paused and reached for his mouse again. Freemasons.

Bringing up all the cryptic emails he’d received onto his screen, he scoured them in the hope of seeing some recognition of Masonic symbolism before quickly feeling that this was surely going to be a non-starter. Apart from the phrase ‘Square and Compasses’, he had no idea what might, or might not, constitute a hidden Masonic reference in any of them. What about the locations, then? Maybe if he could find some link to

Freemasonry, it could be an indication that at least he was on the right lines and to persevere. 'Let's start with the first murder,' he muttered. 'The statue of Queen Victoria.'

A few clicks of the mouse later, he was leaning forward intently in his chair, reading the screen with keen interest.

The most pivotal Grand Master in British Masonic history is the Duke of Sussex, favourite uncle of Queen Victoria. After his death, Edward, Victoria's eldest son, was installed as Masonic Grand Master; on becoming King Edward VII, the position was transferred to his brother Arthur.

As Paul opened up a Microsoft Word document and copied and pasted large chunks of text into it, he could feel the hairs at the back of his neck prickling slightly.

Now what about the second murder, the cemetery chapel, designed by the architect James Pigott Pritchett?

A cursory Google search revealed no obvious Masonic connections to the architect. What about the chapel building itself? A bit more typing and a few more mouse clicks.

The chapel at York Cemetery features a portico of four Ionic pillars. It is believed to be based on a rendition of King Solomon's Temple in Jerusalem.

The hairs on the back of his neck really started to prickle and rise as he read on.

Freemasonry springs from the murder of the chief architect of King Solomon's temple. The architecture of the building is believed to have many references in ancient Masonic symbolism.

Murder. Masonic symbolism.

Was it a coincidence? Just one possible fly in the ointment could ruin this theory though: the discovery of the body at the basketball court in Hull Road Park. As expected, the phrase "Hull Road Park" didn't reveal any striking Masonic connection.

As for "basketball" then this was surely going to be the undoing of the theory. Paul couldn't for the life of him see how Freemasonry could have anything even remotely to do with basketball. A couple of minutes of research on the internet proved him surprisingly wrong.

The game of basketball was invented by prominent Freemason James Naismith, master of Lawrence Lodge, Kansas. The Basketball Hall of Fame is named after him.

He considered phoning Karen or Gene Garland, then reconsidered. *No, not yet.* He would do more research before coming forward with his theory. It was time to try to learn a bit more. More online searching gave him a telephone number he thought would come in useful. He noticed his hand was trembling slightly as he picked up the handset, took a deep breath, and steadied his voice.

'Ah, good afternoon, is that the master of the York Masonic lodge? It's Paul Dobson here from the York Press. I wondered if I could have a bit of your time, please. I'm writing an article to promote Freemasonry in and around York, and I wondered if I could interview you?'

The answer was more forthcoming than he could have hoped for.

'Oh, that's excellent,' Paul replied. 'See you at seven o'clock this evening at the hall, then. Thank you, that's very good of you. Yes, no problem. See you there.'

Paul collapsed back in his chair, his mind in so much of a whirl he barely noticed Linda Reader coming back into his office.

'OK, Paul, here's some good news for you. I've been busy on your behalf today.'

She put the paperwork she'd been holding back into in tray and stood back with a satisfied beam on her face.

'I filled out your expenses and took them into accounts. They're a couple of days late, but I told them to stop whingeing and get them paid in today. Your car is booked in next Wednesday morning for its MOT. Send the bill in to me when it's done, and we'll pick up the tab. It's the least we can do. I've also sorted out an appointment with your solicitor and I've pencilled you off that afternoon, so you don't have to worry about that either.'

'Wow, thank you,' responded Paul. 'I really appreciate you organising this for me.'

'Don't mention it.' Linda smiled. 'Organising is my job. Organising is what I do.'

Chapter 19

At the same time Paul was on the telephone to the master of the local Masonic lodge, Professor Dawn Robinson was on her feet, addressing the team of detectives in the incident room.

'Hi, everyone. I'm very keen to do everything I can to help,' she started. 'I've come up with a couple of theories I thought I'd run by you to see if they have any merit.' She picked at a bit of nail polish on her left index finger while she composed herself for her next sentence, then continued. 'I started by thinking about the concept that the killer's latest quatrain suggested clues symbolised in the message.'

Once again, several pens in the room started scratching. DC Snow made a mental note to look up the word 'quatrain' when he was somewhere private.

'I ran through some ideas of things that have a beginning and an end and arrive at a "destiny" or "destination" that's suggested in the first line – and that gives us the notion of a journey. But what kind of journey? If it's York, with all its railway history, then that draws you towards a train journey.'

Turning to the whiteboard behind her upon which Garland had attached a large printout of the verse, she pointed to the second line. 'So let's take a look. "Feeling the pressure".' She quoted from the verse. 'On what type of train would you particularly have pressure?'

It was DC Snow who got it straight away. 'A steam train,' he said. 'The pressure of the steam in the boiler powers the train. I stood on the footplate of one at the Railway Museum. The engineers' cab is full of pressure gauges.'

'Exactly.' Professor Robinson smiled. 'Yes, I know that diesel-electric trains can have oil pressures and so on, but it's not quite so clearly linked, is it? Now there's one other thing I noticed which may be significant: "starting at the beginning and going to the end" and wondered if that was a coded reference to what we might find if we wrote the killer's message backwards. I put it into my laptop to reverse the text of the verse and it gave me this back.'

She took a sheet of A4 paper from the desk in front of her and turned around. Garland handed her four button magnets, which she used to attach the paper to the whiteboard, and she then stood back to let the room see the output.

gniydyallliwenotxenehtthginotfodneehtybgniyrtuoyfoenoyrevenu
fevah
uoytagnikoolmisreppocdnasretropereulcymslobmysymegassemy
mkcarcuoynac
ezirpruoysnomelehtcinoristiwohesilaerwonuoyerusserpehtgnileef
niagaecnoliafotdenitsedyleruseruoydneehtotpudnagninnigebehte
cnis

The roomful of detectives silently scanned the text.

'I'm not seeing anything immediate,' confessed DS Jamshedji.

'No, neither did I,' agreed Professor Robinson, 'so don't feel too bad. But to be on the safe side, I ran the reversed text through the computer again, this time searching for words, and I did find a few interesting elements.'

Everyone craned forwards a little to concentrate as Professor Robinson attached a second piece of paper to the whiteboard, almost identical to the first but in which several portions of text were highlighted.

gniydyallliwenotxenehtthginotfodneehtybgniyrtuoyfoenoyrevenu
fevah
uoytagnikoolmisreppocdnas **retro** pereulcymslobmysy **megasse**
mymkcarcuoynac
ezirpruoysnomelehtcinoristiwohesilaerwonuoyerusserpehtgnileef
niagaecnoliafotdenitsedyler **user**
uoydneehtotpudnagninnigebehtecnis

'You will notice in the text that it contains various English words. The ones containing only two or three letters we can possibly ignore as there is a high probability that they occurred purely by chance. So what I was really looking for were words with four letters or more and in particular words of seven letters or more. The mathematical probability of getting words of seven letters purely by chance is low, and therefore any word we do find should be treated with some statistical significance. So if you look closely' – she indicated with her varnish-chipped index finger – 'we also have about two-thirds of the way along in the second line the seven letter word "Megasse". Anyone?'

She looked round the room to be met by a shake of heads.

'No, me neither at first, which is why I was glad the computer contained a dictionary with a larger vocabulary than mine, and you can bet I've filed this one away for future quiz nights. "Megasse" is apparently the pulp that's left behind after the extraction of juice from sugar cane or similar plants, and a principal use of megasse was to fuel steam locomotives in many countries.'

DC Goodier had his finger raised. There goes the terrier with a rat yet again, thought Garland. Go on, say what's on your mind.

'When you say "statistically significant",' Goodier asked, 'can you put a figure on just how statistically significant it is? One per cent? Ten per cent? Twenty-five?'

Professor Robinson nodded. 'Excellent question. Well, as you can imagine this is the first time I've had to do this, so there are no official figures, but I asked myself the same question and since there was no existing answer to it, I worked it out.

Goodier's eyes widened in genuine appreciation. 'Wow.'

Professor Robinson smiled modestly. 'It's actually not as hard as you might think. There's an old trick us computer mathematicians use that was invented by a mathematician working on the Manhattan atom bomb project. He couldn't calculate the probability of winning a game of patience, so he just programmed a computer to play hundreds of games instead and see what happened. I replicated his experiment. I lifted a hundred pieces of text from random song lyrics of about the same length as the clue, then got the computer to reverse them and search them for words of seven letters or more. This happened twenty-five per cent of the time. So, it's not exactly an earth-shatteringly rare occurrence, which is why we need to treat it with some caution, but the fact it relates directly to steam engines and the fact that York is famous for a museum full of steam trains just adds to the weight of its significance.'

'I see it now,' noted Jamshedji. 'If we look at words of four letters or more which you've highlighted you get the phrase "*Retro megasse user*" buried in the backwards rhyme. The perfect definition for an old steam train. If I remember correctly from the files, didn't our first victim Alec Hopkins work for British Rail and did he not have a photo of himself stood next to a steam train on his mantelpiece?'

'One more thought,' added Jason Brown. 'One of the most famous steam trains in the collection is the Southern Railway's *Sir Lamiel*. It was used a few years back in a BBC film adaptation of *La Bête Humaine* by the French playwright Émile Zola. I remember watching it. Quite enjoyable it was, too. Significantly, the plot of the film is about a string of murders.'

* * * *

Jack Horner was glad to get home a little early after a tiring day. That afternoon, he'd carried out the post-mortem on Kirsten McNally, not that he'd ever been in any doubt as to the cause of death. Before opening the chest cavity to examine her internal organs and retrieve the expected 9mm bullet, he'd taken, in accordance with guidelines, a blood sample to send off to forensic toxicology. Given the current lead times and backlogs in the system it would take at least two weeks to come back, by which time this whole murder and Kirsten McNally, together with her unexceptional life, would be reduced to a long distant memory. He already knew his report wouldn't add anything of value that wasn't already anticipated. He'd developed the knack over many years of being able to predict, with a high degree of accuracy, what the toxicology report would say simply from his observations of the condition of the body. In this particular case, you really didn't need to be an experienced pathologist to notice the very visible needle marks on the skin and make your own prediction.

Making his way over to his hi-fi, he crouched down to select a record from the oak cabinet below. While many audiophile enthusiasts had gone the way of digital streaming, he preferred to keep things very traditional. To that end, he'd invested a considerable amount of his income into a high-end turntable, arm, cartridge, and stylus, all of which he'd proudly but painstakingly set up himself using an array of specialist measurement protractors. He selected a record.

Ah yes, this would do, Supertramp, one of his favourite bands.

He delicately extracted the vinyl from its sleeve like a jeweller handling a priceless Fabergé egg, and placed it carefully on the turntable.

An image of Kirsten McNally's needle-ravaged skin flashed briefly through his mind. Such a waste. At the time of her death, she'd probably already become a cog in the ruthless, uncaring machine of drug dealing that perpetuated its callous misery onto others. It was time for a drink. *Cognac, maybe? No, not tonight. Gin?*

Casting his eyes over his sideboard, he saw that he was out of tonic water and a slice of anything to put in it. *Whisky, then. Ah yes, you could always rely on a good Scotch.* Pouring himself a substantial glass of Talisker single malt, he placed the stylus on the record and settled back in his armchair with a contented smile broadening across his face as the sounds of Supertramp's famous album from 1974 filled the room.

Chapter 20

DS Jamshedji persisted with the recent line of thought. 'OK, let's just play devil's advocate. I buy the idea that the clues are a great fit to the National Railway Museum, but if the killer sticks to their traditional modus operandi of using a silenced gun, even a well-silenced gun is pretty loud indoors. In that main hall where the steam trains are on display, it would echo and make a distinguishable noise. Add to that, that so far all the killings have occurred at night and the Railway Museum is closed in the evenings.'

Jason Brown stroked his moustache again while he pondered this. 'Not necessarily,' he said. 'There's an open area outside called the South Yard which is used for picnics, a little miniature steam railway, and various odd bits of rolling stock. Whether any steam locomotives like the *Sir Lamiel* are stored out there in the open at this time of year is another matter, though.'

'Hang on,' interjected Garland. 'I've just got a satellite view of the area up on my laptop. Can someone pass me that cable from over there please so I can beam it up onto the screen?' With the cable plugged into Garland's laptop, the detectives were able to view the satellite image from Google Maps on the large TV screen.

'Here we go' – he stood up to point – 'you can even spot some of the rolling stock parked out here from the satellite photo. Mind you, I can't tell what time of year this image was taken. Anyway, look, you can see there are plenty of access points off Leeman Road here' – he indicated with his finger – 'and off Cinder Lane here. I don't know how popular the area is with late-night walkers, but it looks like there are paths that take you along the boundary of the yard right along where the rolling stock is stored.'

'It's also far away from populated streets,' Jamshedji noted. 'And with the added advantage that the traffic on the main road might cover up a bit of unwanted noise. You could make your way up the side of the railway line from up by the rail depot. There'd be nobody to see you and no houses with CCTV cameras to catch you making your way in and out. Now I see it on the screen. It's perfect, in fact.'

'Doctor Tennant,' Garland said. 'You mentioned that sometimes with serial killers there's a causal link and if we can find that link, we could be onto something?' Dr Tennant nodded. 'Jason, you mentioned seeing this film' – he looked down at his notepad – 'Bête Humaine? Can you remember the murders in the film and what the motives were?'

'Not off the top of my head,' replied Jason. 'It was a few years back. But give me a second, I'll look online to jog my ageing memory.'

He pulled his mobile from his inside jacket pocket, lifted his spectacles up onto his forehead, and narrowed his eyes underneath his bushy eyebrows to help him read the small print on the screen at close range. 'Ah, OK here we are. There are a few in there, some successful murders, some unsuccessful attempts. Of course, you won't be surprised to hear the film's a bit different from the book.'

'Go on,' encouraged Garland.

'In chronological order, we've got the following – the first murder was of someone who worked for the railways, for which the motive was revenge for an affair.'

'That's interesting,' noted Garland. 'The first victim, Alec Hopkins, once worked for the railways.'

'The second murder was of an accomplice also involved in the first murder and for which the motive was to get rid of them as a threat or rival. Then there's a third murder, the motive for which was the killing of a lover. The book ends in a fourth murder – though in the film the victim survives – which is about a fight resulting from a dispute. The victim is a fireman. And the fight is on the footplate of a steam train.'

* * * *

The brutish industrial-looking building that once housed the Clock Cinema in the Oakwood area of Leeds seemed to be bracing itself defiantly against the stinging drizzle and bitter cold evening wind. With architecture more reminiscent of a power station than a cinema, the square brick building with a flat roof, upon which now sat a phone mast, stood just off a busy urban arterial route in and out of the centre of Leeds. The cinema, like so many of its kind, was long gone and the building which had brought movies from *Casablanca* to the *Carry On* films to Leeds had subsequently been a bingo hall, then an electrical store, and now housed outlets such as coin-operated laundries and kebab shops. At one end of the building, sticking out like a strange, misplaced afterthought of design, a tall white Art Deco clock tower, which had given the building its name, looked down on the headlamps of the passing cars and buses below.

The stocky man standing under the clock zipped his rainproof coat up a bit further against the cold and wet. He checked his watch impatiently one more time and gazed across the busy junction to a similar brick building now home to an ethnic supermarket but which he remembered back in the day as the notorious Fforde Grene pub.

Christ, there's been some bloody rough nights in there, he recalled.

A once popular music venue, the pub was as famous for its fights and riots every bit as much as its acts. In its glory days, home to concerts by bands such as the Sex Pistols, U2, and Dire Straits, its lasting memory was that of violence and crime. He recalled how on one occasion, a fight there had left the interior completely annihilated, broken chairs and tables and sharp shrapnel shards of broken pint glasses filling a floor soaked with cheap lager and bitter.

He smiled grimly. A lot of that had been a little before his time, but he'd known of its reputation long before he'd been called to run-ins in there several times before it finally closed its doors several years ago. Some bloody rough arseholes there. Still, nothing a hefty belt with a truncheon couldn't sort out before they were thrown in the back of the police van. He afforded himself a smile at the memories. Followed by another good bloody belting when they got dragged out at the other end.

His reminiscence was cut short by the appearance of the figure he'd been waiting for, and he turned his head.

'You're late.' He stared at his new companion's face and laughed. 'Hey, look at you, you've got yourself a nice shiner since I last saw you. What happened? One of them skinny teenage prostitutes in Holgate you fancy gave you a smack, did she?'

'Shut it.' The man turned his face as if to hide his recently acquired black eye in the shadow of the clock tower, and clenched his right fist into a ball.

'Oh no, it wasn't, was it? Hang on, I remember now. It was an old codger that couldn't fight his way out of a fart gave you a good decking, that's right.' He scoffed at the man's sudden startled expression. 'What? You seriously didn't think word wouldn't get back? Well, it has and frankly I'm not bloody impressed, so put your hands back in your poncey leather jacket and listen. I have a job for you this week that might, I mean *might* redeem you.'

* * * *

'Any more for any more?' asked Garland. 'While we're all together let's take the opportunity to get everything out on the table. Jason, did you have anything?'

'One idea I had,' answered Jason Brown, 'was around this idea of "Beginning and end" which reminded me of a Bible quote: "I am the Alpha and the Omega, the First and the Last, the Beginning and the End. Blessed are those who wash their robes, so that they may have the right to the tree of life and may enter the city by its gates".' He gave the last six words a particular emphasis. Then paused and coughed. 'Revelation 22.'

Enter the city by its gates. Everyone's eyes darted around at each other. Jason Brown sensed the mood.

'Yes, I'm sure I don't need to remind you that York is a walled city with streets called gates,' he elaborated slowly. 'Now all we have to do is work out which of them could be the place for a murder. York's got four old city gateways, as you know: at Bootham Bar, Monk Bar, Walmgate Bar, and Micklegate Bar. Incidentally, there are six secondary entrances, but let's put those aside for a minute.' As he spoke, Garland brought a Google Map of York onto the large TV screen for reference.

'Before I continue,' cautioned Brown, 'can I just mention that the Tree of Life mentioned in the Book of Revelation isn't just a Christian concept. It's featured in many religions, notably

Norse mythology, and once you've seen what it looks like, you'll recognise it all over York in shops and printed on T-shirts and hoodies on sale all over the city.'

The detectives were making notes at this news. York was famous for its reputation as a Viking settlement and many local company and society names featured the word Jorvik to attest the fact.

'So, let's see if any other pointers can narrow it down,' continued Brown. 'First off, we have this reference to the washing of robes. Now, it might be pertinent when you find out that the area around the Micklegate bar area in olden times was principally concerned with the industry of fullers. As it happens, my mother's maiden name is Fuller, so I already knew this and didn't have to look it up, but for the rest of you, a fuller is someone who washes wool. We've also got references in this verse to destiny, irony, and feeling the pressure, and all these phrases point to a famous citizen of York from the sixteenth century, by the name of Margaret Clitherow.'

'I've visited her house,' prompted DC Ward. 'It's in The Shambles. They turned it into a shrine which you can visit.' He laughed. 'The wife was nervous about going in. She's heard tales it's haunted.'

'Tell her not to worry,' Brown reassured him. 'The street got renumbered in the eighteenth century, so Margaret Clitherow probably lived in the house opposite. Anyway, you'll know the story: she was put to death for hiding Catholic priests in her house. What was ironic about it was that after successfully helping so many people evade capture, the one person she couldn't save was herself, poor lass.'

He stroked his moustache again, thought for a little while, and then continued.

'Her destiny, then, was to be put to death by literally "feeling the pressure" in a form of execution known as being "pressed to death". A door was placed on top of her and then rocks and boulders were piled on top until the pressure broke her back and killed her. Apparently, it was so grotesque and horrific that the soldiers who were given the task couldn't go through with it and paid some beggars to do it instead.'

'Good God.' exclaimed Garland. 'And whereabouts did this execution take place?'

'Going up towards the Minster and the city gates there,' replied Brown. 'Near where it's believed Guy Fawkes was living at the time, so he might actually have seen it. Two of his mates were Margaret Clitherow's nephews, so Guy Fawkes teamed up with them and, well, we all know how that turned out.'

* * * *

The figure in the leather jacket stomped off angrily into the night, the stinging rain and the harsh critical stare of his handler lashing down on his back. When that tough bastard DCI Brown had retired a couple of years back, he'd cheered and popped open a bottle, but now this new bastard they'd given him seemed even worse.

Chapter 21

'You did mention you had a couple of possible lines of enquiry,' Garland asked Professor Robinson. 'What was the other one?'

'It's sketchy I'm afraid,' she replied, 'but you did say there were no silly ideas, so here goes. That phrase "Since the beginning" put me in mind of the Old Testament opening in the book of Genesis. Well, as it turns out, there are a set of buildings in York called the Genesis Buildings.'

'Really? Where?'

'On the university science park, near the junction at Alcuin Way.'

Garland scrolled the Google map on the screen to York University.

'Here we are,' Professor Robinson pointed, 'they're used by the Plasma Institute research laboratories.'

'Plasma?' interjected DC Snow. 'Never heard of it.'

'You have,' answered DC Parkinson before she could stop herself. 'You were literally playing that song 'St. Elmo's Fire' in the car the other day. St Elmo's Fire is a type of plasma.'

There was an embarrassed silence. 'What?' DC Parkinson demanded curtly in mock indignation. 'I happen to have A-level chemistry. And?'

'OK, OK,' Garland interjected, raising his hands to dampen the guffaws in the room. 'Jason, any thoughts on this idea?'

'Yes, a couple,' Jason Brown responded. 'Now that we're talking about buildings off Alcuin Way. Alcuin was a scholar from York. He invented a method of writing messages in letters and symbols which does rather take us neatly to the third line of our verse "*Can you crack my message, my symbols...*". The second thing is that Alcuin was famous for coming up with ingenious riddles.'

He nudged his glasses back up his nose where they'd slipped down a little and carried on. 'It's rumoured he was the guy who came up with the problem of where you have to get a wolf, a goat, and a cabbage across a river, but you can only fit yourself and one other item in the boat at any time. Anyway, one of his puzzle books was called something like *The Joy of Cleverness*. Would make rather a fitting inspiration for someone who gets joy in setting riddles for the police, don't you think? And what better irony than to meet your end and your destiny than at a place named after the beginning?'

* * * *

Like the majority of the population, Paul Dobson had never been inside a Masonic Hall and although he normally considered himself a generally unshakeable individual, as he pulled up outside the intimidating building, his insides felt like he'd just reached the head of the queue to go on a tall but dilapidated roller coaster. He switched off the engine of his Volkswagen Golf and let a couple of minutes pass for him to regain his composure before climbing out to stand in the car park beside a laurel hedge and to gaze upwards at the imposing structure. Passing through the large door, above which an impressive square and compasses had been carved into the stonework, he had to admit to feeling uneasy as his feet stepped off the crunchy wet gravel outside and into the unknown.

As the entrance hall swallowed him up, his eyes darted around. The foyer was large with oak panelling on one side, upon which hung several paintings of grand-looking men dressed in bright Masonic regalia. On the opposite wall were two more paintings, one of the queen in her slightly younger days, and the other of the Duke of Kent. Despite this though, on closer inspection as he adjusted to his surroundings, some of the paintwork on the skirting below had a few chips and the wallpaper on the wall opposite the oak panelling had peeled a little. The whole place had an air of slightly faded grandeur. It immediately reminded Paul of a grand old Edwardian hotel at the seaside he'd once stayed in with Amanda, which had given the impression of having been absolutely regal in its day but was now wearing the passing of its years.

As he made his way forward, a tall, athletic, crisp-looking man with short dark hair and an upright bearing burst out of the doorway at the other end of the hall.

'Ah, you must be Paul Dobson from the press. Pleased to meet you. How are you?'

Paul stepped forward, and the man extended his arm in welcome and shook Paul's hand vigorously. Paul had been mentally preparing himself for the handshake to stay alert and use the opportunity to see if he could determine what a Mason's handshake felt like and was disappointed to find he couldn't discern anything unusual.

'I'm Alan Brook, master of the lodge. My word, you look freezing, come on through. Come on through.'

Putting a hand on Paul's shoulder, Alan Brook ushered him to a convivial warm bar area. They were the only people in the room save for a young blonde lady in a grey sweatshirt who was setting out dishes of crisps and peanuts on the tables. She was humming a tune but broke off and came across when as they entered.

'Oh hullo, Major,' she greeted them. 'Have you got someone joining you this week? Hope we've got enough chips and peas to go round.'

'No.' Alan laughed. 'Let me introduce you, though. This is Paul from the York Press. He's come to write some flattering words about us, at least, I hope they will be. Paul, this is Louise. She's responsible for running the bar and keeping us all under control.'

'It's a tough job but somebody's got to do it.' Louise offered Paul one of the bowls with a grin. 'Salt and vinegar crisps?'

Paul realised he hadn't eaten all day and was, in fact very hungry. 'Go on then. Thank you.'

'Major?' asked Paul, turning back to Alan.

'My nickname here,' Alan replied. 'It's my proper title when I'm at work, but I don't make a song and dance about it. If you want my full title, I'm Major Alan Brook from the 4th Battalion Yorkshire Regiment.' He paused to regard Paul's blank expression. 'Infantry.'

'Ah,' realised Paul. 'Are you based at…?'

'The garrison on Fulford Road.' Alan leant across and plucked a huge handful of crisps. 'You know the place? It's next to the police station.'

'I know it well…' Paul replied and then stopped himself. It might not be a wise idea to acknowledge that the reason he saw it frequently was because he was a regular visitor at the police station. 'Anyway, thank you for agreeing to meet me at such short notice.'

'No problem at all. In fact, you're lucky tonight. We're having a little practice run-through for our monthly meeting in a couple of nights, so I was going to be here, anyway. If you're still here in half an hour, some of the other lads will be arriving.'

'Can I stay for the meeting?'

'Sorry, young man, no can do. We're opening up a lot more to the outside world, but there are still some limits, you understand. You can come and see our special meeting room, though.'

'I can?' Paul was taken aback. He couldn't have been more astonished if he'd just been invited into the room where all NATO's secret nuclear codes and the big red launch button were kept.

'Why not?' Alan shovelled the crisps down his throat and stood up. 'Follow me.'

Brushing crumbs from his lapels as he went, he marched up a short flight of stairs with Paul following on eagerly behind. Arriving at a wooden door, he swung it open and put his hand round the door frame to switch on the lights. 'Here you go.'

Paul's widening eyes as he peered through the doorway were greeted by a spacious rectangular room with chairs laid out around the perimeter. In the centre of the floor, the carpet was tiled black and white like a giant oblong chess board. Three sides of the room each had a larger chair raised up on a small plinth with a wooden lectern in front of it complete with candlestick. The ceiling was reminiscent of a planetarium, depicting various constellations and planets. Paul's eyes scanned the room, looking for hidden signs of iconography, but, just as with the handshake, he was frustrated to realise he couldn't identify any. He pointed to the candlesticks on the lecterns. 'You still use candles?'

'Shh,' grinned Alan, raising a finger to his lips. 'The ones we use here are battery operated. We've gone electric. Like Bob Dylan did at the Rhode Island Folk Festival, much to the disgust of the traditionalists.'

‘So this is the room where it all happens?’ Paul was slightly unnerved by the echoey stillness of it all. ‘Can I ask what does happen?’

‘Well, it’s where we hold our monthly meeting. It’ll last about an hour and then we’ll go downstairs for a pint or two and a slap-up meal. It’s steak and chips with all the trimmings tonight, and apparently blackberry pie and custard for afters.’

‘What kinds of things do Freemasons discuss?’

‘You’re not supposed to know the details, but I can tell you it’s a lot to do with charity work. You might want to mention in your article that Freemasons in the UK typically donate about fifty million pounds to charity each year and do millions of hours of unpaid voluntary work.’

‘And those stories I’ve read on the internet about what happens in initiations?’ Paul ventured hesitantly.

‘Most of them are all bollocks, pardon my language.’ Alan smiled. ‘Seriously, take no notice of them. For every one bit of real information, there’s a hundred bits of made-up twaddle by conspiracy theorists and fantasists. Of course, you could always find out for yourself by coming to join us, if you ever fancy making the commitment.’

‘I’ll consider it,’ Paul hedged politely. His mind recalled the recent murders. ‘Can I ask though, are there really Draconian penalties I’ve read about that can happen to people?’

‘We promise faithfully not to disclose certain secrets,’ Alan said solemnly as they descended the stairs back towards the bar and the entrance hall, ‘and we do take it rather seriously, so you’ll just have to come and join us, and you’ll find out for yourself.’

They descended the stairs and arrived back in the entrance hall. ‘Well, it’s been fascinating coming along and thank you for giving up your time,' said Paul appreciatively. At that moment, a group of men strolled in through the entrance doors laughing with each other at some private joke. 'Anyway, I'd better let you get on with your evening.'

'The pleasure's been mine. Very happy to help with anything I can and if you have any further questions, just give me a call and I'll answer them.' He paused. 'If I can, of course.'

He shook Paul's hand again. This time Paul wasn't expecting it and kicked himself for not being ready to pay attention. As he started to turn away, one of the men who had just arrived came up to Alan.

'Evening, Major, sorry about this, but I've got an apology for absence for you tonight. We're going to have to find another Senior Deacon for the evening's proceedings.'

'Why? What's happened?'

'Didn't get the full story, but apparently some police operation's happening tonight, and his boss has insisted he stay on at work for a long briefing meeting. That's all I know.'

'That's OK. I'll ask one of the other lads to stand in tonight.' Alan turned to smile at Paul for the final time. 'Got to go, sorry, things to sort out. Good luck with the article.'

* * * *

Many hours had now passed since Karen Parkinson had, at long last, returned home after the evening's briefing meeting. She stole a look at her watch. Nearly midnight. Beside her on the sofa, *Pride and Prejudice* lay untouched for yet another night. Thoughts were bouncing round her head like a manic pinball table that wouldn't turn off, and the concept of any kind of sleep that night had been a complete non-starter, right from the minute she'd come in through the front door and kicked her shoes off. Out there tonight she knew Garland had organised firearms-trained officers to be waiting at all the locations they'd discussed that evening.

Her laptop screen cast a glow across her face as she hunched over the keyboard. She'd watched YouTube videos of the Railway Museum, then spent ages walking around the city gates of York in Google Street View while a plate of microwave pasta had gone stone cold.

And now onto the last location they had discussed at York Science Park. The website for the York Plasma Institute filled the screen. Scrolling down, she noticed a button: "Take a virtual tour". *Well, why not? Let's have a nosey around inside from the comfort of the sofa.* She clicked the button.

Inside the Plasma Institute, the laboratories were modern, bright, and pristine. Her mind was flooded instantly with memories of the last time she'd been in a laboratory in the sixth form at school. This place was a far cry from the comprehensive school lab, with its old desks inscribed with biro-gouged graffiti and its tattered black curtains ravaged by years of pupils carrying out unofficial tests of their fireproof qualities with a Bunsen burner, and Mr Herrington in his white lab coat at the front holding up a three-dimensional model of a methane molecule. *Just imagine*, she thought, *I could be working in a high-tech plasma lab instead of spending my days worrying myself sick in a room where your work colleagues chuckle at you just because you know what plasma is and what a molecule looks like*.

The posters which brightened up the walls of an otherwise clinically white environment were of a different calibre to the school ones, too. She paused her virtual expedition to zoom in and read the words on one of them. It was titled *The Design of the Synthetic Aperture Microwave Imager*. Below the heading was a series of mind-bogglingly complicated looking graphs and formulae. *Hmm, or maybe not*, she thought. *I'll stick to my current job.*

She could still remember the poster in her old school lab, though. A huge Periodic Table of Elements which adorned the section of wall next to the decrepit fume cupboard. For her A-level she'd had to learn the chemical symbols off by heart. Some of the symbols had been easy: H for Hydrogen, O for Oxygen. Some of the Latin ones she recalled had been a little trickier. Na for sodium. Pb for lead. Cu for Copper.

'Sorry, Mr Herrington,' she uttered aloud. 'You did your best, but instead of being a scientist, I ended up a copper. Or as the symbol on your Periodic Table would say, a Cu – but not next Tuesday.'

Symbol.

The beginning and up to the end.

A chill ran down her back. She grabbed her notepad with the latest verse written on it and started furiously writing. Five minutes later, her eyes widened. She flung the notepad onto the table and her hands dived for her mobile phone.

Shit.

Karen's fumbling hands struggled to operate her phone while frantically pulling on her trainers, her heart pounding out of her chest.

Chapter 22

Everyone who has learnt their perception of what our solar system looks like by looking at diagrams in textbooks would be shocked to discover just how spectacularly wide of the mark they are. Faced with the unenviable paradox of having to create a legible diagram that fits across a double page spread, every textbook illustrator has been forced to make such incredible compromises that the scale of the resulting picture has no bearing on reality whatsoever. In 1999, three scientists from York devised an innovative way to put the record straight.

Laid out along a cycle route running south from the outskirts of York, an accurate scale model of the solar system had been constructed, and many of those who experience the joy of walking or cycling along it return with their perspective forever changed. Scores of motorists drive up and down the busy York bypass without ever noticing the colossal golden metal sphere that hangs beside one of the bridges, marking the sun at the start of the trail. The planets of the solar system are laid out along the route, each represented by a small metal sphere in an accurate scale of both size and distance. Earth, by comparison to the vast sun, is roughly the size of a marble and is a few minutes' walk away. An hour's walk would take the intrepid hiker to the football-sized Saturn three and a half miles down the track. Those with tenacity and a good pair of walking boots, or a bicycle, would arrive at tiny Pluto – still a planet when the trail was constructed – more than six miles from their starting point.

None of this was on Karen Parkinson's mind as she rammed her foot on the brake pedal to bring her car to a screeching, skidding stop. Yanking out the keys with trembling hands, she leapt straight out of the car to sprint down under the bridge below the bypass. The beam of her torch bounced erratically off the garish spray-paint graffiti that decorated the concrete supports as she raced underneath, panting heavily.

Around the bend in the track, the scenery opened out to fields on both sides and as Karen hurtled round the corner with her lungs on fire, she could make out two standing figures in hi-vis jackets on the path ahead, each pointing a torch downwards. The sight that made her blood run cold was the ominous, dark third shape lying motionless on the ground.

She came to an abrupt halt by the figures and saw that they were PC Charlie Atkinson and PC Gabby Janowski, the police officers who had also been first on the scene in the cold hours of the morning for the killing of Kirsten McNally in Hull Road Park. She stared down aghast at the lifeless form illuminated in the harsh light of the torches, her breath coming in huge gulps which sent large visible clouds of condensation into the freezing night air.

'We rushed straight over as soon as you'd called it in,' explained Atkinson. 'I'm so sorry.'

Karen clenched her eyes shut momentarily while she collected her thoughts. There was one more thing she just needed to check for her own peace of mind.

Turning the beam of her torch to her left, Karen's suspicions were confirmed. Atop a dark grey tubular plinth, a metal sphere like a ball bearing, not much larger than a frozen pea, was held aloft on a triangular support. The shiny metal ball reflected the light from the torch bulb and dazzled brightly against the rustling obsidian backdrop of the hedge behind. Painted on the side of the plinth, the solitary word burnt its way into Karen's eyes.

MERCURY

PC Janowski's radio burst into life and she turned her face away from a quick flurry of wind to fire an update to whoever had called. She turned back to Karen. 'Garland's on his way, he'll be here any minute.'

'I'll give you a hand taping up the scene,' Karen offered. Anything to take her mind off the frantic, deafening clamour that was blaring incessantly inside her head.

Oh my God, how could none of them have seen it?

A voice and sprinting footsteps behind them heralded a new arrival. Spinning round, Karen struggled at first to identify the figure and it wasn't until it was up close that she recognised the familiar trademark black jacket of Gene Garland. Despite the cacophony going on in Karen's head, she paused to appreciate how deceptively athletic he was, and to come from his home in Dunnington in such a short space of time, he must have floored the throttle like a rally driver.

As he approached Karen, she turned to him and clenched her fists. 'Shit!' She paused, then burst out again in frustration. 'Shit. Bugger and shit.'

'You did an excellent job,' Garland reassured her. 'Far better than all the rest of us in fact.'

He leant slowly and carefully over the body on the path beside the planet Mercury. A middle-aged man in a blue hiking jacket lay slumped on his side, a pool of blood underneath him and his sparse hair, now wet from the damp morning air, blew unflatteringly over his pallid, lifeless face.

Garland stood up and turned to the two constables. 'Thanks, Gabby, Charlie, for getting here so fast. Sorry it couldn't have been a different outcome, but that's how it goes sometimes.' As he turned back to Karen, the sky was becoming illuminated by a display of distant flashing blue lights. 'While we wait for the forensic circus to turn up, you can tell me how you cracked it.'

'With pleasure, boss.' Karen took a deep breath and addressed Garland, wondering how he managed to keep a calm head at a time like this. 'But if you'll excuse me for just thirty seconds, there's a little something I want to do first.'

* * * *

Paul had turned in early to bed that night, having stayed up long enough to watch the late night local news programmes, and was relieved to see they didn't contain any information he didn't already know. He realised that he was feeling burnt out with everything going on with a serial killer at large and the barrage of enigmatic clues, on top of all the already oppressive domestic paperwork he needed to get through in order to try to bring some peace and order to his personal life.

He shoved his pile of divorce documents over to the left-hand side of his modest coffee table, the pile of papers concerning the serial killer to the right, closed the lid on his laptop, and headed into the bedroom to try for a solid night's sleep.

It was not to be. It seemed like only a heartbeat since he'd fallen into a peaceful slumber when his mobile phone on the bedside table was jolting him awake with a buzz. When he snatched up the phone and read the terse message from Karen on the screen, he knew instantly that any thoughts of any more sleep that night had been blown apart.

* * * *

'It's one of those things that in hindsight, you just can't believe how none of us twigged it,' Karen sighed. She fumbled in the right-hand pocket of her tracksuit top that she'd pulled on hurriedly as she'd bolted out of her house. Garland nodded patiently, flashes of blue in the sky from beyond the underpass flickering off his hair. Karen retrieved the crumpled piece of paper she'd torn out of her notepad and unfolded it to display the clue along with her accompanying hand-written jottings.

Since the beginning and up to the end; you're surely destined to fail once again

Feeling the pressure, you now realise how it's ironic the lemon's your prize

Can you crack my message, my symbols, my clue; reporters and coppers I'm looking at you

Have fun every one of you trying. By the end of tonight, the next one will lay dying

'The opening statement "Since the beginning and up to the end..." is a hint to take the first and last letters of each line in the clue,' Karen explained. 'That gives us "Sn", "Fe", "Cu", and "Hg" for the four lines of the poem. There's a reference in the third line of the clue for "my symbols" – and these are all chemical symbols.'

Garland stared at the piece of paper and nodded. 'I see it now. They're the symbols for tin, iron, copper, and mercury.'

'Yes,' continued Karen. 'The thought dawned on me after I'd been looking at York Science Park for a possible location for the murder and remembered they were on the periodic table.'

Garland drew in a slow whistle. 'Go on.'

'When I looked at the verse again, it struck me that the first line contained the word "destined". Des-TIN-ed' – she emphasised the middle syllable – 'and the chemical symbol Sn is the symbol for tin. The next line contains the word IRON-ic and Fe is the symbol for iron. The third line contains COPPER-s and Cu is the symbol for copper. The final line of the clue mentions "every one" and every line of the verse contains the metal referenced by the symbol made up of the first and last letter of that line except the final one. The symbol "Hg" made up from the letters of the fourth line points to the thing we need to make "every one" of the lines complete which is MERCURY – and here we are.'

'Oh, bloody hell.' Garland grimaced as the facts sunk in. 'I've just realised something else now you've said that. Didn't the clue that came with the lemon also say something about "grasping the mettle" – and these are all metals? Oh God, this gets worse.'

He stared back down at the body on the ground and shuddered as the breeze picked up again, blowing the corpse's hair into even more disarray.

Chapter 23

Jack Horner was a meticulous and highly regarded pathologist. As soon as the body had been brought from the Solar System Trail into the mortuary, his first job had been to collect a further set of scrapings from under the victim's fingernails and fibres from the clothing, even though he was sure there would be nothing of any forensic value to be found. Still, there were procedures to be adhered to and professional standards to maintain. He'd taken photographs of the body from a variety of angles before he'd commenced work, carefully removing the clothing from the victim while he still lay in the body bag so as not to lose any potentially vital forensic evidence. He was also convinced there would be nothing here to connect the clothing to the killer, but the rules and procedures were laid down to be followed. As he removed the jacket from the victim, he noticed the 9mm bullet lodged in the fibres in the back. He'd taken a series of photographs with a scale ruler in place before removing it with tweezers and sealing it in a forensic bag for the ballistics lab.

'So everything we are about to do now is just going through the motions,' he found himself saying an hour later to DS Jamshedji, who stood at the other side of the mortuary table. The now unclothed corpse lay face up between them. 'But we still have to do it. Ready?'

Sniffing the Vicks VapoRub on his top lip, Jamshedji raised himself up and down on his toes, a technique he'd been told would help him stop feeling faint and queasy but in his case seemed to have no effect. It always seemed to be him who ended up at the post-mortems. He wondered if and how, somewhere along the line, Garland had come to the conclusion he actually enjoyed going to these things.

'You look a bit tired, Dattaram old chum. Are you all right?' Jack asked, sounding concerned as he cast his eyes over Jamshedji's weary features.

'Oh, this case is wearing us into the ground.' Jamshedji sighed, wishing it wasn't quite so noticeable. 'We're working round the clock. None of us is getting enough sleep, and it's playing havoc with any kind of family or social life. Just the other evening I was supposed to be going to a social meeting, but ended up on duty trying to catch this killer. I take it this is another in the same series of murders?'

Horner grinned. 'Well, technically, the remit of my job is simply to tell you how this poor chap died. Whether a criminal offence has been committed and who did it is your responsibility to decide, not mine. But between you and me – I reckon so, yes. Anyway' – he continued without pause, sweeping his hand towards the victim's lowest extremities – 'what do you think of this then?'

'This is a new one on me,' answered Jamshedji. They both looked down at the victim's left leg, or rather to where the left foot and calf should have been, but which had been replaced from below the knee by a shiny gloss high-tech looking artificial limb.

'Do you have any information about that at all?' asked Jamshedji.

'I'm pulling up the guy's medical records which should give us more detail,' replied Horner, 'and although I'm not supposed to make any assumptions until I've got the facts, I recognise this make of prosthetic limb from other incidences I've seen. Put that together with the fact that this chap has a fit and physically active looking body and you start to get a picture. I'd bet my car and my hi-fi that this chap has had his leg blown off by a landmine somewhere in the world that's hot and dusty.'

Horner showed Jamshedji the victim's other leg. 'Here's a bit of supporting evidence for you.'

Jamshedji looked at the tattoo on the victim's right calf. '"Per ardua."' he read aloud. 'You'll have to help me, we didn't do Latin at the police training college.'

'It means "Through adversity",' explained Horner. 'The full quote is "Per ardua ad astra" which translates as "Through adversity to the stars". It's the motto of the Royal Air Force.'

'The "ad astra" half might have been on his left calf,' suggested Jamshedji. 'I'll make a note to check with his family.'

They both turned their attention to the bullet entry hole in the victim's chest. 'Strange world, isn't it?' mused Horner. 'Poor bugger's spent his career being shot at all over the world, survives something blowing his leg to bits, and then gets shot and killed after he's come home for some peace and quiet and goes for a late night stroll. Not that it's any of my business, but have you any idea what he was doing out at that time?'

'Nothing as yet. We're making enquiries about that. Maybe he just couldn't sleep and took a walk to clear his head.' As Jamshedji answered, he raised his polished Grenson brogue shoes up on tiptoe and back down again one more time to alleviate his nausea.

'I'll take some photographs and some swabs of that entrance wound first,' continued Horner, picking up a photo evidence ruler and holding it aloft as if proposing a toast, 'and then get some blood for toxicology before I open up the chest.' Sensing Jamshedji's burgeoning discomfort he added, 'You really don't need to stay for that bit if you have some more pressing business to be getting on with.'

'Thanks,' responded Jamshedji with relief, thankful for being proffered a convenient excuse to get out. 'Things are rather busy as you can imagine, so I'd appreciate being able to get away.'

'No problem at all. Spare me a thought on your way out, won't you? Even though the fellow had a bullet lodged in the back of his jacket and has a very obvious bullet hole in his chest, I've now got to take out all his organs and examine them minutely so I can include in my write-up all the unremarkable ways he didn't die.'

* * * *

Gene Garland sat quietly in his office, turning his model of *Thunderbird 2* over and over in his hands to help him focus his thoughts. He cast his eyes over the mind map upon which he'd just added the latest information.

So far, despite every concerted effort to crack the killer's codes, including drafting in an expert academic team, he was frustrated that they were making little, if any, headway, and the killer had gone out last night and added another death to the total. This time, he knew, there would be mounting pressure both from certain parts of the media who were not all going to be as accommodating as the York Press, and from his superiors to account for what was going on. His mind was once more thrown back in time to being a young boy sat on the living-room carpet, *Thunderbird 2* swooping through the air in his hand while his mother and father listened to the voice on the phone they believed to be the Yorkshire Ripper. The voice came into Garland's mind as clearly as if he'd only heard it yesterday.

I'm Jack. I see you are having no luck catching me.

A scenario he honestly believed that with all the advances in technology, CCTV, and forensic techniques, he would never see the likes of ever again.

A rapid series of images flashed through his mind, fleeting snatches of the Yorkshire Ripper killings of the 1970s seen through the eyes of a schoolboy watching the evening news. Hostile press conferences. Angry protest marches. Politicians demanding answers. Public enquiries. Police chiefs vilified.

Turning *Thunderbird 2* over in his left hand, he breathed out slowly. As he did so, another series of recollections flowed through his mind, this time more sombre. There had been children left without mothers. Parents attending the funerals of their daughters. Each victim an innocent woman, their lives snatched away decades too early. And those lucky enough to survive being deeply scarred mentally and physically by their experiences.

Come on, Garland, he rebuked himself brusquely with renewed determination. What's a bloody good bollocking from everyone compared to losing a loved one? Frame yourself and square up.

He reached across for the files on the victims and what his team had uncovered from phone records, bank statements, and door-to-door interviews in order to review them again thoroughly for anything he or his team might have missed. After all, he acknowledged to himself, the Yorkshire Ripper case had finally been solved, not by sophisticated techniques, but by good old-fashioned coppering.

Forensic evidence – a 9mm bullet retrieved from every scene, which the ballistics lab told him were all shot from the same gun. DNA evidence – none. Eyewitnesses – none. CCTV footage – nothing of any apparent use. Traces on the email address test.article@…used by the killer had so far come up against a dead end. Searches for connections between the victims had thrown up nothing that appeared significant. Psychological profiling – useful, granted, but it hardly narrowed the killer down in a city population of nearly a quarter of a million people. He frowned. Draining his coffee mug, he placed *Thunderbird 2* gently back on the desk while he considered his next move.

* * * *

The pale shaft of insipid sun managing to peek its way through the overcast autumnal sky glinted off the garish blue and yellow glass panels that made up the front of the Reginald Centre on Chapeltown Road in Leeds. Built relatively recently, the building stood out among the older brick and stone houses and parades of shops that surrounded it in a haphazard, eclectic fusion of architectural styles. It had the unique distinction of housing the unlikely mix of a library, a job centre, and a sexual health clinic.

Not a bad time to get out and get some fresh air to blow away some cobwebs, thought the man in the leather jacket as he strolled from the centre of Leeds towards Harehills Lane. As if to contradict his thoughts, a passing van covered in dirt belched out a cloud of black exhaust fumes, leaving an irritating smell in its wake.

His phone vibrated in his pocket. Pulling it out and looking at the display, he grimaced and involuntarily clenched his right hand into a fist.

For Christ's sake, leave me alone, can't you?

He needed to answer it, though. He swiped his finger aggressively up the screen. 'Yes?'

The voice at the other end was direct and to the point. 'Everything going OK?'

'Yes, thanks. Just on my way up to the next place now. I'll let you know what I find out.'

As he spoke, a flatbed truck rattled past, the bumps in the road jangling the loose pile of scaffolding equipment in the back.

'Say again.'

He sighed and spoke up. 'I said, I'll let you know what happens.'

'Yes. That would be an excellent idea. Good luck,' and with that, the caller hung up.

Suddenly, the day didn't seem quite so bright and pleasant. 'Just piss off and let me get on with it,' he muttered aloud to himself as he shoved his phone back into the depths of his pocket.

Chapter 24

When Paul got the call from Karen to attend a briefing that afternoon, he made sure to be very punctual. As he arrived in reception, Debbie looked up in surprise. 'Good grief Paul, I'm sure it seems less than a week since I last saw you. I hope this doesn't mean I'm having even more fun at this job than I already thought I was.'

Paul chuckled at Debbie's banter 'I had you worried for a moment there, didn't I?'

'I've just seen DC Parkinson pop out a couple of minutes ago,' smiled Debbie. 'She told me she was just going to get some things from her car, so I'm sure she won't be long.'

Paul took a seat on one of the hard plastic chair bolted to the floor of the reception area and idly perused the familiar A4 posters giving the visitor a panoply of crime-related advice such as a reminder to lock your car properly and where to go for drugs counselling. After a couple of minutes, Karen walked back into the police station. As she approached the entrance doors, Paul could overhear her talking on her mobile.

'... and thank you for the huge bunch of flowers, they're really gorgeous ... you really shouldn't have but they're lovely ... OK, got to go now, got a meeting to get to ... OK Bob see you soon ... love for now ... and you too, take care ... bye.'

At that, she hung up and pushed through the door into reception and immediately saw Paul. 'Oh hello Paul, you're a bit early. Never mind, come through with me and I'll go and make you your usual while you set out your things in the meeting room.'

Sitting alone in the room, Karen's phone conversation still fresh in his mind, Paul's mind was cast back to memories of not so long ago when he used to buy flowers for Amanda. It had been a simple joy of his, and he was sure to do it regularly and spontaneously, not just on birthdays and anniversaries, but usually for no reason at all other than to show affection. He sighed at the realisation that this was another pleasure missing from his life right now. Paul concluded that "Bob" – whoever he was, as he'd not heard Karen mention him before – was in a lucky position.

And then his thoughts clouded over at the memory from a couple of years ago when Sue from the office had celebrated her fortieth birthday. Everyone in the office had had a whip-round and collected money to buy her a large bouquet of flowers from them all. Paul, being helpful, had offered to take the money and go the florist to organise it. A couple of days later, Amanda had found the receipt in his pocket and had gone ballistic. She'd refused to believe his innocent explanation, had shouted at him, and accused him outright of having an affair with Sue. The argument had ended with Amanda picking up a vase containing flowers Paul had bought for her a few days earlier and throwing it across the living room floor before storming off, leaving him to clean up.

Karen returned bearing two mugs, her regular "Keep Calm and Let Karen Handle It" mug, and another for Paul, which sported the red and black "UK Action Fraud" logo.

Paul took his mug and tried to banish his depressing train of thought by focusing back on the killer's clue. 'Thanks Karen. So ... you cracked the rhyme then? Well done, I'm impressed. Now it must be your turn to tell me how you did it.'

'I was doing the online tour of the labs at York University when it got me thinking about chemical symbols, and I realised the killer's rhyme had a reference to symbols, then it just sort of fell into place.'

After she'd explained in more detail how the clue had been cracked, her face fell a little. 'It didn't do any good, though. According to the pathologist, we might have only missed it by fifteen minutes as well. But fifteen minutes was plenty of time for the killer to get far away from the scene by the time we arrived.' She took a sip of hot coffee. 'Garland even considered scrambling the police helicopter to see if it could pick up anyone with its thermal-imaging camera, but by the time it would have arrived it would have been no use.'

'What do we know about the latest victim?'

'Forty-year-old male, name of Mark Langridge,' Karen replied. 'Army veteran. According to his wife, he'd gone out for a late stroll, as he often did. Interestingly, he had part of his leg blown off by an IED in Operation Volcano. I had to look that one up. Apparently, the operation was to clear the Taliban from around a hydroelectric dam in Helmand Province in 2007.'

'I know that name,' Paul said. 'We've done several articles on him in the past. Over the last few years, he's raised thousands for military disability charities doing sponsored half marathons in the York area. I'll dig out some articles for you. Does he have any family?'

'Wife, parents, and a brother. Didn't have any kids.'

'Have the police picked up any leads from the murder scene?'

'We're limited in what we can release to the media, so I'm not allowed to divulge that,' explained Karen, simultaneously shaking her head slowly and deliberately, to which Paul briefly nodded in conspiratorial acknowledgement.

She continued. 'I'm guessing that since you've not said anything, you've had nothing in your inbox today?'

'No,' replied Paul. 'I've been looking at my phone every five minutes as well. I don't mind telling you I've been pacing up and down with it all day.'

Karen frowned. 'I honestly don't know which feels worse – when you get an email or when you don't. Whether this means that the killings have come to an end or if this is just a temporary reprieve before it all kicks off again. Our profiling expert said that sometimes you can get a hiatus when the killer is otherwise detained, for example in prison for another crime. Maybe our killer is simply busy doing something else tonight, so has held off.'

'I know. It's giving me almost unbearable anxiety.'

'Relax. Remember, you've given your email password to the forensic IT lab, so if anything does come through, they'll get to see it, anyway. Try to put it out of your mind and just concentrate on getting your press article written up for the next edition. If I get to hear anything newsworthy that I'm allowed to tell you, I'll give you a call.'

* * * *

It was seven o'clock in the evening. The November skies had already been dark for some considerable time and about an hour and a half earlier, the clouds had opened to send buckets of rain cascading onto the roofs and streets of York. None of it, however, was visible from inside the large windowless meeting room at the Masonic Hall that Paul had visited earlier that week. At one end of the room, standing behind a large wooden lectern, Major Alan Brook, the master of the lodge, squared his shoulders, adjusted his tie, and cast his gaze over his companions assembled in front of him, all dressed in similar dark suits and blue and white Masonic aprons. As the last notes of their song died away in the air, he briefly exchanged glances with the two individuals standing at similar-looking lecterns, one to his left, the other at the far end of the long chequered carpet. He cleared his throat and addressed the room.

'Brethren. I begin tonight on a very sad note. It is with deep and great sadness I must inform you all that in the early hours of this morning, Brother Mark Langridge of another lodge in York was killed while out taking a late-night walk. I'm sure you're all already aware of his tireless work in supporting a range of charities. I've therefore amended the summons for this evening's meeting to include the opportunity for us to give special thanks and remembrance for his selfless service.'

The assembled group of men nodded solemnly in agreement.

'So, Brethren. Assist me to open the lodge for the evening's business.'

He turned towards the man standing behind the lectern to his left.

'Brother Jamshedji…'

Chapter 25

Paul hadn't needed his alarm to wake him in the morning. In fact, his sleep had been so light and disturbed, it barely felt as if he'd slept at all. His first instinct was to grab his phone. It stared back at him impassively. He laid it back down.

Heart beating uncomfortably, he prised himself out from under the duvet, padded his way across the hall into his tiny bathroom, and pulled the cord to switch on the light. He squeezed a blob of shaving gel into his palm and as he looked back up at his reflection in the mirror above the basin, he was able to witness his own facial reaction to the sound of an email notification emanating loudly from his mobile phone in the bedroom.

* * * *

The sun hadn't fully risen, and the harsh fluorescent tubes reflected the anxious faces of the detectives in the windows of the incident room as they filed in. Garland ushered them impatiently as they took their seats. At the front of the room, criminal profiler Luke Tennant, local historian and ex-police detective Jason Brown, and mathematics Professor Dawn Robinson were already seated. The latest email was projected on the large flat TV screen behind them, on view for all to see as they entered.

Come from the beginning, look to the end; your continuing failure's not a blip, it's a trend

Soon will lay dying some pathetic low slob; there'll be no mercy shown when I'm on the job

Ancient Queen Vicky or current Queen Liz; glib, weak, and useless is what the police is

As soon as everyone was settled, Garland went straight to business. 'As you can see, we've got another one. It arrived in Paul Dobson's inbox at quarter to seven this morning.' He gestured towards the screen. 'Now before we go any further, remember that the greatest error is not to have tried and failed, but that in trying, we didn't give it our best effort. Stay motivated, everyone.'

The tension in the room relaxed a little. Somehow, Garland being in charge seemed to radiate an infectious, determined confidence. 'Remember folks, thanks to the excellent work by DC Parkinson, we came within a few minutes of catching our killer red-handed. It proves beyond doubt that this can absolutely be done, so chins up everyone, and let's get our brains in gear. I need you all to consider this clue in a positive way. Why? Because it's another ripe chance for us to get a step ahead and catch the perpetrator. So, let's seize that opportunity.'

Everyone in the room sat up just a little more straight in their chairs with renewed concentration. *Excellent*, thought Garland, *that's what I want to see*.

He cast his eyes round the room. 'Where's Portland and Hayward?'

'Visiting Mark Langridge's property and interviewing the family,' answered Jamshedji. 'And I'll have to dash after an hour, there's his post-mortem to attend to.' He grimaced at the thought.

'OK, we've all got our plates full at the moment but let's not lose sight of the fact that cracking this riddle for tonight still represents the fastest way of catching the killer and preventing another death. Professor Robinson, over to you first,' continued Garland. 'Can you quickly take us through the points for discussion?'

Dawn Robinson slid her chair back and stood up to the side of the screen. In her gentle but clear voice, she began to address the detectives.

'Morning, everyone. For the last hour, the three of us together with DI Garland have been investigating some possibilities. The first factor that jumps out to us is this opening comment "Come from the beginning, look to the end", which is similar to the opening line of the last clue which was "Since the beginning and up to the end". With that in mind, the obvious approach is to repeat the method which was used in the last clue – take the first and last letters of each line of the poem and consider them as symbols for chemical elements.'

Turning to a flip chart on an easel, she picked up a marker pen and wrote the first and last letters of each line of the poem: *Cd*, *Sb*, and *As*, before standing back to let everyone see.

'Just as with the last riddle, these are all chemical elements. Cd is cadmium, Sb is antimony, and As is arsenic.' She paused as she noticed Karen looking intently at the screen while chewing the end of her pen and wrinkling her nose. 'DC Parkinson?'

'I'd tried that myself,' she explained, 'but unlike the last clue, the words cadmium, antimony, and arsenic aren't hidden anywhere in the words of the poem like they would be if the killer had followed the same technique.'

'True,' agreed Professor Robinson, 'but maybe that's where the similarity ends, and this clue then branches off in a different direction. It's possible that getting the three elements is a hint from the killer that we're on the right lines. We just need to then figure out an alternative way they fit together to reveal a location. One obvious connection is that they can all be used as poisons, but so can many chemical elements – and in any case our killer has always used a gun, not poison. However I did discover another link. Cadmium is used in rechargeable nickel-cadmium batteries, which are typically used for electronic gadgets in our homes. Antimony is used as an electrode in liquid-metal batteries. These are specialist batteries so you won't find them in household gadgets – their intended use is for huge scale energy storage for renewable electricity generated by wind farms, solar power systems, or hydroelectric dams, for example.'

Hydroelectric dams, thought Karen. *The last victim lost part of his leg in a military operation at a hydroelectric dam.* Her eyes flicked across to DI Garland, who nodded to her in silent acknowledgement that he'd just had the same thought.

'Likewise, arsenic can be used as a material for an anode to replace graphite in high capacity rechargeable batteries.' concluded Professor Robinson. 'The fact that all these elements are used in batteries is so far the strongest connection that I can find.'

'Can I just remind everyone,' cautioned Garland, 'that we need to be very careful going down the road of the killer repeating a method previously used for a clue. But with that caveat in mind, Jason, please brief the team on any connection between batteries and York.'

Jason Brown got to his feet, adjusted his glasses, and straightened his checked cotton shirt. 'Well, any internet search involving the words "battery" and "York" will throw up no end of shops where you can buy batteries for your household appliances and plenty of garages and vehicle accessory dealers where you can get batteries for your car,' he began. 'But that's too vague. I also discovered that the University of York carries out research in rechargeable battery technology, so that takes us back to the possibility of York Science Park again. At that point, however, the trail runs cold, so if anybody gets any new information or flashes of inspiration, please share them.'

'On the topic of warming up old ideas,' Garland commented, 'we did have a go at running various words and phrases through the What Three Words website to see if anything came up.'

He reached across to grab a computer mouse as he continued talking. 'Given that the clue referred to "beginnings and ends", we didn't just use words that were necessarily in consecutive order, but also those at the start or end of lines or phrases. Frankly, there wasn't much, and we hadn't really been expecting anything. What we learnt is that "Glib Queens Trend" is in Kazakhstan and "Blip Queens Glib" looks like some remote backwoods in Russia.'

He clicked the mouse, and the poem disappeared from the screen to be replaced by a satellite image of a road bordering a lake.

'Now at first "Trend Jobs Soon", which we're looking at here, looks like a bit of a non-starter. It's on a road on the north shore of this small lake near Denver, Colorado. It's got housing around the other side of the lake, and a school down at the western end. However, thanks to modern technology, keep looking while I overlay the satellite view of Rawcliffe Lake in York.' Another click of the mouse and the Denver Lake faded into a satellite view of Rawcliffe Lake. It fitted almost exactly. When Garland indicated the similar-looking housing and the school at the western end, there was a murmur around the room.

‘There’s one more idea we’ve had so far,’ added Jason Brown, ‘and it’s to do with the line about Queen Victoria and Queen Elizabeth the Second. You’ll remember the first murder took place right in front of a statue of Queen Victoria.’ Everyone in the room nodded.

‘Well, it’s no far stretch to think the shooter is referring to that kill and therefore, the mention of Queens Elizabeth could indicate that’s the next location.’

DC Dave Snow raised his hand. ‘Great idea,’ he said, ‘however there’s one problem with that. York doesn’t have a statue of Queen Elizabeth the Second.’

Jason Brown smiled. ‘Not right now,’ he replied, ‘but there have been plans in place to build a life-size statue of her at the west entrance to York Minster as part of quite an ambitious scheme to develop that area into a public square. What more cunning way of fooling us all than to commit a murder in front of a statue that isn’t there yet?’

‘OK, folks, that’s where we’re up to,’ concluded Garland, clicking once more to return the poem back onto the screen and placing the mouse carefully back on the desk. ‘What are your thoughts then?’

A light bulb switched on in DC Parkinson’s head. ‘Just going back to what you were saying about a battery. What if we’re thinking about the wrong type of battery?’

It was DC Ward who cottoned on first. ‘You mean like a military battery?’

Brown gave an appreciative thumb-up sign. ‘Ah yes. What a brilliant thought, and what’s more, there was one. West Riding Heavy Battery used to have its brigade headquarters right here in York. It was based at Lumley Barracks.’

‘Lumley Barracks?’ queried DC Ward. ‘I’ve never heard of it. In York?’

‘You wouldn’t have,’ replied Brown. ‘I’m going back to the years between the wars. It’s all modern housing now, but I bet DI Garland’s walked past it to get to the turnstiles. It’s almost slap bang next to what used to be York City’s Bootham Crescent football ground.’

The sun had begun to creep over the horizon as they’d been talking, and the view from the incident-room window had started to appear from under the cloak of the early autumnal darkness and into the pale morning light.

Garland stared out over the awakening vista of the police station car park and beyond that to the buildings of York garrison. *Now what sort of person would know that there used to be a military battery in York a hundred years ago?* he mused.

Chapter 26

Below Paul's office, the shutters over the shop windows were being raised for the day of trading ahead, the lights inside the shops blazing and the street filling up with the citizens of York going about their morning business. He watched them with a blank expression as they navigated the pavement, their feet avoiding the puddles left from the downpour the previous night. For a moment, he wished he could swap places with any one of them.

He'd telephoned the email in to DC Parkinson as soon as he'd received it, but as yet had heard nothing back from her and didn't want to call as he was sure she'd be up to her neck in the hectic work of trying to sort it out.

Like DI Garland and ex-DCI Jason Brown, the reference to Queen Victoria and Queen Elizabeth the Second had stood out to Paul. Something niggled his tired brain; he could have sworn he'd seen an image of the Queen somewhere recently, not necessarily a statue but something. And had he seen anything that connected with the planet Mercury? He gave his head a quick shake. He was tired, burnt out, and not thinking too clearly. Working as a journalist at the York Press did have its advantages, though. Like Jason Brown, Paul knew a statue of Queen Elizabeth had been proposed some years ago because he could remember the York Press covering the story at the time. It should be ready for completion any time now. Maybe that warranted some further investigation. Logging into the York Press database, he pulled up the relevant press release onto his screen and started to read.

The article was dated a few years back, and some of the ideas put forward at the time were extremely ambitious. At the time that the statue of Queen Elizabeth had been proposed, there had also been additional ideas to create a pedestrianised square, a "landscaped ceremonial space" – whatever that meant – and a sensory garden. Gradually, more recollections came tumbling back into Paul's tired mind. To announce the launch of the proposals, there had been an evening buffet held at the York Guildhall, an impressive building in the city centre dating back to the fifteenth century and backing onto the River Ouse. He recalled that Linda Reader had been invited, and he'd felt envious as the functions there had a reputation as something to behold. She'd taken Jane, one of the press photographers, so there should be pictures of the event somewhere in the archive.

Paul navigated into the photo archive and located the appropriate folder. It contained sixty-three photos. Paul gave a dry smile. All those who had never worked in journalism would be amazed at the thousands of photographs that are taken at events of which only one or two, or in many cases none at all, made it into the day's edition. He idly scrolled through the photographs of the black-tie function.

Despite York Guildhall's impressive stature and provenance, many visitors to York simply pass it by blissfully unaware of its presence. Only a few yards from one of the main shopping streets, it is hidden away behind a discreet archway. Only the rear of the building is visible from the opposite bank of the river, where it blends into the multitude of constructions that make up the waterfront. Even most long-standing residents of York have never been inside, but if they were to enter, they would be in awe of its superlative interior which houses a colossal stained-glass window and towering columns supporting an outstanding wooden ceiling.

Paul scrolled through the photographs of all the local "worthies" as he always referred to them, men dressed in suits, women in black evening dresses sipping from champagne flutes. At each passing photograph he became slightly less envious as he realised how dull and boring the evening must have been. There would have been business people hovering around like vultures, trying to pitch for contracts, talking self-important hot air with a joviality as genuine as a three- pound note, all pretending to be friends with people they would happily prefer to not exist.

He paused, seeing a photograph of Linda. She had a glass of something fizzy in one hand and was raising what looked like a cream cheese and smoked salmon canapé in the other, smiling to the camera. Paul grinned. He hoped the wine and buffet had been good enough to compensate for having to spend an entire evening of your life with all those incessantly tedious bores. Like that bland-looking idiot standing next to her. How she managed to keep a politely interested expression on her face while he droned on about some terminally dreary topic like declining gross return on investments in bulk gravel, he would never know.

Hang on a minute, though. Didn't that face look familiar?

He was sure he'd seen it somewhere recently before. *Think, Paul, think.* In a moment of inspiration, he dug out the press article he'd written the previous week about the first murder victim, Alec Hopkins. Accompanying the article was an old photograph of him which had been provided to the press by the human resources department of the company where he used to work. The photograph was several years out of date and showed a slightly younger man, but as Paul rearranged the windows on his computer screen to put the images side by side, he was sure the man standing next to Linda was Alec Hopkins.

* * * *

In the incident room, DI Garland continued the morning's briefing. 'Doctor Tennant, I'd be grateful if you could give us your perspective on this latest clue and what it might tell us about the writer, please.'

'With pleasure.' Luke Tennant got to his feet. 'Despite the primary objective of the clue being to hide the next location, the killer still manages to include the usual taunts and jibes. We need to watch out for a ramping-up in the use of the press and media if this killer doesn't get caught soon.'

Dr Tennant moved over to the desk in front of Garland and, taking the mouse in his hand, replaced the poem on the screen with a map of Napa Valley, California. Across the bay from San Francisco, the city of Vallejo was circled.

'What I'm going to tell you now is about one of the most infamous American serial killers of all time. He operated in the San Francisco Bay area in the 1960s and 70s and called himself the Zodiac Killer. He's linked to at least five known killings and possibly as many as thirty-seven. We studied him a lot at Quantico.'

The room was silent as this sank in. Karen scanned the other detectives, aware that the only sound she could hear was that annoying humming fluorescent tube. Tennant continued.

'The victims were all shot at close range, outdoors, at night, after which the killer vanished into thin air. The most overwhelming similarity of all, though, is this: the Zodiac Killer sent a string of clues and cryptic messages in cards and letters to the police – via the press just like now – ridiculing and teasing them saying the clues would reveal his identity and other information.'

'Can you show us some examples?' asked DC Goodier.

'Sure can.' Tennant clicked the mouse again and the image on the screen was now a grid of handwritten letters, numbers, and various geometric shapes written in black ink. The detectives studied the screen intently as Tennant explained.

'There was no email in those days, so the press got handwritten stuff in the regular mail. There's an obvious difference though, our killer sends us intellectual poetry whereas the Zodiac Killer was sending crude substitution ciphers like the type that school children use to send secret messages to each other.'

'And it was the killer sending them and not some crank?' Goodier asked.

'Initially, there were three letters which went out – in sharp similarity to our situation – to each of the local newspapers,' Tennant replied. 'Each letter included one-third of the cryptogram on the screen, which the killer claimed would reveal his identity when cracked. What you're seeing here is a composite which makes up the full message. A few days later, the press then got a further letter containing details about one of the killings which hadn't been made public and which only the killer, or someone involved in the investigation, could have known.

'There were further letters, Christmas cards, Halloween cards, drawings, you name it. To give you an idea of what the police faced, we've been suffering murders in York for about a week. The Zodiac Killer's spree lasted *five years*.'

'Were any of the clues ever cracked?' asked DC Dave Snow.

'Some. It wasn't as easy as you might have thought because there were many different characters in the messages and in some cases, the letters were rearranged before encryption. A different cipher was used each time, meaning that if you cracked one, it was no use in solving any of the others. The first one was solved by a couple of amateur code breakers working from home – here, have a look.' A click of the mouse changed the contents of the screen to reveal a meandering perversely sinister diatribe full of spelling and grammatical errors.

'So not revealing his identity at all, then,' confirmed Snow.

'No, and neither did any of the others that were cracked. Some of them remain unsolved to this day.'

'You mentioned earlier something about ramping up the pressure?' asked Garland.

'Yes, I hate to break it to you, but things could get a lot worse if our case follows the same trend as the Zodiac Killer.'

'In what way?' DC Ward responded uneasily.

'He became hungry for publicity, making increasing terror threats if certain demands weren't carried out. For example, he demanded that his letters be published in the newspapers, or he would, "cruise round killing people in the night". He wanted people in the city to walk round wearing badges of his "Zodiac" symbol – it looked like a circle with a cross through it – or else he would carry out more atrocities. Worst of all was when he said he threatened to shoot out the tyre of a school bus and then pick off the children as they came running out.'

'Jesus Christ,' Ward exclaimed.

In the stunned silence, it was DC Karen Parkinson who was next to speak. ‘So, the million-dollar question then, is how did the police finally catch him?’

‘That’s the thing,’ replied Tennant, spreading his hands apologetically. ‘He never ever was. One day, about five years after he began, the killings and messages just stopped. It’s now over fifty years since the murders and still nobody knows who he is or was. In fact, given the sheer amount of time that’s elapsed, it’s entirely feasible that he could have died of old age by now and nobody will ever know.’

Chapter 27

On quiet patrol of the dark evening streets around the old site of York City football ground, Pete Ollerenshaw from North Yorkshire Police Firearms Unit reflected that each side of the ground looked like it was in a different city. Along one side lay the magnificent nineteenth-century brick building of an old school, now desolate and quiet. Along the next, football turnstiles were built into a high stone wall full of advertising hoardings. Round the corner was a long, narrow street with smart terraced housing and cars parked on both sides.

To the west where he was now pacing was a wide, pleasant road with grass verges, modern houses, and a variety of trees, many now bare. Scattered on the verges were piles of fallen leaves which had long since lost their autumnal crispness and had turned to clusters of soggy, brown pulp.

As he walked, his senses highly tuned, he recalled the night he'd been expecting to come face to face with a serial killer and instead found only a lemon. Now he was patrolling the other side of town where the old military battery had been, wondering what he would come face to face with that night. His thoughts drifted to Jim Hancock, his friend and a fellow rugby player in the unit, who was putting his life on the line patrolling the area around the front of York Minster, the other identified potential murder site.

At what sounded like the snapping of a twig close behind him, Ollerenshaw's eyes darted round the trees that lined the road, looking for signs of movement. His right hand moved instinctively to grab the Glock pistol in its holster beneath his jacket. False alarm. Ollerenshaw continued noiselessly and vigilantly on his way.

* * * *

Not far away, another individual was also patting the gun in their inside pocket, this time with a sense of heightened nervousness. Tonight was going to be tough, easily the riskiest one yet. Since the first killing, each murder had brought along new levels of confidence until it was almost becoming second nature, but tonight was a concern: definitely the biggest challenge so far.

If only this one could be somewhere else, but no, it absolutely couldn't be. The Sequence was determined. The Sequence had to be followed. Besides, the clue had been written and sent, so what remained was to fulfil its destiny. Just stay focused. Deep breaths.

Maybe some music before leaving the house would help calm the nerves and boost the spirit? Yes. But what should it be? Ah, just the thing, Wishbone Ash's "Phoenix". Perfect lyrics.

A few seconds later and music filled the room, accompanied by a voice, faltering at first but growing in assurance as it sang along. As the song developed, the tempo of the guitars grew faster and the voice in the room singing along grew louder and faster with it to an all-consuming crescendo.

* * * *

As the closing credits to the film rolled up the screen, Paul stuffed his last slice of four seasons pizza into his mouth and turned to his companion on the sofa.

'Thanks for inviting me round tonight. What an unexpected surprise. And thank you for the pizza. That's two meals I owe you now.'

‘No problem,’ replied Karen, grinning. ‘It was just a spur-of-the-moment thing. If I’d given it a bit more planning, I’d have done roast venison with saffron and truffle, but never mind. What with everything going on, would you believe I completely forgot to order my weekly Harrods hamper? Thank God for the local takeaway twelve-inch special with chips.’

Paul started chuckling at Karen’s obvious sarcasm, at which point she broke into a smile and laughed along with him. It was the first time either of them had laughed in several days, and the release of tension in the air felt refreshing. Karen reached across for the remote and turned off the television. ‘What did you think of the film, anyway? I never knew until I looked it up this afternoon that they’d done a Hollywood movie about the Zodiac Killer.’

‘I’m still trying to get my head round it,’ confessed Paul. ‘Absolutely unbelievable. And you say they never found out who it was?’

‘Nope,’ replied Karen. ‘But that’s where we’re going to be different. We’re going to get this cracked between us. I’m serious. We can’t come so close on two occasions and not win eventually. I’m convinced of it.’

In front of them on Karen’s coffee table, taking centre stage with *Pride and Prejudice* pushed well to the side, lay a printout of the latest clue. Beside it was an A4 pad full of jottings in two sets of handwriting, displaying the evening’s efforts of a multitude of ideas that had not worked out.

‘We haven’t failed,’ Karen said. ‘To paraphrase the famous words of the inventor Thomas Edison, we’ve just found ten thousand ways that *won’t* work.’

She stood up and tossed the pad into Paul's lap. 'So, it's time for one more crack at it if you're not too tired?' she suggested. 'I'll get the kettle on.'

* * * *

Along Precentor's Court at the front of York Minster, the firearms officer on patrol that night, Jim Hancock, made his way deftly through the shadows. Although only half a mile away from the old football ground, his was an altogether different environment. Precentor's Court was an open space; a "killing field" with nowhere to hide, caught in the light of the ornate ancient lamps that cast their yellow glow across the wet paving slabs. Turning his back to the Minster, his eyes surveyed the scene. To his left, a thin solitary tree planted in the middle of the pavement offered precious little in the way of concealment. In front of him, opposite the Minster, set into a stone wall across the court was the archway to a small private hospital, and beside it, a tiny, narrow street which some locals would refer to as a "ginnel" and others might call a "snickelway" ran straight ahead. Hancock was relieved to see that there were no obvious hiding places in the ginnel and its linear shape meant there were no corners behind which to hide.

To his right, an unlocked gateway led through to the open area which, in the summer, was a pleasant place for a relaxing stroll, with well-trimmed grassy lawns, beautiful trees, and several benches upon which to sit and admire York Minster and its architecture. He, his wife, and their ten-year-old daughter loved to come to this part of York on a Saturday afternoon. Sometimes they would stop for a coffee in one of the cafés that bordered the open grassed area and have some quality family time together in the sunshine. Tonight, though, it offered a much more foreboding and sinister prospect. The shadows of the lofty walls of the Minster would provide opportunities for a killer to move around undetected.

Jim Hancock completed his short patrol to stretch his legs and tucked himself into a dark alcove at the corner of the Minster, which he hoped would provide some cover, yet offer him a clear view of the scope of his surroundings. He folded back the cuff of his jacket, checked his watch quickly, then pulled his cuff back down again. It was well into the early hours and the energetic evening streets of York had long since fallen quiet, the tourists and night-time revellers having been sound asleep in their beds for some considerable time. Yet even in these still, lonely hours of the night, Hancock observed, the city was never entirely deserted; occasional far-off footsteps or the rumbling of a car engine somewhere in the distance could still be heard faintly from time to time and he observed how even a small, provincial city never entirely went to sleep.

From his vantage point, with his back up against the Minster, Hancock's eyes and ears stayed alert for any minute signals that might herald any new arrival. The glistening slabs of Precentor's Court lay empty. Somewhere in the depths of the night, an owl called out, then the familiar comforting silence descended again.

Pop.

Putting concerns for his own safety to one side, Hancock was up and moving. *Where the hell had that sound come from*?

Not near the entrance to the Minster. His hand pulled his Glock out of his holster, and his eyes darted around. The sound seemed to have come from the river a couple of hundred yards away across the other side of the courtyard. Hancock sprinted across the court to look down the streets opposite. His eyes frantically scanning up and down each street, he spied a dark, uneven lump on the pavement about a couple of hundred yards down Duncombe Place and he hurled himself towards it.

As he approached the shape on the ground, his worst fears were confirmed. In a widening pool of blood, the man lay dying. The man gave a distraught gasp when he saw Hancock, but his breath was already faint and fading rapidly. Hancock threw himself down and tried desperately to apply pressure to the wound to stop the bleeding while he barked into his radio.

'Hancock. Duncombe Place. Request ambulance immediately. There's been a shooting. Man down here. Repeat. There's a man down. Man down.'

Chapter 28

The two police estate cars, their high-visibility Battenberg markings punctuating each end of Duncombe Place, blocked off the now taped-up street. In a couple of hours' time the city would start to awaken gently – unlike DCI Garland who had been woken just over an hour ago to make his now regular dash from his cosy bedroom into the centre of York for an urgent appointment with yet another corpse. Beside him, their breath steaming in the cold early morning air, were Karen Parkinson, Dattaram Jamshedji, Jim Hancock, and Pete Ollerenshaw who, on hearing the news of the shooting, had run the half mile from where he had been patrolling near the old football ground. A plain forensic van parked opposite them had its rear doors open and a figure in coveralls was rummaging around in the interior. The ambulance beside it had long since turned off its blue lights and would be shortly making its way back to the hospital, its high speed journey to the scene having been in vain. The pathologist, Jack Horner was talking to one of the paramedics.

Garland surveyed the area. Beside the forensic tent where the body still lay was the Catholic Church of Saint Wilfrid. A remarkable ornate stone building, it looked far older than the hundred and fifty years of its actual age, and taller than the nearby Minster tower although Garland knew that was just an optical illusion. From above, the gargoyles on the church stared down on the scene.

Behind the tent was a set of painted iron railings that connected the gates of the church to the adjoining Dean Court Hotel, an attractive brick and stone building that in the summer would have its beautiful floral window boxes spilling their bright colours to enhance an already charming street. The hotel sign above Garland's head swung in the wind and creaked, and as Garland lifted his head towards it he noticed that the gargoyles were not the only things keeping a sentinel eye on the road. Was that a security camera?

Jim Hancock kicked the iron railings in frustration.

'Bugger and bollocks,' he swore. Turning towards Garland he continued, 'We got the clue right all along and I missed the murder. So sorry, boss.'

'No, we didn't,' Karen said. The words escaped her mouth before she realised and as everyone's heads snapped round to look at her, she bit her tongue.

'She's right you know,' Garland concurred. 'I agree. We didn't get the clue right at all.' At these words, Karen relaxed.

Garland continued. 'No. It was sheer luck, or misfortune on our part, depending how you want to look at it, that the actual location in the clue is just a couple of hundred yards away from where we thought it could be.' He nodded at DC Parkinson in acknowledgement. 'Think about it. The clue to the cemetery resulted in a killing in the cemetery. The What Three Words clue was to within a few feet. Saint Nicholas Fields was likewise spot on. Our last victim was lying at the foot of Mercury where the clue said he would be. If the clue had actually pointed to York Minster, then the murder would have been at York Minster. We didn't crack the clue.'

Then Garland started to smile. 'But the fact that we were close by, albeit for completely the wrong reasons, could still be made to work to our advantage.'

Hancock's face looked relieved. 'You're right, boss. I hadn't thought of that.'

'Where were you standing when you heard the gunshot?'

'In a recess next to the entrance, boss.'

Garland smiled at Hancock warmly and put a hand on his shoulder.

'That would have been the perfect spot if the location was supposed to be where the statue was to be placed. Relax, Hancock. You've done nothing wrong and everything right in risking your neck running down to save this poor guy.'

His eyes scanned up and down the street, taking in his surroundings. 'This leaves us with the question of how this specific location was actually encoded in the verse,' he said. Pulling his York City scarf to one side to unzip his combat jacket, he retrieved a small notepad and pen from the inside pocket and made some notes as he spoke aloud.

'We're on Duncombe Place, standing between Saint Wilfrid's Church and the Dean Court Hotel. I'd like to see how any of those words fit into the clue. Maybe now we know the location, one small consolation is that we might be able to reverse-engineer it and find out what the clue was really about.'

'It won't bring this poor sod back,' said Jamshedji disconsolately.

'No, but it'll satisfy my bloody curiosity.'

At that moment, Jack Horner, having finished talking with the paramedics, strolled over. 'OK chaps I'm done for now.' He removed his glasses, and gave them a quick polish before replacing them and inhaling a couple of deep breaths of the cold air. 'I don't think there's anything particularly different to the other killings that I can tell you at this stage. Shot at close range just over an hour ago, but of course we all knew that. Male in his late twenties to early thirties. I retrieved a wallet with some ID and a mobile phone and handed them to one of the forensics team.'

'Yes,' confirmed Jamshedji. 'From the wallet, his name's Ryan Christian. Lived in one of the terraced houses behind the racecourse. We'll need to find out why he was walking this way at this time of night But the fact that he was a young athletic guy and he didn't put up any resistance or even try to run off tells us he must have been taken by surprise. Hancock, did you hear any kind of scuffle or shouting prior to the shot?'

Hancock shook his head.

'So let's think about this,' said Garland. 'There's no confrontation involved. No discussion with the victim prior to the shooting, no arguing, no pretending to befriend him to gain his confidence and trust. Just step out in front of him, pull out the gun, bang, and then scarper.' He pointed up to the CCTV camera on the corner of the hotel. 'I'm hoping we can get some footage from that which might shed some light on exactly what happened.' He smiled. 'I'll get a fingertip search organised. Our killer had to disappear in a sprinting hurry, so there's always the possibility that they could have dropped something. If we're very lucky, the CCTV footage from that camera on the side of the hotel might even show us what route the killer took up to and away from the scene.' He paused. 'And I know it's not exactly the height of the tourist season, but we'll need to interview everybody staying in the hotel overnight to find out if anybody happened to be awake at that time to see or hear anything significant.'

He thoughtfully looked up and down the street. 'There's something about this location, though. Unlike all the others, this one's close to the city centre on quite a well-lit road. The killer was taking one hell of a risk.'

'Maybe they're becoming emboldened,' suggested Jack Horner. 'I'm no expert on that kind of thing though, so it might be worth bending the ear of that criminal-profiling chap you mentioned.'

Garland furrowed his brow. 'Jack, can you do me a quick favour? Based on the entry wound you saw and the way the body was lying, how do you fancy sticking your neck out right now and saying in what direction you think our victim was facing and where our killer would have been standing when the gun was fired?'

'I'll have a damned good go,' replied Horner. 'I'd say, based on what I've seen, that it's consistent with our fellow here walking past the front of the hotel. As he passed directly underneath the hotel sign, he was shot by our killer standing in the doorway of Saint Wilfrid's Church'

Garland's phone rang. Pulling it out of his pocket, his eyebrows rose when he saw the name on the screen. 'Professor Robinson. What on earth are you doing calling at this unearthly hour?'

'I'm fine,' assured the voice. 'I've just been up nearly all night with this latest clue not letting me sleep. Anyway, I think I know where the next location is. It's—'

'I'm really sorry to tell you it's too late. I'm at the murder scene now.'

'Oh no. Is it outside Saint Wilfrid's Church next to the Dean Court Hotel?'

'Yes. Got it in one. You really did crack it. I'll be calling a briefing meeting later today in the incident room and I need you to come in. In the meantime, don't let this prey on your mind and try to get some rest before then because I'll need you to be on top form in the meeting. For now though, please tell me how you solved it, it's been driving me mad as well.'

He listened to Professor Robinson's response.

'Well, at least that's my curiosity satisfied,' he exclaimed with a grim expression on his face.

Chapter 29

Paul Dobson sat alone on Karen's sofa watching the television and clutching an uneaten bowl of granola, trying to force his brain to cut through the almost painful fog to concentrate on the morning news. As yet, there had been no mention of anything relating to any shootings. He couldn't remember flaking out into unconsciousness through sheer mental exhaustion, but he did remember waking up still on the sofa in the early hours of the morning. Karen must have thrown a blanket over him before leaving him in peace, his notepad still open on the coffee table. It had been dark, and he'd been awoken by the sounds of Karen trying to be quiet to not disturb him and failing.

'Got to go. There's been another one,' she'd whispered, throwing a key onto the coffee table. 'Don't get up. There's tea and coffee over by the kettle and plenty of bread and cereal if you want some breakfast later. Here's my spare key. Just lock up when you go and I'll collect it from you later.' With that, she'd disappeared. Since then, he'd not heard a thing. He'd not slept another wink either.

As his mind struggled to focus through the net curtain that seemed to have descended between his brain and the outside world, he marvelled at how emergency workers, particularly medical staff, managed to survive a career in which working all hours of the night was a regular occurrence. He recalled how Amanda had once told him that she'd spent a year at a nursing college and the whole reason that she'd quit before finishing her course was that she couldn't reconcile herself to years and years of having to work through the night. Sitting huddled on the sofa, his brain screaming out for some restful sleep, he had to concede he could see where she was coming from. Then his thoughts went out to Karen; if he was feeling rough just sitting here on the sofa, he couldn't imagine what kind of time she'd endured somewhere out in a cold York night dealing with a dead body. He looked around the kitchen for at least something he could do to make life easier for her on her return. He washed up and tidied around the living room, picking up some leaves and petals that had dropped to the floor from some flowers in a large vase by the fireplace. When he was done, he sat and read the clue again. *What secret had it contained?* he wondered.

* * * *

At the morning briefing Gene Garland stood at the front with a determined look on his face and his shirt sleeves rolled up ready for business. When everyone was seated, he started.

'OK people, we've a lot to get through this morning. You'll already know that the victim, thirty-year-old Ryan Christian, was found shot outside St Wilfrid's Church and Dean Court by a member of our firearms team who was on duty outside the Minster. CCTV footage from various cameras in the city has shown images of our victim walking from the north of town and then along past the theatre. We also have some interesting CCTV from the camera at the junction between Duncombe Place and Museum Street, which I'll show you in a moment. We're also recovering CCTV footage from the hotel. Now, before we go any further, I daresay you'll be wanting to know what the clue meant, so for that, I'll ask Professor Robinson to explain.'

Dawn Robinson got to her feet, and Garland passed her the mouse. She put the clue up on the TV screen.

'I'd been thinking about the Zodiac Killer's codes that we looked at yesterday,' she said. 'Where letters were turned into other letters, or numbers or symbols, and looked at the possibility that our killer had done something similar.

'The challenge was working out what type of cipher had been used, and in fact, the killer has already told us in the first line: "*Come from the beginning, look to the end*". We misinterpreted that to think of letters making up chemical elements again, but that's not what the clue is telling us. It's telling us to literally put the beginning at the end and vice versa.' She clicked the mouse, and at this, the screen filled with a picture of the alphabet A-Z with the reverse alphabet Z-A printed underneath.

'So you reverse the alphabet, put the first letter to the end and vice versa and you now have a cipher in which A becomes Z, B becomes Y, C becomes X, and so on. Then you use the cipher to decrypt the message. OK, a lot of the words you get are gobbledygook as you'd expect, but some aren't. Let's take a look at that clue again.'

Come from the beginning, look to the end; your continuing failure's not a blip, it's a trend

Soon will lay dying some pathetic low slob; there'll be no mercy shown when I'm on the job

Ancient queen Vicky or current queen Liz; glib, weak, and useless is what the police is

'And now let's run it through our cipher. I've taken it each line at a time and then put some highlighted words in capitals for you.' Another click of the mouse followed to reveal the deciphered text on the screen.

Xlnv uiln gsv yvtrmmrmt ollp gl gsv vmw blfi xlmgrmfrmt uzrofivh mlg z **YORK** rgh z givmw

Hllm droo ozb wbrmt hlnv kzgsvgrx **OLD HOLY** gsvivoo yv ml nvixb hsldm dsvm Rn lm gsv qly

Zmxrvmg jfvvm Erxpb li xfiivmg jfvvm **ORA TORY** dvzp zmw fhvovhh rh dszg gsv klorxv rh

'York, old holy oratory,' she concluded. 'Which is…' She turned to Jason Brown.

'It's Saint Wilfrid's Church next to the Dean Court Hotel,' he replied.

'Excellent thinking' Garland reassured Professor Robinson. 'You cracked it and that's one hell of an achievement. Remember, everybody, that the killer has to be lucky every time. We just need to be lucky once. Now let me put another idea to you all. I'm coming round to the conclusion that since we've struggled to find any connections between the victims, that the real connection has to be not between the people but the places.'

At this, he turned to the board in the corner of the room behind him, which was plastered with photographs of each of the scenes.

'All the previous murders were in places that were quiet at night. This is the first one that was in anything approaching a populated area and they nearly got caught as a result. Doctor Tennant, have you any idea behind why the killer might change their typical choice of location?'

Tennant got to his feet and removed a ballpoint pen from his inside jacket pocket. The killer's cipher disappeared from the screen to be replaced by a series of photographs of various serial killers: Jeffrey Dahmer and Joel Rifkin through to Dennis Nilsen and Peter Sutcliffe. At the sight of the image of Sutcliffe, Garland's lips pursed and the corner of his eyes narrowed.

Tennant identified each killer in turn.

'Dahmer and Rifkin both stated for the record that their first murder was by far the hardest one. With each successive murder, it became easier and more mundane – so routine indeed that their confessions to the police were as matter of fact as if they were admitting to doing ten miles an hour over the speed limit. There's a logic behind their increased confidence. First, as with any task, the more you do the better you become. They perfected their technique like a craftsman would to the point that it became second nature.

Secondly, some killers start to believe that having evaded capture for so long, they have some kind of invincibility. They might even believe that a divine force, for example God or Satan, is protecting them by moulding events in their favour. One can only imagine how the West-Yorkshire-accented Yorkshire Ripper felt when the police suddenly got a tape with a Geordie voice on it.'

Garland internally groaned. That tape. Memories came back again. His parents listening on the phone to the voice. Sitting in the front of his father's Ford Cortina driving into Leeds past the hoardings displaying handwriting samples. His older sister Ruth running in through the door of the house late one night, panicking and in floods of tears, sobbing that she'd thought she'd heard someone following her back home.

He shook it off and sat up straight to focus as Tennant continued.

'A serial killer motivated by thrill-seeking may also find that the rush is diminished as the killings go on. So, in order to get the adrenaline, they notch up the risk to chase a high - which is when they can get careless and make mistakes'

'What if the killer knew the risk but was somehow compelled that they had to be there?' asked Karen. 'Like the location was somehow predestined? What might cause that to happen?'

DC Goodier spoke up. 'Here's a thought. If our latest victim was on his way to his home behind the racecourse, then there will have been other points on that route that were more discreet and with better opportunities for a hasty, unobserved getaway.'

DS Dattaram Jamshedji was next to speak. 'If that's the case, then suppose the locations are linked in a sequence, boss? We don't know how they're linked and how they form a sequence but for the killer they have a personal significance which they feel compelled to follow.'

Garland beamed and pointed his index finger triumphantly at Jamshedji. 'Yes. Excellent thought. I want everyone to spend some quality time considering what that sequence might be.'

He continued. 'I've got some other news to lift our spirits. First of all, I've received the statement from our firearms officer, Jim Hancock, who was patrolling the west entrance to the Minster and heard the shot. He is convinced that it sounded like the gun was fitted with a silencer – or suppressor to give it its proper name. And not only that, but for a suppressed gun it was still especially quiet compared to what he may have reasonably expected to hear from that distance. And that's not all. We also have this. Watch closely.'

Another click of the mouse and the view from the CCTV camera at the top of Museum Street appeared on the screen. There was a slight, exasperated grunt around the room at the realisation that it was pointing not up Duncombe Place towards the murder scene, but down towards the bridge over the River Ouse.

'Yeah, I know,' Garland said, 'life's not perfect, but it's not all bad either. Keep watching.'

For a few seconds there was nothing but a static image of the street with nothing changing but the timestamp in the corner, then from the edge of the screen, a figure dressed from head to toe in black appeared and sprinted until it reached the bridge then exited the screen as if to run down the steps from the bridge to the river bank.

'I've requested that to get enhanced,' Garland informed them. 'Although I'm sceptical of how much it can be improved and unpixellated to show anything more of interest. Hopefully, the CCTV on the hotel will show us more. But chins up, everyone. We've both heard and seen our killer for the first time. Until last night, we were dealing with a silent, invisible phantom.'

Chapter 30

Garland and Jamshedji sat at Garland's desk deep in concentration, watching the footage which had been recovered from the Dean Court CCTV camera. As misfortune would have it, the positions of both the killer and the victim meant that the moment that the shot was fired had not been caught on camera. The footage showed someone dressed in a black hoodie with the hood pulled up tightly emerge from the right-hand side, disappear briefly off the screen, then reappear a few seconds later running in the opposite direction. There was no writing or image on the front or back of the hoodie to make it identifiable, and no facial features were visible. After pausing and rewinding a couple of times, Garland reckoned it was possible to put an estimate on height and build: under six foot tall, slight to medium build, and clearly fit enough to be able to run the distance from the site of the murder down to the river. A frustrating fact was that the fingertip search of the escape route had once again failed to produce anything of forensic value.

'I once read this theory,' contemplated Jamshedji, 'that any person is less than six social connections away from anybody else in the world. Well, from what our database is telling me, or rather not telling me, I'm starting to doubt that very much. From all the phone records, interviews and enquiries, I'm struggling to think how you could find a set of victims so unconnected to each other.'

Garland shifted his eyes over to the paperwork laid out on his desk. Pushing aside his model of *Thunderbird 2* and an uneaten cheese and pickle sandwich, he turned again to his mind map to add the latest details from the previous night's shooting. Alongside it lay another large sheet of paper upon which he'd ruled a line vertically down the middle. At the top of the page, on the left-hand side of the line, he'd written the heading "What we know" and on the right-hand side "What we don't know". Depressingly, the right half contained far more content, but the left-hand side was starting to fill up, so there was some reason, however slight, for encouragement.

'What thoughts have you had for connections in terms of motive?'

'Various ideas, boss. I looked at a possible military connection but couldn't join up all the dots. Then I wondered about an association involving alcohol. I even started thinking that there was a connection with the Oranjeboom lager can found in Alice Morton's house and the Oranjeboom that Kirsten McNally was selling, which links to the lemon in St. Nicholas Fields. It's not spelled the same but – *Oranje* and lemon? Oranges and lemons, the bells of St Clements? There is a St. Clements church in York too, but then the latest murder was near St Wilfrid's church which is nowhere near to that.'

Jamshedji leaned forwards in his chair. 'I feel like I'm going slightly mad, seeing connections everywhere where they don't exist. The only other idea I had was something to do with astronomy – Alec Hopkins had a photograph of himself next to a train called the Evening Star, Alice Morton had a crescent moon necklace, Kirsten McNally had a horoscope app on her phone, Mark Langridge had a tattoo of a motto relating to the stars ...'

'Not mad at all,' Garland reassured him. 'I'd say that was bloody good detective work. But if all that turns out to be a non-starter then we're left with the conclusion that the answer must lie in the comment you made in the meeting earlier. That it's something to do with the sequence of locations themselves.'

Between them lay a map of York upon which Garland had marked the murder sites in numerical order. They studied it intently.

The first location in West Bank Park was to the left of the map. The second, in front of the chapel at the cemetery, was to the right of that and lower down just below the centre. The murder at the basketball court in Hull Road Park was slightly to the north and east of the second murder. From there, the fourth location – the lemon in Saint Nicholas Fields – was just above Hull Road Park and the fifth location on the solar system trail was down at the bottom centre. Back up again and slightly to the left, just to the west of the city centre was the latest one.

What the hell connected them? Places where someone had spent their life story being dumped by successive lovers? Places where they suffered an injury? An injustice?

'Can you get the team to have a search through HOLMES and pull out the details of any crimes, solved or unsolved, with links to all the murder locations? I'm wondering if the killer might be revisiting spots which hold some significance to them based on previous crime scenes.'

'Will do, boss.'

Garland took a pencil, and, treating the locations on the map like a dot-to-dot puzzle, he joined the dots to see if any picture emerged. If it did, it wasn't immediately obvious; the first three locations made a wide, broad V shape; the latter three locations making a second "V" shape, this one long and narrow. 'Does that shape signify anything to you? ' he asked Jamshedji.

Jamshedji shook his head. 'Nothing immediately jumps out at me.'

Garland thought back to the clue referring to symbols which led up to the killing on the Solar System Trail. Could the word "symbols" have a double meaning in addition to chemical symbols? Could the locations be tracing out some kind of design?

He grabbed his mobile and called Dr Tennant. After a few rings, Tennant answered. Garland put his phone on loudspeaker so that Jamshedji could hear the conversation.

'Hi, Luke, it's Gene. Just a quick one. Do you have any information or experience about killers that have used symbols and icons as part of their crime?'

'Oh God, yes,' replied Tennant. 'Loads. I guess the most obvious one is the Zodiac Killer about whom I was talking the other day. If you remember, I mentioned that he gave himself a very distinctive emblem consisting of a cross through a circle. It looked a bit like a gun sight. Then there was another guy in America called Dennis Rader who became known as the "BTK" killer because all his letters were signed with this weird logo made up of the letters B, T, and K. Some have suggested it stands for his modus operandi: blind, torture, and kill. The letters were arranged in a very distinctive pattern that looks like a naked woman laid on her back. If you look it up on the internet, you'll see exactly what I mean.'

Garland furiously wrote down the names while Doctor Tennant was speaking. 'Excellent. Any more?'

'Yeah, honestly there's no shortage of them. I can think of this guy who would draw his trademark pentagram in the dead woman's lipstick at the scene of each murder. One of the weirdest was an American who signed off all his correspondence with a "smiley". There'll be plenty more, I can guarantee. I'll have a dig around for you this afternoon, but those are the ones I can think of off the top my head.'

Garland wrote these down. 'Thanks, Luke. If you would please, before I go, are there any common sources of inspiration where killers get their ideas for symbols? I know I'm grasping a bit here.'

Tennant laughed. 'If only. Despite years of research, we still don't fully understand what goes on in these messed-up minds. Devil worship is probably the most obvious one, and if you're going to be looking any up any Devil-worshipping signs on the internet, then I reckon the best search term would be the word "sigil". Outside of that, it could be anything and everything. A lot of rock bands have emblems that look like sigils, as do logos for several computer games. Inspiration can come from anywhere around you. But what's strikingly different in this case is that if the killer is drawing a symbol, then unlike those I've just mentioned, yours hasn't announced the symbol up front and associated it with themselves from day one. Instead, it's being painted over a period of time, if indeed that's what they're doing.'

'OK, understood. But stay on this line of thought. I'll email you across the diagram I've just drawn of the pattern of our recent killings. I need you to pull together every possible angle linking serial killers and patterns and get straight back to me the second you get anything you think relevant. Thanks again.'

'Don't mention it. Any time.'

Garland hung up the phone and turned his attention back to his sketch as if mentally trying to coax an answer out of it. Another idea materialised, and he grabbed the computer mouse.

* * * *

Jack Horner completed his post-mortem on Ryan Christian and

as he scrubbed his hands, his thoughts turned to writing up his official report. He'd taken fingernail scrapings and samples from the clothing with forensic adhesive tape, although since there had clearly been no physical altercation, they weren't going to reveal anything of forensic value. He'd taken a blood sample which would go for more detailed analysis. Of course, he'd found the 9mm bullet and bagged it for ballistic examination. This one had taken a bit of finding. After its initial pass through the heart it had struck the scapula at an angle and bounced around inside, making somewhat of a mess before finally coming to rest.

He glanced up at the clock on the wall. Just about midday. Making a quick mental calculation, he reckoned that a couple of hours should be enough to finish the report, which would allow him some space in the afternoon in-between his other work to concentrate on the next part of his personal project. If that went well, then that might even allow him to leave work on time and call at the cemetery, have some quality time there, and quietly give a progress report.

* * * *

Karen and Paul strolled along the bank of the Ouse along the wide, airy promenade named the Dame Judi Dench Walk in honour of the award-winning actress who had been born in the city. They each clutched a small white cardboard box, the hot contents of which they were trying to shield from the wind.

'Thanks for coming out to meet me.'

'No problem. Here's your key back. Glad I could buy you lunch.'

Karen looked down into her carton with a smile. 'Peas and scraps too. You know how to spoil a girl.'

Paul gazed up and down the promenade.

'So, this is where you think the killer ran?'

'Probably. Everyone's gut feeling, mine included, is that they ran away from the city centre rather than towards it.'

They stopped and turned to face the river. A few pleasure boats were tied up at the side.

'It's not such a bad escape route,' observed Karen. 'You've got these railings on one side of the path blocking any view of you from your right, you've got a wide river on the other side. These old street lights are probably enough to guide your way so you don't fall over, but aren't bright enough to illuminate you too much, and I can't see a single CCTV camera along the whole stretch.'

At that moment, an inflatable orange dinghy powered by an outboard motor came cruising up the river, breaking the silence. A flock of ducks which had just landed on the water scattered, responding angrily, quacking their displeasure loudly at the dinghy's solitary occupant for disturbing their peace. Paul and Karen both laughed loudly, at which the occupant of the dinghy, an old fellow in a red hiking jacket and a white knitted bobble hat, heard them, and gave them a cheery wave in response as he went past. As she returned the wave, Karen's mobile phone vibrated in her pocket. Pulling it out, she gave it a cursory glance and then thrust it back.

'You mentioned something last night about going round to the Masonic Hall,' Karen began as they turned to retrace their steps. She scrunched up her now empty fish-and-chip box and dropped it in a nearby bin. Noticing the reaction on Paul's face, she laughed.

'Don't worry, we've searched the bin already, it's safe to use. Where was I again?' – she paused – 'Oh that's right, the

Freemasons, how did it all go? Did you have to roll up your trouser leg?'

'I wouldn't know anything about that,' Paul said. 'But it went very well, thanks. I met the master of the lodge, a very pleasant chap, actually. In his day job, he's a Major at the garrison next to the police station. I even got to see the inside their secret meeting room,' he said with an undisguised air of prestige.

'Seriously?'

'Yes. They're not as secretive as you think. They've even got a website. Look.'

Pulling his mobile out, he brought up the website of the local lodge and showed Karen the screen.

'Wow. I didn't expect that. What's the logo?'

'That's the square and compasses,' replied Paul, glad for the opportunity to demonstrate his new-found Masonic knowledge. 'Two original stone masonry tools which their members apparently use as a metaphor for daily conduct in their lives.'

They'd reached the foot of the steps which would take them back up onto Lendal Bridge.

'Garland told me he once met Judi Dench at a charity bash,' remarked Karen, pointing at the sign for the "Dame Judi Dench Walk". 'He told me she's a lovely person and he absolutely admires her to pieces as an actress, but given that Garland's an ardent York City fan, he was mortified when he found out she supported Everton.'

Chapter 31

The two men strolling through the rough, untended grass of the overgrown field above the Neville Hill Train Depot in Leeds paused and turned to look at the view below them. For anyone interested in the railways, which one of them was and the other most certainly was not, it was an impressive sight. Alongside a colossal set of engine sheds that sprawled beneath them lay dozens of railway lines, fanning and swelling out in front of them into a bulge of steel and wood . Ultimately, they converged back in at the other end of the works into the set of railway lines going out. On many of the tracks, an assortment of ageing trains and carriages sat in the autumnal damp, awaiting maintenance or scrap.

The taller of the two men scanned the rolling stock. 'Shame,' he said disappointedly. 'I picked this spot for our meeting this time because I was hoping to see an old Intercity 125. Now that was a great piece of British engineering from my youth.' He sighed fondly. 'Made your heart swell just to look at it. Now we've moved on and there's another bit of our nostalgia gone in favour of bland foreign-made stuff.'

His companion spat into the grass. Frankly he couldn't care less. *Things came. Things went. So what?*

'Anyway, shame to disrupt this lovely walk by talking about business, but here we are,' continued the first man. 'At least out here there's not much chance of bumping into any undesirables. Other than you and me of course.' He gave a conspiratorial grin. 'So, go on then, how did it all go?'

'Everything went fine, trust me. I'm nearly there with it all.'

'And this evening? You made sure you're properly prepared for it. I don't want this operation cocking up with any slackness.'

The eyes scanned the railway tracks once more, still seeking out an Intercity 125 in the crowd of trains. No, none there. His eyes suddenly narrowed and he rapidly swung round aggressively to face his cohort. 'Fail to prepare and prepare to fail and all that.'

'Relax. It's all in hand. But you've got to promise to honour our deal. Just this time and then we're done, right? Yes?'

The face softened just a little. 'You've got my word. I might be a bastard, but I'm an honourable bastard. Now go and do a good job.' Then, with an uncharacteristic smile, 'Good luck.'

They turned and made their way back towards the road to part company.

'Shame about not seeing an Intercity 125, though. I'm right pissed off about that.'

* * * *

Karen and Paul crossed the busy Lendal Bridge on their way back towards the car park where Karen had left her car. Karen had a thought.

'You also mentioned last night that you'd seen a photo of what looked like our first victim at a corporate event at the Guildhall. Have you found out any more about that?'

'Not yet,' replied Paul. 'In fact, you're the only person I told about it.'

'I need to mention it to Garland. He's very keen to not miss out any detail. You want a lift back to the office?'

'No, it's OK, thanks.' Paul's mind was jerked back to the unsavoury appointment. He'd been deliberately trying not to ruin the occasion by thinking about it. 'I've got the afternoon off to see my solicitor. It's about...well...you know...' His voice tailed off reluctantly.

'It's OK you know. You can mention her,' Karen reassured him. 'In fact, it'll probably do you good. How long were you together?'

'I was married to Amanda for six years.' Paul broke into a smile, feeling more relaxed. 'Although I must admit, sometimes it felt like longer.'

'I've never been married, but I once had a long-term relationship that went to the dogs. Total nightmare he was in the end. He's long gone now, thank God. I'll tell you about it some time when all this mess is over. What did she do?'

'Got angry a lot for no reason.'

'No, you chump. For a job, I mean.'

'All sorts, really. When I met her, she was working in an admin job at the university. She didn't really enjoy it. I think she always felt the role was beneath her ambitions. Anyway, after three or four years there the job came to an end and looking back, that's probably when the cracks started appearing, or maybe it just brought on the inevitable. By that stage, I was getting tired of making all the effort but always being in the wrong. Sorry, that sounds bad.'

'No, not at all. So, then what?'

'Well, she applied for quite a few jobs, but she struggled to find anything she thought was at her level and when she did, it didn't last. It put a bit of a strain on things financially. I was just a general-purpose journalist at the time. Sometimes I wonder if I was patient and understanding enough.' He shrugged and then said, 'She even applied to the police once, but nothing came of it.'

'If I know you, you'll have had the patience and understanding of a saint,' Karen replied. 'Anyway, suppose she'd got the job in the police, how would you have coped with going out with a copper?'

'I rather think I like that idea a lot,' replied Paul.

There was a pause in which the only sounds were the passing traffic across the bridge and Karen and Paul's footsteps on the wet pavement.

Karen looked up at him. 'Really?' she smiled.

* * * *

Garland had always made a consistent effort to be computer literate. Indeed, it was a source of pride that many of his friends and family, including his teenage son and daughter, no less, came to him with technical issues such as with the family's cantankerous inkjet printer. He'd always considered technology to be such an integral part of modern life that he was rather withering of colleagues with a lack of technical expertise, proclaiming it to be simply down to nothing more than laziness on their parts to make the effort to learn.

It had taken him less than five minutes to open up the Microsoft Paint drawing app on his computer and draw the logo traced out on the map by the locations of the murders. He saved it as an image file and then, opening up his web browser, he uploaded the file into Google Image Search to see if he could find any close matches on the internet. He wasn't disappointed. He rubbed his hands in anticipation and grabbed his pen, eager to make notes.

The first symbol on the screen was the Sigil of Lucifer. Garland's eyebrows rose. Originally meaning "Light Bringer", he learnt, the name Lucifer had become synonymous in Christian theology with Satan, the Devil. Theology wasn't one of

Garland's strong suits, but a few minutes' research revealed information about Lucifer's fight with Michael the archangel who cast him down from heaven. Garland added this latest information to his mind map before turning back to the computer. He wrote a memo to get one of his team to investigate the possibility of satanic organisations as a matter of priority. He also saw that Lucifer was considered to be synonymous with the morning star and he briefly noted the point that the name Morning Star is a misnomer as it is, in fact, the planet Venus, the next planet out from the sun after Mercury.

The second symbol was also interesting. The Sigil of Azazel. Soon Garland had brought himself up to speed with Azazel, a name associated with the ancient biblical rite of the scapegoat. In the rite mentioned in the book of Leviticus, two kid goats were presented to the priest, who, invoking God's name in the Hebrew form of the Tetragrammaton, decided the fate of the goats by lots; one to be a sacrifice, the other, the escape goat or scapegoat, to be sent out into the wilderness.

Garland leant across his desk to his mind map and added the word "SCAPEGOAT" in large capital letters. Had the killer once been scapegoated over something?

The third and final symbol of interest was Aleister Crowley's Hexagram of Thelema. From what Garland could see, the path traced out by the murders so far roughly made up the lower half of the hexagram. Did this suggest that there were more murders to come to complete the top half?

Aleister Crowley was probably Britain's most famous occultist, with such eternal notoriety that he even appeared in the collage of faces on the cover of the Beatles' *Sergeant Pepper's* album. He'd enrolled in the secret Hermetic Order of the Golden Dawn, an organisation dedicated to the research of the occult, divination, and the paranormal. The three founders of the Golden Dawn had all been disillusioned, renegade Freemasons.

* * * *

Karen and Paul stood beside York War Memorial. Bright red Remembrance Day poppy wreaths adorned its base. The sight of the memorial and the wreaths pricked Paul's conscience, and he realised that, distracted by the ongoing chaos in his life, he'd neglected to buy a poppy. Remembering the sacrifices that others had made was important to him, and he made a mental note to purchase one on his way to the solicitor's. Even just thinking about the meeting again gave him a horrible, knotted feeling in his stomach. If it hadn't been for Linda having the good sense to organise it for him, he thought, he might have procrastinated forever. It had to be faced.

'My car's this way.' Karen pointed. 'Good luck with everything this afternoon. You feeling alright?'

'I'll be fine,' Paul reassured her.

'Of course you will.' In a moment of complete spontaneity, she leant across and gave him a parting peck on the cheek.

It would have been an absolutely beautiful moment if it had not been accompanied by the noise of Paul's mobile phone in his pocket announcing that an email had arrived.

Chapter 32

Jack Horner completed his report on Ryan Christian's post-mortem and saved the file on his computer. He always derived a solid personal satisfaction in completing one thoroughly even if, as was the case in this instance, there was little enlightenment to be found other than what had already been immediately obvious to everyone. With no physical contact between killer and victim, there was no new forensic information to link the poor fellow on the table to his murderer. Anyway, the report was done, which was the main thing. It meant he could give his full attention to the project, which he'd been quietly itching to look at all day.

Reaching behind his chair, he hefted his soft black leather briefcase up onto his lap, opened it, and retrieved a memory stick from one of its many internal zipped pockets. Handling it carefully, he inserted the memory stick into the USB port on the side of his laptop. There was no way he was going to save this particular file on a work's computer or on an official network.

He opened the file and examined its contents diligently on the screen. It was a spreadsheet. Down the left-hand column, a list of names was ranked in alphabetical order. In the remaining columns, alongside each name, were various pieces of information and annotations. Some of the spreadsheet was still incomplete, but the gaps were filling up. He was now in desperate need of a confirmation email – which he was expecting any time soon, hopefully that very afternoon, which would mean he could look forward to a rewarding conclusion to something that had involved much fastidious planning and execution.

* * * *

Paul left the solicitor's office, making his way back through the reception room past the bubbling tropical fish tank. His meeting had overrun by a quarter of an hour due to his soon-to-be ex-wife Amanda digging in her heels and disputing the split of matrimonial assets in the financial settlement. Disappointingly, it seemed there was going to be very little consent in their so-called "consent order". It was rather a blow, as Paul had always hoped to resolve matters amicably and quite generously on his part, but it looked like Amanda was determined to extract as many pounds of flesh as she could grasp. Stepping out into the overcast afternoon, he retrieved his phone from his pocket and, switching it back on, noticed he'd had a missed call from Linda ten minutes ago. He called back.

'Hi, Linda. Is everything OK?.'

'Yes, fine. Look, I don't mean to intrude, but I just wanted to give you a bit of moral support and hoped everything went well at the solicitor this afternoon.'

'Hmm. Could have been better to be honest, and we've some way to go yet.'

'Chin up, Paul. Trust me, it might feel like hell on wheels right now, but in the long-term it'll be worth it. My divorce a year back was awful, but I'm so glad to be able to put it behind me now and spend the rest of my life looking forward. I've been able to plan and organise some really good things this year.'

'Thanks, but listen, there's something I need to tell you. Between you and me, I got another one of those emails just before my appointment. The police already know – in fact DC Parkinson was with me when it arrived – and I've been asked to go round to the police station this afternoon. I'll be back at my desk first thing in the morning.' He paused with a sick feeling in his stomach. 'Regardless of what happens tonight.'

'OK but take it easy. Everything's fine here at the office, so just you look after yourself.'

At her desk, Linda replaced the receiver back gently and swung her swivel chair around to where Sue Webb, the office manager, had been standing during the call.

'Paul Dobson.' She smiled, looking up. 'Lovely lad, but so naive.'

Sue smiled back knowingly and shook her head, sending perfumed wafts through the air of Linda's office. 'Oh yes. Absolutely. What are we going to do with him?'

* * * *

The meeting in the incident room had already been underway for about half an hour, with Garland summarising and working through the next steps regarding the murder of Ryan Christian. Karen collected Paul from reception when it was time for him to join them and introduced him to the other detectives and to Dr Tennant, ex-DCI Jason Brown, and Professor Robinson. Professor Robinson motioned for Paul to sit next to her on a chair reserved for him at the front. Garland, shirt sleeves rolled up, one hand grasping a mouse, and the other running through his close-cropped hair, was looking impatient. The large TV screen on the wall was already displaying the latest clue.

Hush! Lights, camera action! I sound so debonair
Iron guns fire lead bullets in my movie premiere
Laugh – this is more comedy gold than a film noir
Wool over your eyes again, I bid you all au revoir

Paul regarded Garland in admiration. He must have hardly slept since this whole spree had started, yet here he was still standing, still fighting, and still determined that failure was never going to be an option.

'OK,' Garland began. 'I'd first like you all to welcome Paul Dobson, the journalist who's been receiving the cryptic emails. I've invited him to attend this part of the meeting as he was successful in cracking one of the clues earlier this week, and I want to bring in everybody of value to work on this latest. Jason, if I could start with you, I know you've had some initial thoughts.'

'Thank you.' Jason rose and straightened the lapels of his checked jacket. 'Well, the things that must scream out from this clue are the metaphors for Hollywood and the film industry. There's a place called Holly Wood in Ryedale. However, we need to get this into perspective; when I say "near" I mean it's about twenty miles out to the north, and all our killings so far have been within a mile or two of the city centre. If this is going to be the location of the next killing, it would be a huge departure from the norm. Let's continue this film theme.'

He nodded across to Garland, who, with a click of the mouse, replaced the clue on the screen with a list of movie titles.

'Here are some movies you might be surprised to learn were filmed in York,' he announced. 'Take the top one, this Harry Potter film. Now, lots of people think that for obvious reasons the railway station scenes are at Kings Cross in London, but many of them were actually shot in York. The Shambles is apparently an inspiration for one of the streets in the books too.'

DC Goodier smiled. His kids had been hooked on all the films, which of course meant that he'd sat through them all as well. He inwardly congratulated himself for spotting York railway station the first time he'd seen it. He raised his hand. 'There's a Severus Street in York – and one of the main Harry Potter characters is called Severus,' he said for those who might not know. 'And I know it'll be in the file, but I just remembered that when we researched our first victim Alec Hopkins, we found out he shared the same name as an actor in one of the Harry Potter films.'

'Well spotted,' Brown said. 'Moving on, York station was also used in *Chariots of Fire*. York was a Roman city and at one time the streets were full of chariots. The Yorkshire Museum contains artefacts from the Iron Age chariot burials and the second line of our poem begins with the word "Iron".'

Brown turned back to the TV screen and the remaining bullet points. 'Other films which have been shot in York include one of the Garfield movies and there's a Garfield Terrace. Anyone familiar with it?'

DC Ward raised his hand. 'I know it well,' he said. 'It's a pleasant street but quite well populated so it's not the ideal place to shoot someone and make a getaway. At least, I suppose, that's what I would have said until last night's rather audacious murder.'

'Quite,' agreed Garland. Goodier shot a glance sideways at Ward. He'd heard Ward come out with many choice words when discussing crimes but this was the first time "audacious" had been one of them.

Brown continued. 'Some scenes in the most recent *Charlie and the Chocolate Factory* were shot locally. There's the connection with Rowntrees chocolate factory which is just north of the city, and there's the Terry's factory to the south. One more thing….'

Brown nodded and Garland brought up a poster on the screen. The image showed a beach with a man holding his arms out and a woman wearing a red hat. It wasn't the picture that made everyone in the room sit up, it was the movie title. *Steele Wool.*

'In the clue we have references to iron, lead, and gold and the last line talks about having the wool pulled over our eyes,' explained Brown. 'Put that lot together with the concept of movies and *Steele Wool* looks interesting.'

He looked out across the room. 'The film is a dark comedy, and the third line of our clue talks about comedy and film noir. And the plot is about an actress who becomes a hired assassin and goes on a killing spree.'

'I've already got a copy for one of us to watch,' Garland said. 'DC Snow, you look like you enjoy a good movie, so this job's yours, but you'll have to provide your own popcorn. I want you to look out for any connections to York or to anything connected with the previous murders, however tenuous. Make a list of all the pertinent people, places and themes in the film and put them into HOLMES to see if any of them make any connections and let me know immediately if anything significant comes up.'

'I've tried to research the location guide on the internet movie database website but sadly it's not too forthcoming,' lamented Brown. 'From what I've been able to learn, the film was shot around Union Station in Los Angeles.'

'Hang on a moment then,' said Garland, leaning forward to reach for the keyboard. He brought a street map of Union Station onto the large TV screen, then dragged the little yellow man icon across and dropped it down. 'Let's see what this place looks like.'

The road outside was wide and busy and Union Station stood just a little way back. It was clean and pleasant looking, with arched windows and a charming clock tower giving it the slight air of a Mediterranean church. Noticeably though, around the clock face and at various intervals along the outside wall, was a set of bright red wreaths.

'OK, time for a break.' Garland consulted his watch. 'Back in ten minutes please, all of you.'

The detectives filed out of the incident room. Paul was somewhat relieved to have a pause in proceedings. 'Which door's the toilet?' he asked Karen.

'Down there at the end on the right. I'll see you back in the incident room. I'll make you a drink.'

She was about to say the line which had become a commonality between then when Paul interjected and beat her to it. 'Yes, I'll have the usual'

Paul made a beeline for the toilet. As he was washing his hands, DS Jamshedji breezed in.

'Hello, Paul.' He smiled. 'Did you enjoy your visit to the Masonic Hall, then?'

Chapter 33

Paul felt the world briefly swim in front of his eyes. He grasped the side of the sink for support as Jamshedji moved to the urinals without a care in the world.

Jamshedji's tone sounded surprisingly warm and jovial. 'The master of the lodge, Major Alan Brook, told me you'd been for a look around. Did you have a good time?'

Paul hesitated in shock at the revelation that Jamshedji knew that he had visited the Freemason's lodge. Best keep it short and simple. 'Yes, thank you. Very interesting.'

'The meeting room upstairs is superb, isn't it? I love the place. Plenty of friends always willing to provide any amount of help, advice, and support any time you need it. There's a great atmosphere, good banter, and lovely grub as well. Hey,' he shouted across, his voice resonating off the tiled walls. 'I've had an idea. Why don't you come along to our Christmas party – it's in a few weeks' time – and see what one of our charitable social events is like? Consider yourself formally invited. How about it?'

'Thank you,' replied Paul. Jamshedji's enthusiastic attitude had knocked him completely off balance. He really didn't know what to say.

Jamshedji washed his hands and as he held them under the hand drier, the loud blast of air from the motor almost drowned out his last words as he shouted them over his shoulder above the noise. 'Excellent. Be great to have you along. Right then, back into the incident room, we've got a serial killer to catch tonight.'

* * * *

As they filed back in, Karen shoved her mobile phone back into her pocket with one hand as the other struggled to hold two large mugs of coffee without spilling.

'Here, I'll take one,' Paul offered as he met up with her in the rather cramped corridor, still bemused by his conversation in the toilets. 'Thanks.'

'OK, let's push on,' announced Garland as everyone took their places and the sound of chair wheels on the floor faded away. 'As you'll have noticed in your files and on this incident board map of locations, we're looking at a possible pattern to the murders. Doctor Tennant, over to you.'

Tennant got to his feet and brushed back his hair.

'The ways in which serial killers select their victims are extremely varied. For the opportunistic types, as we've discussed, it's down to a random urge which results in the death of some unlucky person in the wrong place at the wrong time. So the decision is usually based on the specific person rather than the place.

'If we consider all the motives I talked about the other day, we can see that none of the conventional ones fit, which means we are left with having to consider other possibilities.' He coughed politely before reaching his conclusion. 'It's my firm contention that this killing spree is all about fulfilling a destiny. I'm going to propose that the locations have all been deliberately chosen from day one and the killer is now working their way through the predetermined list in order to fulfil some kind of specific goal.' He paused. Goodier's palm was raised. 'DC Goodier?'

'Do you have any insight at all into how the locations and their sequence could be chosen?'

'There are infinite possibilities. It could be a very personal one, with locations linked to specific incidents in the killer's life. For example, places where they had marriage proposals turned down, places where they were attacked and mugged, the list goes on. However, on that note, DI Garland has an interesting theory which I know he wants to present to you.'

He sat back down and Garland took to his feet again to address the room. A map of York with the murder locations marked on it appeared on the screen.

'I'd wondered,' explained Garland, 'if what our killer is doing is attempting to draw out some kind of pattern or sigil relating to black magic or Devil worship. I did entertain the idea that our killer is driven by the notion that if they trace out a certain black magic symbol with their killings then that will, in their mind, complete a magic spell which will be the key to their acquiring some kind of demonic superpower, like the ability to summon the Devil, become ultimate master of the universe, or some other insane power-crazed idea.'

A glance round the room was met by serious-looking faces nodding appreciatively. Relieved that his idea appeared to have gained credence, Garland continued with his next slide. The points on the map were connected in order by thick black lines and the background map faded away just leaving the motif drawn out by the killings.

'I did a reverse-image search on the internet of what we have here and the interesting ones I came across were these three.' The drawing disappeared to be replaced by three mystical looking symbols. 'These are three sigils associated with black magic or Devil worship. The first one is called the Sigil of Lucifer, the one in the middle is called the Sigil of Azazel which is also a symbol associated with the concept of a scapegoat, and the one on the right is of particular interest as it fits our pattern very closely indeed. It's called the Hexagram of Thelema, as drawn by Aleister Crowley. For those who don't know, Aleister Crowley was a famous magician. And by that, I mean black magic, not the Paul Daniels or Penn and Teller type.'

'So, based on that,' Jamshedji added, 'the idea is that we might be able to extrapolate where the next killing is going to take place. If the theory holds up, all we have to do is follow the points around and calculate where the next one falls.'

'Indeed.' Garland nodded. 'Assuming the theory works, that is. However, in practice it's muddied by the fact that we don't know which of these three sigils, that is if the killer is using any of them at all, is being used, and bear in mind the locations don't land slap bang on the spot you'd get if you simply overlaid any of the sigils on the map, which suggests there may be some other factor that we haven't yet worked out which is also involved.'

Paul sat in silent concentration as the symbols were displayed. They reminded him of another zigzag logo he'd seen recently, namely the shape of the Masonic square and compasses. Glancing sideways in the direction of Jamshedji, who was looking his way, he decided to mention his thoughts to Karen in private.

'Nevertheless,' continued Garland, 'there's some good location-mapping software out there and I've run the coordinates through it.' He brought the map of York back onto the screen. 'Its best weighted prediction according to its algorithm is somewhere around here.' He indicated an area on the map. 'If we consider the city centre to be the middle of a clock face, then the software prediction is somewhere between the nine and eleven o'clock positions on the dial and about a mile and a half to a couple of miles out. That would be the Clifton and Rawcliffe areas. At this point, I'd like to turn to Professor Robinson to take us through her thoughts.'

'Thank you' As she stood up, adjusted her hair band, and smiled at the room; Garland put the clue back up on the screen.

'Going back to the clue. I've taken a look at it, and you'll see I've highlighted some things I believe might be significant. I was struck by the fact we continue to have a connection with metallic elements. In fact the rhyme mentions three of them specifically by name. *Iron* guns, *lead* bullets, and comedy *gold*.'

She paused to let the room take in the rhyme once more, this time complete with her particular emphasis.

> **H** ush! **Li** ghts, **ca** mera **ac** tion! I sound **s**o debonair
> Iron guns fire lead bullets **in** my **mo** vie **pr** emiere
> **La** ugh – **th** is is **mo** re **co** medy gold **th** an a film **no**ir
> **W** ool over **y** our eyes **ag** ain, I **bi** d you **al** l **au** **re** voir

'Taking the first and last letter of every line yielded nothing. We know our killer never repeats the same method, but just take a look at all the letters I've highlighted. Each one is where a word starts with the symbol of a metallic chemical element. We even have complete words like *in* and *au* – which are indium and gold. She sighed. 'Then I ran into a bit of a brick wall. Putting movies and metals together, I discovered on the internet that there was a movie called *The Sound of Metal*, but I'm not convinced about that because it doesn't seem to have any obvious connection to either serial killers or York.' She looked round the room and spread her hands in invitation. 'So I'm looking for ideas about anything connecting metal with films or entertainment in general and Devil worship.'

DC Snow's interview with Kirsten McNally's next-door neighbour and her use of the term "heavy metal" was still fresh in his mind.

'Metal rock music,' he said. 'As in heavy metal. That's metal. It's entertainment and a lot of people associate it with the Devil.'

'Good thought.' Garland smiled. 'So now let's look for a specific piece of heavy metal, hopefully one that will link us directly to one of these sigils like Aleister Crowley's hexagram here.'

'Easy,' said Snow straight away. 'I was listening to this song just the other day called 'Mr Crowley' by Ozzy—'

'Osbourne,' finished Garland. 'It's on his *Blizzard of Oz* album.'

The room fell into a somewhat shocked silence.

'What?' demanded Garland. 'I know some of you younger lot think I'm some old fart, but I'll have you all know that not only does this old fart have the album in question but I even went to some Black Sabbath gigs when I was in my twenties, which I bet is more than any of you can say.'

At this piece of news, the tension broke a little and everyone started laughing as Snow's face turned slightly pink with embarrassment. Everyone, that is, except Karen Parkinson.

'What's the matter, DC Parkinson?' asked Garland. 'Don't tell me you're shocked to find out that your carbon-dated DI actually does have a life, and that Snow isn't the only one in the room who's listened to Ozzy Osbourne?'

'It's not that,' Karen said. 'There's an Osborne Drive in the Rawcliffe area. Right in the spot where your software predicted the next killing.' Her voice rose in panic. 'It's my address, boss. It's the road where I live.'

Chapter 34

Twenty miles away, DS David Edgerton sat at his desk at Stainbeck Lane police station in Leeds. From his chair by the window, he'd watched the lights in the houses across the road coming on one by one as the daylight faded and the cloak of darkness descended. He looked up at the plain, functional clock on the office wall and then down at his "IN" tray. It was getting late and there were still mountains of paperwork to get through before he could call it a day. Still, he reminded himself, this was the job he'd always wanted to do.

Looking back, he reckoned that the decision had been forged in the moment when, as a child, he, his mother, and his father had been involved in a horrific car accident with a seriously drunk driver. They could all have been killed. He and his mother had survived unharmed, but his father had been injured for life and still suffered pain in his hips on a daily basis. The experience had affected him deeply, and he'd realised from that moment on that the world contained people who did selfish, irresponsible, and sometimes evil things, where good innocent people suffered as a result. He resolved that every day he could stop a good person being hurt by a selfish or malignant action was a day in which he made the world a better place. If only it didn't involve so much bureaucracy and form-filling, though.

His mobile lit up on the desk and started ringing. He looked down at the display. His informer.

A bit earlier than I expected, but this should be interesting.

He picked up the phone.

'Edgerton.'

'Hi.' The voice at the other end sounded on edge. 'It's been a success. I've finally got the information you're after.'

‘Excellent. You’re good to talk?’

‘Yeah, very comfortable.’

Edgerton relaxed. “Comfortable” was their previously agreed code word, which meant their conversation was private. Had his contact had said he was “fine” or “OK”, then it would have been a signal that he was under some kind of pressure. Edgerton walked over to his office door and gently swung it shut.

‘Good news. So, go on then, what have you got?’

‘I need to make sure. We still have our deal, right?’

‘Well, that rather depends on what you have to tell me. Do I have to remind you you’ve been in the bad book recently? Three serious cock-ups in less than a week. First you decided to go round to Kirsten McNally’s place just after she’s been murdered. Second, fighting with the murdered girl’s dad instead of just buggering off quietly. And third, you got yourself arrested.’ He sighed. ‘Do you see what a complete all-round pain in the arse you’ve been? Anyway, I hope our little meetings at the Oakwood cinema and the railway depot have sorted your head out. Let’s hear what you’ve got, and I’ll decide from there.’

‘Yeah, look I’m sorry about that. I panicked and I shouldn’t have done. But listen – I’ve got confirmation of the pub that’s dealing in black-market ammo. I also found out which shop is going to be attacked in an armed robbery on Saturday, and I’ve got you a list of names of the people involved.’

‘Excellent, well done.’

As the informer read out the names of the pub, the shop, and half a dozen individuals, DS Edgerton smiled.

‘You got any other proof?’

‘Yeah. I did what you asked and bought some boxes of ammo from the supplier in the pub. They should have the seller’s fingerprints on them. They're in my pocket. I need to arrange to meet up with you to hand them over.'

'Great work. Now listen. I know you think I'm a bastard, but I honour my deals. So here's what happens now. We're going to meet tonight, and you can hand over the evidence. We'll take it from there and you don't need to be involved after that. After we've met, go back home, pack your things, and at six tomorrow morning a vehicle will come and pick you up from home. The driver will have a safe word so you'll know he's legit. Then you and your girlfriend are out of harm's way and can disappear forever. Everything's been organised in advance.'

'Thank you.' The informant's voice sounded like the weight of the world had been lifted. 'Seeing as you've been decent, there's one more thing. I think you'll find this very interesting indeed.'

* * * *

Karen came out of Garland's office and closed the door behind her. The meeting in the incident room had finished a quarter of an hour earlier. Paul was downstairs waiting in reception. Firearms patrols had been organised for the night in Garfield Terrace and Osborne Drive. Palmer and Ward were double checking the previous locations in the police database to see if anything had been overlooked. Hayward and Goodier were now investigating the possible existence of any black magic or Devil-worshipping societies in York. Snow had a movie to watch.

As for her? Garland had ordered her to find alternative accommodation for the night. If she couldn't find a friend or family member nearby to put her up, she was to book into a hotel and put it on expenses. As she had already had precious little sleep the last two nights, Garland had sent her off with immediate effect to allow her the time to organise somewhere to stay and then get some rest. He had also asked her to spend some time in the evening revisiting the clue to see if she could see anything new to what they'd discussed in the briefing. While Garland was delighted with the progress on the latest clue, he was still sceptical, and she knew that deep down he was worried that the real answer had eluded them all just as it had done before.

I should phone Bob, she thought.

Pulling her phone out of her blue canvas bag, she dialled the number. It only rang a couple of times before his voice came on the line.

'Hi, sis. Are you all right?'

Karen's smiled on hearing her brother's voice. 'Hi Bob. Yes, I'm fine. You can stop worrying about me although I know you always do, regardless of whatever I tell you. Just a quick question, how do you fancy putting your irritating sister up for the night?' She decided not to tell him the reason why.

'I'd absolutely love to, but haven't you remembered this is the week the family and I are going down to London for our pre-Christmas shopping break? I'm in the car just passing the junction for Milton Keynes as we speak. I did offer you to come along with us if you remember.'

'Damn. I do remember now.'

'We're back home in three days' time, why don't you come up and visit us then? It would be great to see you, it's been a while.'

'Thank you. I'll check my diary.' Karen sighed internally. *Looks like it's going to be a hotel tonight, then.*

‘And the family here want me to pass on their love to my little sis.’

‘Cheeky sod, I’m only a year younger than you. Oh, and thanks once again for the flowers, you really didn’t need to. I’m just sorry I couldn’t always get to talk or return your texts straight away.’

‘You’ve been a huge help with me getting my dispute successfully sorted out with the builders on my kitchen extension and I felt it was the least I could do to say thanks. And it stops me feeling so guilty for all the times I’ve bugged you on the phone when you’ve been busy this week. If you can’t get over in a few days, we’ll have time to catch up properly at Christmas. You’re still coming, I hope?’ he continued a little hesitantly, as if treading around carefully so as not to accidentally offend. ‘Are you coming up on your own again this year?’

‘Maybe.’ Karen contemplated her answer. ‘Maybe not. We’ll see.’

* * * *

DS Dattaram Jamshedji strode back to his desk. He removed his immaculate jacket, placed it gently on a hanger so as not to crease it, hung it up, then sat down to mull over the afternoon’s events.

He hoped Paul would take him up on his offer of coming along to a Freemasons social event. The young journalist seemed a decent kind of lad who would probably enjoy joining the society and the camaraderie and banter that went with it. It would also provide the opportunity to do some really wonderful charitable work. It was true, he considered, how you could always ask any of them for their help and support at any rough time in your life. *Except the rough time I'm having this evening.*

He sighed. Unfortunately, when it came to hunting down a serial killer, there was little that any fellow Mason could do to help. This was going to be one for him and the team of detectives alone. *Or was it? Maybe one of them could help after all.*

As the idea entered his head, he grabbed his phone and dialled the number already saved in his contacts list.

'Hello. Alan Brook speaking.'

'Good evening, Major. It's Dattaram Jamshedji from the lodge here. Hope everything's well with you? I just wondered if I could quietly pick your brains on something?'

'Yes, no problem, but we'll have to be quick. I'm trying to get the dining room vacuumed before the missus comes back from shopping at the Designer Outlet. Honestly, I reckon if my bank card got pinched, I'd be better off not reporting it to you lot because the thief would spend less than the wife.'

'You love her to pieces, and you know it.' Jamshedji laughed. 'But anyway, let me cut to the chase. You've spent your life in the army, and you've got years of military experience with handguns. There's something I want to ask, just between you and me, in relation to the murders you'll have heard about in the news.'

'Fire away,' replied Major Brook. 'Oops. Sorry. Probably the wrong choice of expression. But go on, what's the question?'

'It's about the weapon which might have been used. Our firearms officer reports hearing a shot from just over a hundred yards away, but took great pains to stress that it was quiet even for a weapon fitted with a suppressor. He's an experienced officer, so I know I can trust his word. I wondered if you had any thoughts on that.'

Major Brook pondered for a moment. 'Well, one thing that he'll know is that guns fitted with so-called silencers are typically anything but completely silent. That'll be why your officer uses the same terminology as me – suppressor rather than silencer. It's not like in the spy films. In reality, there's still an audible and distinctive pop. For your man to make a point that it was particularly quiet seems relevant.'

'Yes, it was to me too. So, here's the big question. If you were to conduct a military raid late at night and you wanted to take something really silent, what gun would you use?'

'Hmm.' There was a slight pause. 'Well, some Ruger handguns are pretty quiet, but to get the least noise out of them, you'd need to combine them with very specialist low-noise ammo. Such stuff exists, but it's not easy for civilians to come by.'

'Just supposing…what if the gun just used standard 9mm ammunition?'

'Let me think. Well, I've got an idea, but it's a bit off the wall.'

'As my boss frequently tells us at times like these, there's no such thing as a crazy idea.'

'There was a pistol specially created for British Special Forces in World War Two. It was deliberately intended for use in clandestine operations such as espionage and sabotage, so it was designed for its extreme quietness. It didn't have a huge range, but that wasn't deemed necessary because its purpose was to take out guards and their guard dogs at very close quarters. I've never fired one myself, but allegedly it's not much louder than a pellet gun. Before you ask, they take 9mm rounds.'

Jamshedji gave a low whistle. 'What's this pistol called?'

‘It’s called the Welrod, because it was designed in a Special Operations research facility near Welwyn Garden City. Quite a few were made.’

‘I think you might be onto something here, Major.’ Jamshedji walked over to his jacket and extracted a fountain pen from the inside pocket. ‘So, just between you and me, if I wanted to get hold of one, where should I go looking?’

‘Given your job, you’ll know the black-market for handguns far better than me. But if I was to take a punt, I’d bet most are going to be Remingtons, SIG Sauers, Glocks, that kind of thing.’

‘Yes,’ replied Jamshedji. ‘In all my years I’ve never heard of a Welrod gun before.’

‘The Welrod’s not going to be a black-market gun,’ Major Brook said confidently. ‘I reckon the best way you’re going to come across one is if your grandfather was in the special forces during or just after the war and you’re clearing out his garage to take stuff to the tip or a car boot sale. And the bullets for it are bog-standard provided you have a suitable source. The 9mm Parabellum is one of the most popular bullets in the world today.’

‘Thanks for your time. That’s been really helpful.’ Jamshedji finished writing notes on his desk pad. ‘I’ll catch up with you at the next lodge meeting. I’d better let you get on with your vacuuming now. Make sure you go right up to the skirting board.’

Before he’d even finished his polite goodbyes to the Major, Jamshedji’s highly polished shoes were already making their way along the corridor to Garland’s office.

Chapter 35

At his desk, Jack Horner tried to occupy his mind with routine bureaucracy while he waited anxiously, like an expectant father, for the email he was hoping would soon arrive. Turning his attention to his in tray, he picked up a letter on a sheet of headed paper and afforded himself a chuckle, as he always did whenever he saw the Caduceus of Hermes, which had been used in the medical company logo. Often used as a symbol of the healthcare profession, two snakes entwined around a winged staff was actually the traditional symbol of liars, thieves, and commercialism. The correct symbol should have been a single snake wrapped round a plain staff; however, the wrong logo was frequently chosen. Contemplating this, Jack snorted. *Medicine is based on the application of sound scientific knowledge, not mythical or magic beings with snake-wrapped flying staffs,* he muttered to himself.

A ping sounded from his laptop. Tossing the sheet of paper unceremoniously to one side, he focused his attention on his email inbox. As he opened the attachment and read through it, his smile broadened, followed swiftly by a decisive frown. He was going to have to inform Garland about this. Taking a deep breath, he hoped that his long-standing friendship and all those hours spent side by side with him over the years cheering on York City every weekend would count for a lot of understanding. He was going to need it.

Horner wasn't a natural procrastinator. It was his philosophy that when things needed to be done, however uncomfortable, it was best to push on and do it. It needed to be done properly, too. He told himself to do an hour or so of research on this new information, then he would pick up the phone.

* * * *

The sky over Walmgate had already fallen pitch-black, and the shops opposite the York Press offices were starting to close for the day. Linda Reader stood in her upstairs office and paused to look out, catching a last view of the street, and checked her watch. A group of shoppers, all laden with bags, passed by underneath, their raucous laughter at some shared joke drowned out as a double-decker bus rumbled by, the colours of its cream and maroon livery barely distinguishable in the pink street lights.

She closed the vertical blinds, drawing a cover over the outside world, and returned to the corner of her desk. She shut down her laptop, glad to see the end of a long afternoon, and closed the lid, giving a long sigh as she did so. *Poor Paul*, she thought. One of the best journalists she'd ever had, but such a rudderless soul right now.

She had to admit she'd felt rather guilty for the assignments both she and the city of York had been able to offer him, dealing with a string of low-wattage news, going along dutifully, Fruit Pastilles, and *Private Eye* in hand, to the police station every week to hear the latest thrilling instalment in The Mysterious Case of the Stolen Lawnmower or The Intrepid Hunt for the Missing Ginger Cat or whatever it was that week. She'd suffered a period where every Monday morning she'd been half expecting him to hand in his notice and go work somewhere bigger and more exciting. Leeds perhaps, or London, or who knows, even further afield. Then his divorce came along, which had put a hold on all that; there's only so much upheaval in life that a person could deal with at any one time. One day though, his divorce would be final, like hers, like they all eventually were, and then he could be off and on his way. She loved having him around, enjoyed looking after him and taking care of him, initially as an employee, then, as she really got to know him, as a friend. He would leave quite a hole if he ever went.

Sliding her laptop into its bag, her mouth contorted into a thin smile. Well, it didn't look like he would be going anywhere soon now. With any luck, he would stay around a bit longer, what with all these goings-on.

* * * *

Paul's eyes lit up as Karen burst through into the police station reception area where he'd been waiting for her. He stood up and rushed to greet her and in doing so, was almost knocked to one side as she hefted her bag onto her shoulder.

'Oops, sorry.'

'It's fine. Are you OK? Is everything all right?'

'Yes, I think so. Just been speaking to Garland. He doesn't think I should be at home this evening, what with the clue possibly pointing to my address. I've just come off the phone from my brother Bob to see if he'd put me up for the night but he's currently on his way down to London. I'm going to take up Garland's offer to find a hotel and put it on expenses.' She laughed. 'I'm tempted to find a really swish one with a pool but I'm that worn out I'd probably fall asleep in the water.'

'Why not stay at my place? It's not far. I'll even throw in drinks and a takeaway.'

Karen immediately looked relieved. 'Thank you, that's brilliant. I really don't fancy being on my own this evening. I really appreciate this. I'll grab some things and come straight round.' She paused and then smiled. 'It's a good job I know you well enough, otherwise I'd wonder if you had an ulterior motive for inviting a girl back.'

Paul returned her smile. 'Well, I do.'

'Really?'

'Yes, I'm hoping you'll stay awake long enough to have one more crack at that latest clue. Indian or Chinese?'

* * * *

If Karen was feeling wrung out and exhausted, Gene Garland was completely rejuvenated and energised by DS Dattaram Jamshedji's news. This could be a badly needed significant breakthrough in the case. It was time for a really strong coffee and then back to the desk. He grabbed his "Apollo 11 Anniversary" mug and was about to head down to the small kitchen at the end of the corridor for a hot refill, when the phone on his desk rang. The caffeine refuelling would have to wait a few more minutes. He snatched up the receiver.

'DI Garland.'

'Good evening, Detective Inspector, it's DS David Edgerton from Leeds here. Hopefully, I'm in for a happier phone conversation this time around rather than the bollocking I got last time. I've got some interesting news for you.'

'Hope you didn't take it too personally.' Garland smiled and sat back in his chair. 'But we had just had your informer in one of our cells overnight for fighting the father of our latest murder victim. Anyway, please spill the beans.'

DS Edgerton was put immediately at ease by Garland's tone. 'It feels like I was destined to become drawn into this case from the off, anyway,' he admitted. 'First of all, my parents and I had been in a car accident years ago involving your first victim,

Alec Hopkins. My father told me some of your team had been round to interview him. Then, if that wasn't coincidence enough, I used to live on the same street as the second victim, Alice Morton, who you found dead at York Cemetery.'

'Really?' Garland had known about the first connection but the second one was news.

'Yes. Bloody foghorn of a woman she was, I can tell you. I wouldn't wish death on anybody, but if there's any small consolation, the world is probably just a bit quieter now. Not only that, but then, as if to prove that fate is determined to connect us, I then find out my old boss, DCI Jason Brown, is working with you. Send my best regards to him, will you please? Anyway, I digress.'

'Yes, come on. I'm all ears here.'

'Well, our aforementioned informer has been working on a nice little case for me here in Leeds in connection with an armed robbery. That is, until they try to go through with it this weekend coming and, well let's just say there'll be a surprise waiting for them. But anyway, part of his investigation was at a pub we suspected was involved in illegal ammo dealing, and sure enough, it was.'

Garland leant forward in his chair and nudged his mug to one side. The coffee could definitely wait. 'This sounds interesting.'

'I don't know if this is in any way connected to your case or not, but apparently in addition to the regular scrotes who've been glowing bright green on our radar for months, there was a new customer in there about a fortnight ago. This person's believed to have bought some ammo but hasn't been seen since. The timing of it all just seemed odd. It would be just a few days before your serial killer started doing their thing.'

Garland could feel the hairs on his arms start to rise. 'What calibre ammo we talking about?'

'Nine mil. Possibly hollow-point. Does that fit with your murders?'

'You'd better believe it does. Now the biggest question of all is...do you have a description of this person?'

'Not a great one,' replied DS Edgerton. 'Not enough for a Photofit or anything. The buyer was only seen the once, was wearing a hoodie, and kept themselves mainly to themselves. But I've been told we're looking at someone medium build, light-coloured hair, and about five foot six, give or take. But one thing I do know. It wasn't a man. It was a woman.'

Chapter 36

Garland propelled himself straight into the middle of the office full of detectives. 'Listen up, everybody, right now.' Conversation came to an abrupt halt, and all eyes swung up from their screens and their desks.

'Change of focus. A couple of things have come to light this evening that I want you to start working on with immediate effect. First, DS Jamshedji has a theory about the handgun and believes it could be a type called a Welrod. The reason behind his logic is that it fits with the extremely quiet sound which was heard by our firearms officer at York Minster the other night. The Welrod was specifically designed for Special Forces' covert operations in World War Two and is one of the quietest guns ever produced. Jamshedji and I have just watched an online video together in which one is fired and I can confirm it is incredibly quiet. We've put a link to the video in your files. When you watch it, you should also notice that the Welrod doesn't automatically eject the spent ammo casing like many modern handguns, but retains it inside the gun to be ejected manually. This is consistent with us not finding any spent cases at any of the crime scenes.

Jamshedji has proposed that since this is an uncommon historical item, and typical black-market handguns are the more common makes which we're all familiar with, you're more likely get hold of a Welrod through a connection to someone that used to be in the military. The Welrod was only ever issued to certain members of the armed forces and was never sold commercially. I want us to start looking for people in York who have been members of the Special Forces, and not necessarily just during the Second World War. This gun's been used up to the Falklands conflict in 1982 and possibly further.'

The once weary room felt like a cloud had magically lifted from it as a palpable energy came flooding through. Instantly, the air was buzzing with conversation. Garland raised his hand for silence.

'Listen up carefully, I've not finished. There's even more good news. I've heard from a DS in Leeds who tells me that about a fortnight ago, a few days before all this mayhem started, an informer of his witnessed a person not already on their radar buying 9mm ammo in a pub in Leeds. The person is described as having light hair, of medium build, about five foot six and, listen very carefully to this everyone, this person was female.'

An excited murmur rippled around the room.

'And yes,' continued Garland, 'I've checked the CCTV footage from the Dean Court Hotel again and it's consistent with the person on the footage being a woman.'

Garland continued to hold his hand aloft for silence.

'I've also just spoken on the phone with Doctor Tennant about what triggers a killing spree, and the one that could be highly relevant in our case is that of opportunity. Just imagine someone who's harboured a desire to go out killing for some time but has been afraid to do so because they lacked an effective means. Then one day, quite by chance, they find themselves with access to the perfect weapon, and that effective means falls right into their lap. It's not so hard to imagine, is it?'

As the detectives took in this latest revelation, Garland's mobile rang. Frustrated by its interruption, he pulled it out and his index finger immediately went to silence the call, but he saw the name on the screen was Jack Horner.

'Just excuse me one minute, everyone.'

He stepped out into the corridor and answered.

'Gene, something personal's come up. I know you're up to your neck in things at the moment with this serial killer, but I'd really appreciate talking to you urgently.'

'Jack, it's going to have to wait I'm afraid, a lot of things are kicking off tonight. Can we do this tomorrow or some other time?'

'I'd rather not,' insisted Horner. There was urgency and anxiety in his voice. 'Please, Gene, I'd be really grateful to get this off my mind. It'll take less than half an hour, not even that. Fifteen minutes. But it's incredibly sensitive. I'd much rather do it face to face.'

Garland groaned. 'All right. But I haven't got the time to travel far to meet you, not tonight of all nights. Things are moving quickly and I'm really under some pressure here.'

'That's OK. Let me suggest something. We'll meet at the cemetery. I have something important to show you there which will make everything clear.'

Garland considered the proposal. Things were pretty tight, but he'd delegated all that he could, and he had to remind himself he had a strong team and everything wasn't resting on him alone. The cemetery was less than a five-minute walk from the police station and Jack was also a good friend going back many years.

'Go on then. I've got some stuff to sort out on my desk here and I'll see you in the cemetery' – he consulted his watch – 'exactly half an hour from now.'

* * * *

Professor Dawn Robinson's black BMW X3 came to rest on her

drive, and she pushed the large button on the dashboard to silence the purr of the engine. A gentle glow filled the interior of the car. Leaning across, she pulled her bag on the passenger seat towards her and rummaged around inside it for her front door keys.

Sitting in the car, keys in hand, she paused in the silence to contemplate the various intellectual projects on which she'd worked during her career in search of everlasting fame. She'd spent untold hours on the famously unsolved Riemann Hypothesis, which had frustrated the greatest mathematicians in the world for over a century. The solution to the fiendishly difficult mathematical problem The Goldbach Conjecture – or even more prestigious still, the notorious P versus NP problem – was, despite many vexing hours in deep concentration and effort, nowhere in sight. Still, she considered, intellectual problems come in many forms.

Where were the police going to be patrolling this evening? Garfield Terrace? Osborne Drive?

She shook her head softly. No. The location wasn't going to be either of these.

* * * *

‘Come in,’ said Paul, opening his front door to Karen. ‘The place isn't very big, I'm afraid, but there are drinks in the fridge and I've put the menus for the takeaways on the table.’

‘Thanks.’ Karen pulled her canvas bag off her shoulder and deposited a black sports holdall on the floor. ‘I'm really grateful for your offer to put me up tonight.’

‘No problem, the pleasure’s all mine. Be nice to have some company on an evening anyway, and I feel better knowing you’re safe. Go through and make yourself at home.’

‘Thanks.’ She went through into the living room, flopped on the sofa, and picked up a newspaper that had been lying on one of the cushions. She waved it aloft. ‘If we need to take a break from looking at this latest clue and I can stay awake long enough, you can try to teach me how to do these stupid crosswords. They might as well be written in Egyptian hieroglyphics for all the sense they make to me. I’ve always been a Sudoku person, myself.’

‘I’ll stick the kettle on,’ shouted Paul from the kitchen, and then, because he couldn’t resist, ‘the usual?’

‘Hey, that’s my line,’ Karen retorted from the living room. ‘But yes, please.’

Paul came back in five minutes later to see her with the newspaper open at the cryptic crossword.

‘Like this clue, for example. *Steve Irwin initially gets directions to tissues*. Six letters. What the hell does that all mean?’

Paul considered the clue for a moment before a smile broke out across his face. ‘Ah, got it.’ he said. ‘Sinews.’

‘You’ve just exactly proved my point.’ Karen laughed. ‘What’s Steve Irwin the crocodile-hunting celebrity got to do with a box of tissues? What’s “sinews” got to do with anything? How the hell did you manage to get the answer out of that lot?’

‘It’s not too hard when you break it down. “Steve Irwin initially” is a hint to take Steve Irwin’s initials which are S and I. The directions bit is a reference to directions on a compass, N, E, W, and S. Put that lot together and you get sinews which are types of tissues – muscle tissues.’

'Right. Okaaay. I'm starting to get it now but we could still be in for a long night while I get the hang of solving the rest of the crossword. Maybe for now we should start by taking another look at this killer's clue.'

* * * *

Garland made his way up the path through the cemetery, his combat jacket zipped up to the top against the cold and his knitted York City scarf wrapped round his neck. As he made his way up, the street lighting from the road below faded away and he fished his torch out of his pocket. As he approached the summit, he could see the outline of the chapel at the top and as he got closer, he could see a dark figure stood in front of it.

'Hi, Jack,' he called.

'OK, where do you want me to fly to?'

It was a tired old joke between them, going back years, whenever they met on a social occasion, based on the greeting sounding like the word "hijack". They were both careful to keep these kinds of jocular exchanges private and they were never uttered in front of colleagues. On this occasion, however, Garland felt that any humour in Horner's voice sounded forced.

Garland reached the top of the slope and stood next to Horner, his torch glinting off the shiny blue plaque on the chapel, dedicated to its architect. He noticed in the torchlight that Jack's face looked strained and heavy with the weight of something serious.

'Follow me,' Horner instructed.

Without another word, they made their way across the front of the chapel, walking past the spot where the body of Alice Morton had lain just a few days ago. *What a hell of a week this has been,* thought Garland, looking down as they walked past it. *It feels like a decade and an exhausting one at that*. They carried on round the corner of the chapel and made their way to the rear of the building. In contrast to the ancient headstones that lined the slope up to the chapel, those here were more modern and recent. It was dark and Garland had to use his torch to light the way.

'Careful you don't trip,' he warned.

'It's OK, Gene, I've taken these steps hundreds of times. I could do it with my eyes closed.'

Jack came to a halt at a black granite headstone and knelt beside it. Garland followed him to the other side of the headstone and picked out the lettering with his torch.

'Pamela Bodenham.' He read the name aloud. There was a brief pause while he took in the rest of the headstone. 'Oh my word. Poor lass died in her twenties. No age at all. What happened?'

'Suicide,' replied Jack. 'Supposedly. But I was never convinced about that.'

Gene looked carefully again at the dates on the headstone. 'Jack, she died over twenty years ago. Why has a twenty-year-old suicide got the pair of us here tonight, old friend?'

Chapter 37

'Let me run an idea past you.' Karen tossed the newspaper aside. 'It's a bit off-piste but hear me out. Garland's been thinking about the murder locations and plotting their coordinates to see if they form a pattern. I had an idea that maybe the sequence isn't to do with the position, but instead what's *at* the locations.'

Paul nodded. 'I'm listening.'

'Here, I've brought my tablet with me.' She pulled it out of her bag. 'I've got a lot of crime scene photos on here, so how about we look through them together and see if we can spot anything that might make a sequence or a link?'

'Count me in,' Paul replied. 'OK, what've we got?'

Karen brought the screen to life and located the folder where various crime scene photos were saved. 'Just remember, if anyone asks, I didn't show you these,' she cautioned.

The first murder. West Bank Park. November fifth. Several photographs taken from various angles showed the body of the prostrate Alec Hopkins. 'I'm more interested in what's around him,' muttered Karen. 'Ah, here we are. Make a note of these.'

'I guess the obvious distinctive thing is the statue of Queen Victoria,' noted Paul. 'There are benches and hedges around too, but you get those everywhere.' He made a note.

'And now the second one.' Karen swiped across the screen through the photo library. 'Alice Morton, York Cemetery. Let's have a look at the exact spot at the chapel building itself where the body was found. Distinctive looking building, isn't it? Looks like a miniature Greek temple.'

'Hang on, just zoom in on that photo,' said Paul. 'It looks like a blue plaque on the wall over the body. What does it say?'

'Can't make it out fully on any of these photos and the edge is cropped off. Looks like it's dedicated to the architect, James Piggot something-or-other.'

'OK, I'll write that down as well. Next.'

'Number three is Kirsten McNally, shot at Hull Road Park next to the basketball court.'

'Oh God, I don't need reminding about that night.' Paul groaned.

'Yes, sorry. It's not nice, but we need to look through all these. Ready?' She swiped at the photos. 'Well, the obvious thing is the basketball court. She's lying practically slap bang under the hoop that's just over the other side of the wire-link fence.'

'Stop a moment,' requested Paul. 'There's a poster on the side of the pavilion behind her. What's that on the poster?'

Karen zoomed in and squinted. 'Looks like a top hat and a wand. I remember now, it was advertising a magic show somewhere locally, earlier in the year, I think. OK onto the next one.'

'That would be the army guy found at the Solar System Trail, then?'

'No, hang on, there was the wild goose chase lemon before that, wasn't there? Let's not leave that one out.'

'Do you have any photos of that?'

'No, since it wasn't a murder, but it was in the middle of Saint Nicholas Fields.'

'Noted. OK. Then we have the Solar System guy.'

'That's Mark Langridge. Victim number four. There's not much around here apart from trees, hedges, and a corn field. The only thing of significance is the model of the planet Mercury where he was found.'

'Right-o. And then that must take us up to the most recent one.'

'Yup. Ryan Christian.' She swiped the screen again.

'That's St Wilfrid's Church behind his body,' observed Paul. 'Can you just zoom to the top half of the screen? What's that dark shape hanging over his body?'

'It's the sign for the hotel,' replied Karen. 'Dean Court.'

'OK then.' Paul put his pen down. 'So, to sum up, we've got Victoria followed by a blue plaque of Piggot someone-or-other, then we've got magic and a basketball court, Saint Nicholas Fields, then Mercury, and then Dean Court.'

Karen stared at the list, hoping that a blinding flash of inspiration would strike.

'Nope,' she frowned, 'I don't see any connection there that immediately jumps out. Maybe some intensive googling might throw up something that's not widely known. If not, then this line of thinking is probably on the wrong track. I'll take a look anyway. While I do, stick the kettle on again. I'll have ...'

'... I know.'

* * * *

In the bleak cemetery, Jack took a deep breath and composed himself.

'Back then I was a junior doctor at Leeds General Infirmary,' he explained, 'and we had an intake of student nurses, as we did every year.' He paused. 'One of them was Pamela Bodenham. She came from York and it was through my relationship with her that I got to know this wonderful city.'

Garland waited beside Horner, letting him reveal the story at his own pace. Eventually Horner spoke again.

‘She was lovely. She had a bright personality, intelligent, and had a lot going for her. I remember some of the other student nurses nicknamed her Kate because she looked a bit like the singer Kate Bush.’

‘You and Pamela. Were you…?’ For someone who’d spent years asking tough questions, Garland found it particularly difficult to question his friend.

‘Yes. I was very fond of her. I loved her with all my heart and I believe she loved me too. I often dream about how life would have turned out had she not died, but that can be a conversation for another day, Gene.’

‘Go on.’

‘I got the feeling in the days leading up to her death, there was something troubling her, like she was in some conflict or argument about something or someone. I don’t know. I should have pushed harder to find out sooner. I still feel I let her down, Gene, I really did. And it’s bothered me to this day.’

‘Tell me what happened the night she died.’

‘I’d arranged to visit her that evening at her room at the nurse’s home, which was on site at the hospital,’ he said. ‘She had told me she had something on her mind, this conflict I’ve just mentioned – some ethical issue about one of the other nurses, she’d said – and she wanted to talk to me about it. I’ve still no idea what it was. I knocked on her door several times, but there was no answer. Had it been anyone else, I might have just thought she’d forgotten and gone out somewhere, but she was always very punctual and reliable and I recall she’d been very keen to talk. I just knew that something was wrong. I called out and when I didn’t get a reply, I opened the door a fraction. It was unlocked. She was lying completely still in her bed. I was too late.’ He stopped again.

Garland put his hand gently on Horner's shoulder. 'You're all right, my good friend. Whenever you're ready.'

'I did the obvious and checked her pulse and there was nothing. She was dead. It was then I noticed the two empty bottles of beta blockers in the bin by her bed and I felt frozen in my stomach.'

'Just help me here, Jack. What are beta blockers used for?'

'Slowing the heart rate. Slow it enough and it stops altogether. Of course, it looked obvious for all to see that Pam had taken her own life.' He sighed deeply.

'But that's not the end of it though, is it?' Garland prompted gently. 'If it were, we wouldn't be here now on a cold night twenty years later.'

Horner nodded. 'To make it worse, of course, the only way she could have access to the kind of tablets in those bottles was by stealing them from the hospital supplies. So, to add insult, she died with her reputation in shame. But still something niggled away inside me. You know how you just get, how shall I put it, a nose for something not being quite right?'

'I certainly do,' replied Garland. 'I've relied on it nearly every day of my career. What wasn't right and what did you do that night, Jack?'

'I just had this instinct that she wouldn't have taken those tablets of her own accord. Would someone in a suicidal state of mind have had the presence of mind to be so tidy as to put the used bottles in the bin? The choice of medication niggled me as well. It's a good tablet of choice to put into someone's drink if you wanted to make it look like suicide. These particular beta blockers would be tasteless, therefore impossible to detect, and wouldn't need a high dose. They're highly soluble, making them easy to administer covertly, and once anyone had taken them, they'd just go listless and collapse without any noise or commotion.' He looked directly at Garland. 'Looking back, maybe it was on that evening that my career in forensic pathology was decided.'

'Was this angle ever investigated?'

Horner shook his head. 'No. At the inquest, things came out, some of which Pam had told me, and one or two things she hadn't. In her younger years she had been diagnosed with a period of depression and on one occasion, about a year before starting her training in Leeds, she had tried to take her own life. At that point it became simply an open and shut case of a tragic suicide and that was the end of it.'

'But not to you, was it?' persisted Garland. 'You did something?'

'I picked up one of the empty bottles of tablets and hid it in my pocket,' confessed Horner. 'When I got back home, I sealed it in a plastic bag and kept it safe in a drawer. I've moved house twice since then and it's come with me every time.'

'Because...?'

'Touch DNA tests didn't exist in those days, the technology wasn't sufficiently developed, but something inside me made me faithfully keep hold of the bottle in the hope that one day some technology would come along and we might be able to do something. Then a few years ago, it actually became possible.'

'So, you've recently extracted a touch DNA sample from the bottle. Why now, Jack?'

'Well, as you can imagine, you need very specialised lab facilities. However, who better to have access to this kind of thing than a forensic pathologist? But it's not been easy, and this has been a long time in the planning. I don't want to break any confidences, but let's just say I've had to call in a few favours.'

He saw the look cross Garland's face. 'Nothing illegal, mind,' he added hastily, 'but it might be better if this wasn't widely publicised.'

Garland nodded. 'Understood. Then what?'

'I sent the sample off to an ancestry and genealogy DNA company. You know how they work, Gene?'

'Yes, I do. From what I understand, you can use them to find ancestors and relatives you never knew you had. Every person who sends in their DNA has it stored in their database. Every new sample arriving is checked against the existing database for potential matches, and they inform you if anyone has a partial DNA match for you.'

'Exactly. This afternoon I got an email back from them with this letter attached. Here, I've printed it off.' He reached into his coat pocket and retrieved two folded sheets of A4 paper, which he handed over. Garland unfolded the pages and held up his torch to read the letter's contents.

'To Dr Adrian Horner,' he read. 'Bloody hell. I've got so used to calling you Jack over the years that seeing your real name written down still comes as a surprise.'

'Yes,' admitted Horner. 'I've had that nickname since I was about ten. I didn't care for it at first, but I've got used to it.'

'That's nothing,' grunted Garland. 'Trust me. Try being a teenage schoolboy with the surname Garland and imagine what nickname you get. Think about it. It's probably how come I got so handy in a fight early on in life. Anyway…' He scanned the rest of the letter, reading aloud. 'Thank you very much for your…blah, blah, blah…we are delighted to inform you…blah, blah, blah…'

As Garland's eyes scanned down the page, they suddenly widened. 'They found an ancestral match in their database.'

'This is why I wanted to see you tonight. If we can link this DNA match to somebody who was at the hospital that year, then we might be able to discover what really happened that night. I believe we could be looking at a murderer.'

Garland gave a rapid intake of breath. 'I'd like to think so, Jack, but bloody hell fire, you've taken some liberties here. How we can make anything of this I really don't know. I'll need to see who this match is and then I'll have to go and think this over on a night when I've not got a serial killer stalking the streets.'

'It's on the second sheet, Gene.'

'Let's have a look.' Garland turned to it. 'It's saying there's a familial match to a Lieutenant Derek Coll.' He turned his head to Jack who looked solemnly back at him.

'Yes.' Horner spoke calmly in a measured voice. 'The letter from the lab tells us that the touch DNA samples from the tablet bottle belong to a close relative of this Lieutenant Coll fellow. If we can find a relative of this Coll fellow who was at or had access to the nurses' home in those same years, then we've got forensic evidence linking them to killing Pam.'

'Have you found anything more out about this Lieutenant Derek Coll yet?'

'Not much. I've only had this information a few hours. From my research on the internet, I've learnt he was in the Commando Regiment in the seventies. He was awarded a Distinguished Service Order too, for his courage in the ground assault retaking the Falkland Islands.'

'Commandos? Falkland Islands?' Despite his thick scarf keeping out the cold evening air, Garland felt an unnerving chill envelop him. 'Where is this Lieutenant Coll now?'

'He lived not far from here, a few miles out in a village to the west of York. But talk about bad luck with timing. He died about three weeks ago. I found out about his DSO from his obituary.'

Garland handed the sheets of paper back to Horner, the voice of his intuition growing increasingly loud in his ears.

'Thank you for this, Jack,' he said. 'I promise I'll do whatever I can. But what you've told me tonight may be even more important than you think. Now, if you'll excuse me, I've really, really got to dash.'

Garland had never been so glad that he'd kept himself physically fit into his middle age. It enabled him to run at full speed all the way back from the cemetery to the police station.

Chapter 38

'Let's try this one,' Karen suggested, propped up comfortably in the corner of the sofa, newspaper in hand. '"I rang them awkwardly for a nocturnal terror". Nine letters.'

'Hang on.' Paul grabbed the notepad and pen and started scribbling. After a few seconds, he looked up. 'Nightmare,' he exclaimed.

'Explain yourself.'

'It's an anagram of "I rang them". Anyway, I should know all about nightmares. After all, I was married to one for long enough.'

Karen giggled. 'Was Amanda really so bad?' She took a long gulp of coffee. 'God, that was nice. I needed that.'

'Absolutely, she was. Although, if you were to meet her, you'd come away thinking she's the sweetest person you've ever met and I'm talking a load of nonsense about her.'

'Hey, don't bank on that after the week I've just had.' Karen wagged a finger in feigned admonition. 'You know that profiler Doctor Tennant? He was telling us about some of the psychopaths he's interviewed, and said that you'd be amazed at what warm and inviting personalities they have. He told us you'd find it impossible to believe that someone so charismatic could be capable of even returning a library book late, let alone murder. Now what phrase did he use? Oh yeah, "superficial charm". He reckoned that's how so many of them can get away with being undetected for so long.'

'Superficial charm seems about right,' Paul replied. 'Maybe that's how I got hooked on Amanda to start with. Now I think about it, she was really good at making new friends, it was keeping them she had a problem with. Eventually, she'd fall out with them over some minor issue or other and whenever she did, she went into annihilation mode.'

'She was like that?'

Paul nodded slowly. 'She could bear a grudge and when she did, she didn't care one iota about how much she had to lie and cheat to get back at someone.' He grimaced. 'On top of that, she had absolutely no feelings of guilt for any innocent person who got damaged in the crossfire. To her narcissistic world view, everything was focussed on proving her point and winning, and sod anyone else that got hurt in the process.'

'How did it end, if you don't mind my asking?'

'Not at all. It's good to get it all out.' Paul sat back on the other end of the sofa. 'It had been going downhill for a while. She was becoming increasingly demanding and equally angry that nobody in town wanted to recognise what she considered her vast potential. In return, I suppose, I was getting increasingly wary of her behaviour.'

Karen placed the newspaper on the sofa armrest and listened. She'd learnt from her police interviewing skills when not to butt in.

'It all came to a head at a visit to Madame Tussauds down in London,' continued Paul eventually. 'We'd gone down for a weekend to see if a relaxing couple of days away would help re-float a sinking boat. The trip round the waxworks started out well enough. I took some photos of her posing with the models of various celebrities – you can stand right next to them nowadays – and it was all going fine.' He paused, replaying that day's events through his mind.

'Then I must have done something that pissed her off. Whatever it was, I still don't know, so it must have been something relatively trivial. It was often like that. She did her normal trick of going from zero to a hundred in less than five seconds and she had this blazing rant at me, and it all came out. She told me that I'd dragged her to live in a city that didn't appreciate her talents, that she was tired of everybody she met here falling out with her, and that we were through. She stormed off and left me standing in the middle of the waxworks and made her own way back to York.'

'And you?'

'There was a time when I would have followed her straight back,' Paul admitted, 'but you know what, I'd paid for the hotel room, and I decided I was going to enjoy my stay in London. That night I went out for some drinks on the South Bank. On the Sunday morning I went to the Science Museum, which is a place she wouldn't have been seen dead. I think she'd had plans to drag me round Selfridges that day. After a slap-up pub lunch, I went to see *The Fighting Temeraire* at the National Gallery.'

'Good for you,' laughed Karen. 'Although, I bet she didn't like that one bit.'

'When I got back home on Sunday night, I was dreading a commotion of nuclear-bomb proportions, but when I walked through the door, the house was empty. She'd gone, and taken her stuff with her. Frankly, I was glad to have a peaceful evening without her.'

'Where is she now?'

'Back living in our old house while it's up for sale and our solicitors are arguing the toss. Which means I'm renting here until it's all sorted out.' He laughed. 'It's not much, but with her not around at least the noise level in the house is consistently below that of Concorde's jet exhaust.'

Karen snorted with laughter. 'Seriously though, if there's anything I can do to help you through this, just let me know. I'm here for you. Anyway, how can I not admire a man who appreciates *The Fighting Temeraire*?'

* * * *

'I need you to help me with something right away.' Garland came to a stop next to DS Dattaram Jamshedji's desk, panting slightly.

'Bloody hell, boss. Are you OK? What is it?'

Garland caught his breath. 'About three weeks ago, a Lieutenant Derek Coll who was in the Commando Regiment died. A descendant of his might be linked by DNA to a historical crime. I don't know about that yet. What I do know is that he's a prime candidate for someone that might have a Welrod in his garage that might just have happened to be found by a relative doing a garage clear-out. I'm putting this Coll guy right at the top of my list as of now.' He panted again to regain his breath. 'What I need is—'

'—is to get his details, plus those of any relatives who live locally,' finished Jamshedji for him. 'In particular, any who happen to be female, with light hair, and about five foot six inches tall. I'm on it straight away, boss.'

* * * *

After having got his story off his chest, Paul felt more at ease. Karen was a patient and understanding listener. 'Enough of Amanda anyway,' he said. 'Let's not bring the evening down going on about her. But thanks for the ear.'

'It's not a problem at all.' Karen smiled. 'Wait until you hear some of the crap I've been through in life, but yes, let's save that for another evening. For now, though, let's get this crossword finished and by the time we're done, I might, and mean might, have started to get a handle on how these stupid clues work. OK then, here we are.' She picked the newspaper back up. 'Six down. "Most appropriate article on quiet examination".'

'How many letters?'

'Six.'

'Hmm.' Paul twirled Karen's pen in the air while he pondered the clue. Then a light bulb seemed to come on. 'Aptest,' he answered confidently.

* * * *

Garland tore across the corridor from Jamshedji's desk, pulled off his scarf, flung it onto the chair, and sat without bothering to remove his jacket. Firing up his laptop, he started to look for Lieutenant Derek Coll and any links that could lead him to the killer. He'd not been searching long when his mobile rang. Pulling it from his pocket he saw it was Professor Dawn Robinson calling. He answered.

'Garland.'

'Hi, Detective Inspector.' Professor Robinson's gentle voice came on the line. 'I need to tell you something about the case. Have you got five minutes?'

'If you've got information about the case, then you've got my attention. What's up?'

'It's about the latest clue. I've had another really detailed look at it.'

'Excellent. Go on.'

'Well, all my life I've dreamt about solving an important problem,' she began. 'I think all mathematicians do. But what better problem for me to solve than one where people's lives are at stake?'

'And you're uneasy about the theories we've come up with for this latest clue so far, aren't you?'

'Here's my issue. All these theories about Garfield Terrace and Osborne Drive are all well and good, but the previous clues have had the answers buried in the actual letters and words of the clue. Sorry to sound negative, Detective Inspector, but I just don't see either of these being the location.'

'Do you have an alternative? One that fits more closely with your theory?'

'No, but I've discovered something striking I think might unlock it for us. I've applied some of the work I've been doing recently with a software team at the university. It's on an algorithm for what we aim to be the most powerful stylometry software available. This evening I ran our clue through it.'

'Excuse my ignorance, Professor. Stylometry is…?'

'It might be the next big thing in forensic analysis. Remember where you heard it first. Stylometry is the analysis of linguistic characteristics. The theory is that every writer has a certain personal style, for example, based on preferences for certain adjectives they use, a subconscious bias in words they put together with each other, use of abbreviations, lexical difficulty, and so on. Put these elements together and it means that every writer has their own unique "fingerprint" as it were. It's been used to conclusively verify the authorship of the works of Shakespeare with a high degree of success.'

'OK, I'm not sure where this is going, but what have you found?'

'Well, we can't directly identify a specific author of these clues. Sorry to disappoint you there. But the software did throw up the very notable observation that the last word in each line of the clue is French and the probability of that happening purely by chance alone is less than one in a million.'

Garland found the piece of paper on the desk and read it again.

Hush. Lights, camera action. I sound so debonair
Iron guns fire lead bullets in my movie premiere
Laugh – this is more comedy gold than a film noir
Wool over your eyes again, I bid you all au revoir

'I see what you mean.'

'So I started out,' Dawn continued, 'taking the French word at the end of each line – *debonair, première, noir*, and *revoir*, and translating them into English. That gives us—'

'Stylish first black goodbye,' finished Garland. 'Although you could argue that *revoir* is more like "see you again".'

'Ah, Gene, vous parlez Français?'

'Je le parle couramment,' replied Garland to her surprise. 'Mais je ne peux rien voir. Toutefois…pas une mauvaise idée.'

'*Je vous en prie*,' exclaimed Dawn Robinson, taken aback by Garland's fluent grasp of the French language. 'Yes, I couldn't make out anything from those words either. I've researched combinations online but so far, I've got nothing I can propose with any confidence.'

Garland picked up his model of *Thunderbird 2* from his desk and examined it in his hand as he gave the clue some extra consideration. *Oiseau de tonnerre numéro deux*, he thought. *Doesn't have quite the same ring to it as in English.*

'OK, professor. If we're convinced that translation is the way forward, then let's stick with this line of attack and see what we can come up with.'

At that moment, Jamshedji burst into Garland's office. Garland looked up. For a typically extremely calm and unruffled man, Jamshedji looked like he was fizzing with energy.

'Oops, sorry, boss, didn't see you were on the phone. I need to show you this piece of paper as soon as possible. I've just found a very interesting familial link to your Lieutenant Coll. Make sure you're sitting down when you read it.'

* * * *

'Aptest,' considered Karen. 'As in most appropriate. I get that bit. So walk me through the rest.'

'You just have to pick through the clue and then put the bits together,' Paul explained. 'Usually there's a set of rules that crossword compilers use, and you just have to learn them.'

'OK, so break this one down for me.'

'Here we go. It's straightforward, really. The word "article" in a crossword clue is usually a reference to either the indefinite or definite article in English grammar, which is either the word *a, an,* or *the*. *Quiet* is a reference to how it's written on a music manuscript, the musical term *piano* abbreviated to the letter *p*. And an *examination* is a *test*. Put that lot together and you get *a* plus *p* plus *test* equals *aptest* which means most appropriate.'

'Oh, for heaven's sake.' Karen groaned, throwing her hands in the air. 'I've got a mountain to climb to get the hang of these. I promise I'll never think of you the same way next time I see you in reception doing a crossword. All this talk of tests and articles is doing my head in. Get the kettle on again.'

Paul collected the coffee mugs, stood up, and started to make his way across the room to the kitchen when Karen suddenly called out.

'Hey. Stop. I've just thought. What was the email address the killer's using?'

Paul slowly turned round. 'It was test.article@...Why?'

'*Test* and *article.*' Karen launched herself across the sofa, seized the notebook and pen, and started writing furiously. 'Oh no. Oh God no, surely not.'

'Karen, you've gone white. You're making me nervous. What is it?'

'Test and article. *Exam* and *a*. It was right in front of our eyes all along.'

Paul felt the room go icy cold. 'Exam and a? What do you mean "exam" and "a"?' His voice rose in urgency. 'For God's sake tell me, what do you mean?'

'Look at the way I've written it. I've spaced out the letters a bit differently. Do you see what I see?'

She turned her notepad around to face Paul to reveal what she'd written.

ex am and a

Chapter 39

Paul froze. 'My ex. Amanda.' His face drained. 'Oh God, no. No way.'

'Paul, maybe there's a reason you were singled out to get those emails.' Karen picked her words carefully as Paul paced the room. 'Amanda has an axe to grind with you and from what you were saying, it sounds like she's developed an intense hatred for the citizens of York. In her twisted mind, it's not her fault she can't get a job or keep friends. It's everyone else's.

Still in a state of numb disbelief, Paul stared blankly at the notepad.

Karen continued. 'You said she'd applied to join the police but got rejected. That won't have exactly made us top of her Christmas card list. What if she's on a mission to prove that she really is too intelligent for you, the police, and this city?'

'Oh no, this is too much.' Paul dropped back onto the sofa beside Karen, his head spinning with confusion.

'What was it you were saying about her? Something about "wouldn't care one iota" about what she'd to do to get revenge and "absolutely no feelings of guilt for any innocent sod that got damaged in the crossfire", wasn't it? Now I'm no Quantico-certified expert like Doctor Tennant, but that sounds like psychopathic tendencies to me.'

Paul felt numb all over. 'So, it's all one big vendetta. Against the city of York, me and York Police in which innocent people are just detestable, throwaway detritus to be used as a means to an end.'

'Doctor Tennant explained that it's as if the victims are like characters in a computer game like *Grand Theft Auto*. They don't really exist or have any value, so they can be demolished along the way without any personal remorse.'

'I'm struggling to take this in. What do you think we should do now?'

'Let's not get ahead of ourselves. It's only a theory at this stage and we've already had enough red herrings in this case to make a Stargazey Pie big enough to feed the Household Cavalry. But there's something we can have a think about right away. Take a deep breath and then look carefully at that sequence of locations again and think of a possible connection with Amanda to see if it makes any sense.'

Paul picked up the notepad, read it again, and thought long and hard. It was a couple of minutes before he spoke. 'No, nothing. Absolutely nothing whatsoever.' He sighed. 'Maybe it isn't Amanda after all, and we've just gone off on a mad tangent.'

'You've not been to these places with Amanda and no memorable events have happened there?'

'No.' Paul shook his head. 'We've probably walked from the Minster to the river together because it's near the city centre. I've walked past the cemetery on my way to the station, but I've never been there with Amanda. And as for the other places, I don't think I've even visited them myself until all this started.'

'Maybe I just got carried away and we're barking up the wrong tree, but we do have some CCTV footage of the killer from the last murder. Just for comparison, can you show me what Amanda looked like? I've never seen a photo of her.'

'Well, I didn't exactly plan on spending my evening with you showing you photos of my ex, but OK.'

'Thanks. The most recent ones would be most helpful.'

'Well, they'll be the ones I took at Madame Tussauds. It's literally a record of our last day together because I've never seen her face to face since.'

He grabbed his phone and swiped the screen. ''Ah yes, here we are. This is her, look.'

He turned the phone to Karen who looked at the picture. There was Amanda, dressed in stonewashed jeans and a short-sleeved aubergine shirt tied at the waist, standing next to a waxwork of Victoria Beckham who was wearing a black cocktail dress. Both women were equally glamorous, Amanda with blonde hair standing alongside the brunette Victoria Beckham as if they were both posing for paparazzi. Karen picked up her own phone and started tapping the screen with an intent look on her face.

'What are you doing?'

'I'm looking to see if I can find Victoria Beckham's height. Hmm. It says she's about five foot four. Assuming the waxwork makers got it right, would you say Amanda is maybe a couple of inches taller?'

Paul looked. 'Yes, I reckon so.'

Karen frowned. Her copper's intuition was working overtime. 'OK, next photo.'

The next picture showed the championship jockey Lester Piggott, standing up in the saddle, crop in hand, riding a bay horse in front of a backdrop of a racecourse, as if he were leading the field. Amanda was standing in front of the galloping horse, adopting a pose of mock surprise as if she were about to be trampled underfoot and was jumping hastily to one side.

'Shame that horse wasn't real,' muttered Karen. 'OK, next one.'

In the third photograph, basketball player Magic Johnson, wearing a Los Angeles Lakers vest, was leaping to dunk a basketball through a hoop. Amanda was mid-leap beside him, as if attempting to block his shot.

'She does look quite athletic, probably able to run from a crime scene,' mused Karen, still churning some thoughts through her mind. 'Next.'

In the next photo, Amanda had her left arm around the shoulder of the actor Nicholas Cage, the fingers of her left hand splayed in a peace sign. In her other hand, she held a can of 7-Up. She smiled at the camera.

'What's on the backdrop behind them?' asked Paul, straining to make it out.

'Looks like the Houses of Parliament and the Eiffel tower,' replied Karen, zooming in on it. I recognise now what film it's supposed to be portraying – it's "National Treasure".'

'Ah yes of course, I remember now,' said Paul, 'Amanda and I once watched it on television together. Amanda was quite a Nicholas Cage fan.'

'Poor Nicholas doesn't appear to be quite as delighted to meet Amanda as she does him though.' Karen laughed. 'Maybe he could sense something about her you didn't. OK, next one.'

Paul scrolled to the next photo, which was Freddie Mercury, singing with all his might into a microphone and punching his left hand triumphantly into the air. Amanda stood beside him, posing as if she were performing a duet and sharing the microphone with him.

'Was she a good singer?'

'Terrible. Like an alley cat sliding down a gravel path on a galvanised dustbin lid. Freddie would have been most put out if he'd ever heard her.'

'OK, I'm getting a good idea of what she looks like now. One more photo and then we're done, and you can make me another coffee.'

Paul swiped his finger on the screen one last time to reveal the ice dancers Jayne Torvill and Christopher Dean performing the Bolero in their gold medal-winning performance at the 1984 Winter Olympics in Sarajevo. At least, Christopher Dean was. Amanda had carefully positioned herself in front of Jayne Torvill, so it looked like it was she and Christopher Dean were performing that world-famous routine.

Karen raised a quizzical eyebrow.

'She couldn't even skate in real life,' said Paul, as if reading her thoughts. 'I once took her out to Bradford ice rink. Big mistake.'

Karen laughed as Paul got up and went through to the kitchen. He'd just pulled a couple of fresh mugs from out of the cupboard when he heard her voice urgently calling him back. 'What is it?' he called. He walked back into the living room to find Karen bursting with nervous energy.

'The list of the locations,' Karen said frantically. 'Here…' She read them aloud and emphasised certain words. 'Queen *Victoria*, the architect James *Piggott*, a *basketball hoop* and a *magic* show, Saint *Nicholas* field and a lemon, the planet *Mercury* and the *Dean* Court Hotel.'

'Yes?'

'Now let's go through the photos you've shown me. *Victoria* Beckham. Lester *Piggott*. *Magic* Johnson playing *basketball,* Amanda holding a *lemon* drink with *Nicholas* Cage in a film in which if I'm not mistaken has a very famous and memorable scene involving *lemons*. Followed by Freddie *Mercury* and then Christopher *Dean*.'

As Paul's mouth gaped wide open, Karen jumped off the sofa. 'That's the pattern we've been looking for. She's recreating and killing your last day together.'

* * * *

Across York, the final preparations had been made for the night's murder. The final one. This would mark the end of the sequence after which...well, she'd just slip back into the shadows for evermore, confident that she'd shown this arrogant, backward city who was really the boss. Everyone in this stuck-up city thought they were so clever. Ha. Not clever enough to crack a few simple clues. Not that simpleton soon-to-be-ex-husband of hers nor those oh-so-haughty lot in the police who'd all probably been laughing as they'd turned down her application. Well, they weren't laughing now, were they?

The Welrod had been the most serendipitous find. Coming just after splitting up, with her dozy husband out of the way, her uncle dying, and her finding that gun in his garage was a gift from heaven. It was such a rare and opportune discovery; it was as if God was sending her a message. The bullets had been surprisingly easy to come by. There had been that cretinous chav from where she went to school in Leeds who carried round his criminal record like a badge of pride. She knew he still desperately had the hots for her. Pathetic, pitiful scum. He was repugnant and so far beneath her she wouldn't lower herself to touch him with a bargepole. Still, he'd been a very useful idiot, and it hadn't taken much flirting for the nauseating brat to drunkenly boast about where he knew you could get bullets with no questions asked. He'd probably forgotten he'd told her by now, the retarded prick.

It had been about twenty years since her first killing. That screwed-up student nurse with the attitude problem that she'd been training with in Leeds. When the cow had started to suspect the little sideline she'd been running selling drugs she'd managed to purloin, she'd had to go. The imbecile had been so gullible it had been easier than expected to take her in with a sob story, pretend to break down in floods of tears, have a "conciliatory" coffee with her, and slip the tablets into her drink.

A steady hand loaded the gun as she reminisced. She'd decided to leave nursing after that incident, just to be on the safe side. Not that she'd been enjoying the course, anyway. Over two uneventful decades then passed, only for a most welcome and timely opportunity to land her way once again.

Gun loaded, she checked the safety-catch. Excellent. Smiling at her reflection in the mirror by the front door, she let herself out of the house with a quiet click of the door. Off she went into the night in which the sequence would be complete, and she knew exactly where to go. Such a pity nobody else did. Hilarious.

Chapter 40

'Stop marching up and down like a palace guard on amphetamines, and come here,' Karen insisted, sitting back down and patting the sofa. 'If we run with the idea that the locations are retracing your day at Madame Tussauds, then all we have to do is look at the next photo you took and it should point to the upcoming one.'

Paul grabbed his phone. 'I only took one more photo that day before she went ballistic, but here it is.' He showed his phone screen to Karen.

The picture showed a waxwork of Bryan Ferry, the lead singer of 1970s and 80s pop group Roxy Music. Bryan, dressed in a snappy suit and tie, was singing into a microphone, performing a duet with Amanda.

Karen looked up at Paul, her eyes gleaming. 'So that's it. Bryan Ferry. If our theory holds up, then the location for tonight's killing will have something to do with a Bryan or a Ferry.'

Paul's mind was buzzing. It was almost too much to take in. He forced himself to concentrate. 'The first thing that comes to mind is Askham Bryan village. It's not far out of York.'

'Good thinking.' Karen wrote it down. 'But it's further out than all the other killings, which have been within walking distance of the city centre. Remember, she's got to get there and back undetected, and besides, all the other clues have been more precise than a whole village.'

She tapped away at her phone screen in concentration. 'Ah. Talking of ferries, there's a boat service on the River Ouse that runs a ferry in and out of the city centre and I've also just found an article about a ferry service that operates just outside York from the village of Nun Monkton. Look.'

Paul craned across to look at Karen's phone screen. 'Well, the landing stage is a clear location,' he observed. 'But like Askham Bryan, it's quite a long way out of the centre for someone on foot. It wouldn't be an easy place to get there and back undetected.'

'There's one more possibility,' noted Karen as she continued to tap away, 'and this is a really strong one. There's a Ferry Lane. It's a short road that runs to the bank of the river to the east of the Archbishop's Palace.'

Paul looked at Ferry Lane on the map and nodded. 'Well, it certainly looks a plausible spot for a murder. It's accessible on foot, provided you don't mind a short hike from the city centre. Getting there and back undetected should be easy as it's a quiet, out-of-the-way spot, but maybe not so quiet that you're not going to get the occasional late night dog walker or someone to select as a target.'

'So that's whittled it down to three possible locations. Ferry Lane, the ferry station at Nun Monkton, and the village of Askham Bryan. Right. I need to call Garland and let him know our theory right away.'

'Whoah, hang on,' Paul protested. 'Let's keep a level head. We're not even sure it is Amanda yet or whether we've just let our minds run away on some crazy theory. Or if this really is a murder sequence or just us stupidly jumping to conclusions based on a string of coincidences.'

'Paul, we can't ignore this however absurd it sounds.'

'Hear me out. I have an idea. The evening's still relatively young. All the murders so far have been late at night. I think we have plenty of time to drive round all the possible places for a quick recce job to see how feasible they really are and then call it in.'

Karen looked at her watch and frowned.

'No, not all of them. I'll reluctantly compromise. Ferry Lane is by far the strongest possibility in my opinion and it's also the nearest. It'll probably take less than ten minutes from here in the car,' she conceded.

'Okay. A ten minute drive to see if it's a genuinely viable location is worth it to put my mind at rest that we're not just stupidly extrapolating on some mad speculation. I'll get my car,' Paul persisted.

'We'll take mine. Amanda doesn't know my car. I'm not expecting anything untoward, but there's no harm in being careful. And when we get there, if it looks anything like a reasonable place to carry out a killing, I'm calling Garland straight away. I'm not as sceptical as you are.'

* * * *

Karen drove as quietly as possible down Ferry Lane. Once they'd turned off the main road and onto this narrow lane, barely wide enough for her car, the street lighting had vanished. It was dark outside apart from a pearlescent autumn moon, which occasionally pierced its way between the passing clouds. Karen found herself nervously wishing that she'd not chosen the colour white when she'd bought her car. *Hardly the ideal colour for a covert reconnaissance in the dark*, she contemplated. Beside her in the passenger seat, Paul stared out like a hawk at the passing scenery caught in the dipped headlights. The low hedge on one side was almost up against the side of the car. There was a low building on the right with space for a few cars to park in front, but it looked deserted.

'OK. I've made a decision. I'm calling Garland right now.' Karen pointed to her phone, which was resting on the centre console by the gear stick. 'Get him on the line for me. His number's on my speed-dial list.'

Paul picked up Karen's phone and fiddled with it with increasingly visible frustration.

'What's up?'

'Can't get a signal.'

'Keep trying.'

The car moved slowly on. The lane became tighter, flanked by the wall and a hedge. After a few more yards, they came to a small clearing by the river. An octagonal wooden building stood in front of them. Karen pulled her car into the shadow of a small yacht which was resting on a trailer, and switched off the lights and the engine.

'Any signal yet?'

Paul looked at Karen's phone once more. The glowing screen seemed to illuminate the whole interior of the car. 'No, none. Never mind, let's have a look around. Two minutes, that's all, and then we're away.'

Alighting from the car and closing the doors gently behind them, they made their way over to the riverbank. In the moonlight, they could see that the river was high, as was typical for the Ouse throughout autumn. As they stood in silence, they could hear the water gently rippling by. Tied up near the foot of a small jetty were a couple of small boats which bobbed gently on the water. Paul and Karen looked at each other. Paul was doing his level best to stay calm and relaxed but inside his nerves were jangling like coins on a tin tray. He struggled to moderate his breathing. He was beginning to think that getting out of the car hadn't been a good idea.

'I think we've seen enough,' whispered Karen, picking up the nervousness which seemed to radiate off his skin. 'We need to go back to the car right now and get to somewhere where we can get a phone signal.'

'Yes, OK,' Paul whispered back. 'I'll check round the left-hand side of that wooden building. You go around to the right and we'll meet up again at the other side at the car and then we're out of here.' Giving a silent thumbs-up to each other they trod gently back up from the riverbank and parted company as they approached the octagonal building, Karen going to the right and Paul to the left.

As Paul emerged from around the left-hand side of the building to head towards Karen's car, he was startled as he almost bumped into the figure in a dark hoodie that was standing there. The figure in the hoodie, however, seemed to be in no surprise at all.

'Hello again, Paul. Fancy meeting you here.'

Paul froze.

'Amanda?'

Pulling the hood back from her head, she let her blonde hair fall down onto her shoulders. She gave her head a quick shake to move the hair out of her eyes. Paul stood immobile with shock. Even in the moonlight he would know that face, the face that he'd slept next to every night for years, the face he'd woken up next to every morning, the face he'd kissed.

The face which had shouted and sworn and spat at him when she was angry. And now that face was laughing.

'Oh, what a great night this is going to be. I really didn't count on you being bright enough to crack my last clue but then again you were stupid enough to come down here alone, so I guess that cancels it out.'

'Amanda. Wait.' Paul moved towards her and in a flash the Welrod was out of her pocket and pointing straight at him.

'Stop right there. Not another step.'

Paul halted in his tracks. Karen's car was less than fifty yards away. He could make out its white shape alongside the dark hull of the yacht on the trailer. However, Amanda was standing directly between him and it. There was no way he could make it there.

'As an unexpected bonus, it looks like with you dead after tonight, I'm going to get all the house and savings as well.' She laughed. 'In all my wildest dreams, I didn't expect it was going to turn out as well as this but thank you so much for making your last night my best one yet.'

The barrel of the Welrod glinted in the moonlight. Paul's eyes were transfixed on it.

So, this is how it all ends.

He resigned himself.

'Hold it.' Paul's and Amanda's heads turned in unison to see Karen walking towards them.

Amanda swung the gun round to point at her and Karen stopped in her tracks. The three of them now stood in the moonlight in a triangle.

'Do yourself a favour,' called Karen. 'You think we've not already phoned this one in? Put the gun down and make it easy on yourself.'

Amanda flashed the gun back in Paul's direction and then nonchalantly swung it back to Karen again. She grinned. 'Sorry. I don't believe a word you say. So, it looks like the last killing is going to have to be a double. What a splendid finale to the sequence.'

'I doubt it,' said Karen, standing her ground. 'You'll never get us both. If you shoot me first, Paul will rush you, and get you before your second shot. If you shoot Paul, I'll rush you before you get a second shot. Either way, you're going down.'

'Who's this then, Paul?' called Amanda, jerking her head at Karen. 'The new tart? Didn't take you long did it, you nasty little piece of shit.' She curled her lip in disgust. 'Jesus Christ, I thought you'd have better taste than this.'

She glared at Karen in the moonlight. The only sound that Paul could hear was the flowing of the river behind him and his own heartbeat pounding loudly in his ears.

'Nice try.' Amanda laughed. 'But I've got considerably better with this thing over the last week.' As if to prove a point, she twirled the gun casually around in her hand before bringing it to an abrupt stop, pointing at Karen.

'So which one of you shall I do first?' Amanda asked. 'The cuckold or the tart?' She played the barrel of the Welrod back and forth leisurely between them as if to prolong the agony.

As the barrel of the gun made its next pass between them, a bulky shadow came cannoning out of the darkness at high speed from behind the yacht behind Amanda, its black combat jacket making it almost invisible in the moonlight.

Too late, Amanda tried to turn but was hit full-on with a sickening thud and knocked to the ground. The Welrod spun away from her hands and as she cried out in pain, the dark figure knelt over her prostrate body and pulled her hands up tightly behind her back.

Paul and Karen stared on in disbelief as the figure turned its face upward into the moonlight. Garland!

‘Parkinson! Get over here. This one’s yours. Come on. You’ve deserved it.’

His voice snapped Karen out of her temporary stupor and at once, the world fell into clear, calm focus.

As Paul surveyed the scene, wide-eyed in shock, he heard Karen’s voice ringing out in a clarion and authoritarian tone he’d never heard from her before.

‘Amanda Dobson you are under arrest on suspicion of murder and attempted murder. You do not have to say anything, but it may harm your defence if you do not mention something which you later rely on in court. Anything you do say may be given in evidence…’

Chapter 41

It was the third week of December. In the entrance hall to the Masonic Hall where Paul had stepped in with trepidation only a few weeks earlier, now stood a ten-foot-high Christmas tree dazzling with gold and red baubles, fairy lights, and tinsel.

'It looks magnificent, doesn't it?' Paul said.

'It certainly does,' replied Karen, 'but I still think I prefer ours.'

'So, what are you both doing for Christmas?' asked Garland. 'Anything special?'

'Next week it's the York Press Christmas party,' said Karen, 'so I'll finally get to meet everyone that Paul works with. You know his editor informed him she's relieved he's found a good reason to stay in York so she gets to keep her best investigative reporter. I told Paul to tell her it's a tough job but I'm glad to be of service.'

'Excellent. That also hopefully means I get to keep the Detective Constable that I don't want to lose either.'

'And then for Christmas Day, we're both going up to see my brother Bob and his family in Durham. It's a bit of a family tradition. Anyway, I'm sure we'll have a relaxing break up there and I reckon everyone will get on like a house on fire with Paul.'

'More Prosecco anyone?' Dattaram Jamshedji, accompanied by his wife Akshata who looked absolutely radiant in a shimmering dress, appeared with a large tray of drinks. 'These are on the house.'

'Don't mind if I do.' Gene Garland lifted a couple of glasses from the tray and handed one to his wife, Marcia, who raised it in toast.

'Cheers everyone,' she said.

Neither Paul nor Karen had met Garland's wife before. She was gorgeous. Garland himself had also scrubbed up well. Dressed in an immaculate dinner suit and sporting a large bow-tie, his exhaustion and world-weariness had disappeared, and he seemed happy and at ease with the world once again.

'Thanks, Dattaram.' Garland thanked Jamshedji. 'It's very decent of you to invite us all to the Masons' Christmas party.'

'No problem at all,' beamed Jamshedji. 'I thought you'd all enjoy it. We're having a turkey dinner and then we've got a local rock band to do a turn followed by a disco. It should be a fantastic night. Anyway' – he smiled at Paul – 'we could hardly not invite the man here who's going to become one of us in January.'

Garland raised his eyebrows. 'You're becoming a Mason, are you, Paul?'

Paul surveyed his fellow partygoers. 'It seems a decent social life,' he replied. 'Dattaram here was very persuasive. Besides, he said they needed me for their team in the cross-country running event in February for the police pensioners' housing charity. Given that it's thanks to the police I'm still alive, it seemed the least I could do. And I've never properly thanked you for that, Gene. So, thank you.'

'You never fully explained to me what happened that night.' Marcia, Garland's wife, nudged him gently in the ribs. 'Something about solving a clue and then racing off down a lane.'

'I don't like to bore you with details,' said Garland modestly. 'And in any case, it was Professor Robinson who did the hard work. To use a football analogy, she'd taken the ball the full length of the pitch and then crossed it over to me conveniently standing near the goal mouth to head the ball into the net.'

'I'm still massively impressed,' remarked Karen. 'Go on, explain.'

'The last word in every line of the poem was in French,' explained Garland. 'Translating the French words into English made no sense. So instead, I took the first word of each line in the poem, which were English, and translated them to French. The first words of each line were *hush*, *iron*, *laugh*, *wool*. In French that's *Chut. Fer Rit Laine* – or as we would pronounce it: *Shoot. Ferry Lane.* As soon as I realised where the shooting was going to be, I drove as fast as I could straight there with Jamshedji following close behind. On the way I called the team back at the station to get on to the Armed Response Unit to come immediately and give us backup. I parked a bit further up the lane outside a building backing onto the sports field and then when I made my way down, I saw this standoff going on. I crept behind a yacht that was parked up on a trailer. When I saw an opportune moment in a split second, I dived out. The rest, we all know.'

'And Amanda?' asked Akshata.

'Awaiting trial. She's also confessed to the murder of a student nurse in Leeds just over twenty years ago.' Garland was glad he'd been able to squeeze that confession out of her without having to go into detail about Jack Horner's DNA evidence. 'As for this latest spree of killings, it appears they were motivated by a psychotic sense of retribution. To paraphrase a quote of the comedian Ruby Wax: "Her whole career's been an act of revenge".'

'Yes,' agreed Paul. 'Which reminds me. I'm kicking myself now for not solving the crossword clue I was chewing over on my way down to my update meeting with Karen just before Bonfire Night. *Facsimiles of Ruby's output*. The answer, coincidentally, was *waxworks*.'

Major Alan Brooks, the master of the lodge, appeared at the entrance to the dining hall. He raised a small brass gong in the air and banged it to gain everyone's attention.

'Ladies and gentlemen. Dinner is about to be served, if you could all please make your way into the dining hall.'

Paul and Karen walked over hand in hand.

'Don't get too drunk tonight.' Karen giggled. 'You can't come for your crime update tomorrow with a sore head.' She winked at him jokingly.

'Is there anything big going on this week?'

'Some very serious crime indeed,' replied Karen in mock severity as she gave his hand a squeeze. 'A broken window at a youth club in Fulford, some stolen hubcaps from a Ford Fiesta, and a significant breakthrough with the missing wheelbarrow mystery.'

ACKNOWLEDGEMENTS

My first thank you is to my partner Julie who supported me throughout the whole process and is the inspiration for Professor Robinson.

A huge thanks also to the author Malcolm Hollingdrake and his wife Debbie for the hours of mentoring and advice. If you have not read any of Malcolm's crime novels, including the wonderful Harrogate series and Merseyside series, then put them on your to-be-read list, they are excellent.

A very special thank you to Paul and my sister Karen Seddon – the real-life Karen Parkinson – for the time, suggestions and encouragement that kept me going throughout the writing process.

A very heartfelt thank you to both my parents who have always supported my creative efforts throughout my life; I just wish you could be both here to read this book.

And finally, but by no means least, to the wonderful crime author community for all their help and encouragement, with a special shout out to Paul Finch, Ann Bloxwich, Donna Morfett, Liz Mistry, Dee Groocock, and Caroline Maston and Samantha Brownley at UK Crime Book Club.

ABOUT THE AUTHOR

Born in Yorkshire, Tom spent his earlier career in a variety of scientific research and engineering roles and now in middle age hopes to share his love of the city of York with his readers – albeit via somewhat dark, intriguing, and mind-teasing scenarios.

When not writing crime novels, Tom loves researching true crime and modern history, playing the guitar, listening to all genres of rock and solving cryptic crosswords with a particular penchant for the one in Private Eye.

Website: tomsibson.co.uk
Twitter: @TomSibsonAuthor
Facebook: facebook.com/tomsibsonauthor

Printed in Great Britain
by Amazon

43750387R10169